Mr

a **MISTER**
STANDALONE

MYSTERIOUS

New York Times Bestselling Author

HUSS

MrMYSTERIOUS

New York Times Bestselling Author

HUSS

Copyright © 2016 by JA Huss
ISBN: 978-1-944475-12-3

Edited by RJ Locksley
Cover Design by JA Huss

DEDICATION

For Mariel Hawthorne
Because she raised a man I could fall in love with.
;)

CHAPTER ONE

M A C

MR. PERFECT'S HOUSE
RIGHT NOW

The sound of a helicopter outside wakes me. Rubbing my eyes, I turn over, find Ellie missing—she's up in Idaho Springs with Ming and Ariel for a spa weekend—and sigh a little, wishing she was here.

But the helicopter sound gets louder. So loud, in fact, the walls start vibrating. Ellie has complained about this in the past when I've come home from a trip using the helicopter, but no one has ever come to the house in a helicopter but me, so I've never experienced it.

What the fuck is happening?

My mind races with all the worst-case possibilities.

Ellie fell off a cliff up in the mountains.

No, that's stupid. They wouldn't Life Flight her here, for fuck's sake. They'd take her to a hospital. I'd be woken up by a phone call, not a helicopter.

Some kind of work emergency.

Equally stupid. Work is twenty minutes away by car. No one but me would fly over here from work. Hell, no one but me has a helicopter at work. We have a ton of jets over there, but only one helicopter. And it's mine. Parked outside. On my helipad.

Nolan. He's my next guess.

1

But no. I just talked to Nolan a few hours ago. He called to ask me if he should threaten or bribe Ivy's OBGYN into telling him the sex of the baby. They just had an appointment the other day and Nolan emailed me some ridiculous blobby-thing picture of their bun in the oven. Ivy has taken the surprise route as far as the baby's sex goes.

Nolan isn't handling that well.

I told him bribery is probably better than threats. So it can't be Nolan outside. He wouldn't leave Ivy alone. Besides, he's too far away for a helicopter ride. He's out at that desert hotel they run.

It's not Oliver. I know he's in New York trying to close some deal.

Pax is the only guess left.

And he makes sense, so I throw the covers off and jog down the hallway towards the front door. Scout barks excitedly, following full speed behind me, ever the faithful farm dog. I don't even know where Pax lives right now. He says he has an office in LA, but I've never seen it. And he's always out here in Colorado with Oliver.

But Oliver called me just this morning wondering if I'd seen or talked to Paxton, and I had to tell him no. Pax never bothers with me unless one of us has called a Mister meeting.

Scout crashes into me as I slide on the smooth polished floors in my socks. The house is chilly now that fall is in full swing. And Ellie likes to keep the thermostat in the in-floor heating turned up, but she's not here to regulate the temperature. So I slip my feet into the boots I wear out to the barn and grab the first thing my fingers come in contact with from the foyer closet, and pull the navy-blue pea coat on as I step out into the frigid darkness.

I try to close the door before Scout can get through, but she's way ahead of me in the escape plan. She wiggles through and starts running towards the helipad, her long silver-blue sheepdog fur waving and bouncing with her short, quick strides.

She runs circles around the new arrival, which is off to the left of my own helicopter, like she can herd this thing into submission. Her bark fills the night and I look around nervously, still not quite accustomed to living in the middle of nowhere with the closest neighbors a mile away.

The helicopter has landed and the engine suddenly stops. The propellers start to slow down, that *womp womp womp* sound fading as two men get out. One stumbles while the other one helps him walk.

I stand there watching.

It *is* Pax. The stumbling one. I can tell by his gait. But I'm more surprised about who he's with than I am about the midnight helicopter appearance.

Five.

Hmmm.

Paxton is loud as they walk towards the large farmhouse-style front porch. I forgot to flip the light on, so everything is dark and still. Scout follows them, circling them like she does the geese we keep in the barn.

Paxton is slurring his words when he stumbles again. Five has a hold of his coat, so he doesn't go down.

"Come on, asshole," Five growls. "Get your shit together."

3

"My *shit*?" Paxton laughs, obviously drunk. "My shit is so together, you Aston motherfucker. And just wait!" Pax yells, pointing up at the sky like he's crying *Eureka*! Loud enough to make an echo off the house. "Just wait! He will blame you too!" He laughs loud and uproariously. "He will blame you *tooooooooooo*!"

"What the fuck is going on here?" I ask Five when he approaches the porch. Pax stumbles on the front stoop, almost smashing his nose on the concrete steps, but stops the catastrophe by slamming one hand, palm down, on the smooth stone. The other hand holds a drink.

I squint at it. A small tumbler glass with ice and something that looks like... mint leaves sticking out.

He didn't spill a drop. It's still three quarters full.

Five sighs, but says nothing.

"What's *going on* here?" Pax bellows, grabbing the railing with the drinkless hand while the other tries to get the rim of the glass to his lips. He takes a long slurp and then waves his hand in the air. A splash of alcohol pops out of the glass and falls in a stream, right into the open mouth of my dog.

"Scout," I say sternly. But she's beyond excited right now. Her little nub of a tail is wagging and bobbing furiously as she hops around Paxton like he's the best thing ever. "What the fuck are you doing here, Pax?"

Ellie would not like this one bit. She barely tolerates Mysterious. He's way too much for her. He's way too much for *me*, to be honest.

"Tell him." Pax laughs. "*You* tell him," he says again.

I look at Five, who rolls his eyes and cops a seat on my porch railing, leaning back a little, like this is going to be a

4

long story and he needs to get comfortable. "Oliver is going to kill him."

"What?" I ask, scanning the road, hoping none of my neighbors across that cow field can hear what's happening over here. "Why?"

"Tell him," Pax bellows again. "Tellllllll h*iiiiii*m."

"No," Five says, checking his fingernails. "I'm not telling him shit. I'm not telling anyone anything. You wanted this to happen tonight, so here we are. You tell him."

Pax smiles, his glassy eyes gleaming in the starlight. "I'm fucking Cindy Shrike."

I shake my head a little, trying to wrap my brain around his words. "What?"

"Have been"—Pax laughs, taking a sip of his drink—"for eight weeks now."

"What the fuck?" I look at Five. "You knew about this?"

"He showed up at my house tonight. Said he needed to borrow my helicopter. But he was drunk on those stupid Kentucky Derby drinks."

I stare hard at the drink in Pax's hand. He downs the entire thing, then slams it on the porch railing so hard, I think he might break the glass.

"I'm gonna need another," Pax says, pushing past me to open the front door. "Where's that ball and chain, Perfect? She here? Because she's not gonna like this, my friend. Not one bit."

And then he lets himself in my house. Scout, who is caught up in his blustering, follows eagerly after.

"Is Ellie home?" Five asks. "Because if she tells Arial what's happening—"

5

"She's not here," I say. "Is he fucking serious? Who the hell fucks a guy's baby sister?"

"He refuses to tell me the story," Five says. "He said you're the only one who will understand."

"Me? I thought he was an asshole before he messed with Oliver's sister. Now? Fuck that. Oliver is not going to like this."

"Oliver is going to flip his fucking lid."

Then I remember who I'm talking to. Oliver and Five go way back. I don't know the whole story, but I know they grew up together.

"Oliver is going to show up at Pax's house—wherever the fuck *that* might be—with a goddamned shotgun. Oliver's father will be there too. And since you've never met Spencer Shrike, I'll just tell you right now, you do not fuck with that guy. He comes off all sweet and charming, but don't let him fool you. Mr. Shrike knows his way around a gun." Five looks at me from the corner of his eye. "And a murder charge."

I let out a breath. I think I was holding it. "What the fuck does that mean?" Jesus Christ.

"It's not important. But you get the idea of where this is heading?"

I nod and we look at each other for a few seconds. "So… why are you guys *here*?"

Five shrugs. "He says you're the only one we can tell. Nolan and Weston kind of hate Pax, in case you haven't noticed."

Oh, I've noticed. "Why tell anybody?" I ask. "Why doesn't he just shut the fuck up about it? Chalk it up to a bad mistake and move on?"

"Well," Five says, heading for the open front door to my home, "he says he loves her and he's not giving her up. So... we need to deal with this. And you, Mr. Perfect, are the perfect man for the job."

"What *job?*"

"Telling Oliver, of course. It's all you, buddy. That's what happens when you're the calm, level-headed one on the team. You get to break all the bad news. So let's go. He said he'd tell us the entire story from start to finish." Five looks at his watch. "And we've only got a couple hours before people notice I'm gone and start asking questions."

"What people?" I ask, following him in. But Five doesn't answer. And I'm not sure if it's because he's hiding things— which he is. No one really knows anything about Five. Except Oliver. And Pax, probably. More than me, anyway— or if it's because Paxton Vance is commanding Five's attention as he pours ice cubes on top of a dish towel in my kitchen and starts hammering it with a can of soup.

"What the fuck are you doing?" I ask, walking over. Five is leaning against the bar, looking bored. Scout is doing that little wiggle leap she does when she can't contain her energy for one more second.

"Crushed ice," Pax says, as if that explains everything. "You want a margarita?" he asks us. "Or a mint julep?"

"Since when do you drink that kind of shit?" I ask, pushing him away from the counter and grabbing the soup can from his hand. "You're gonna crack my fucking granite, asshole. Stop pounding." I look over at Five, confused. "Can people get drunk off mint juleps?" It's such a ridiculous

7

drink, right? The only people who drink these things are old ladies on Derby Day.

"Exhibit A," Five says, motioning to Pax. Who has left the kitchen and is rummaging around at the bar in the adjoining room.

He finds what he's looking for—a bottle of bourbon and a bottle of tequila—and returns to the kitchen, pulling mint leaves out of his pockets.

"Cindy," Pax says, rubbing a hand through his wild dark hair. "Cinderella likes these two drinks. They're *our* drinks."

Our drinks? I mouth the words to Five, who stands up straight and takes his coat off, draping it over a barstool at the kitchen island.

"She's so goddamned perfect, Perfect. You'd love her."

"You cannot date Oliver's sister," I say, snapping out of it. "No. No. This is not happening. If you even looked at my sister—"

"You don't have a sister," Five says.

"Camille counts," I say, defensive. "I'd fucking kill him if he even *looked* at Camille. You need to break this off, Pax. Like now. You can't date a guy's sister. It's like the number one Bro Rule. How'd you like it if Oliver was dating your sister?"

"He doesn't have a sister," Five says.

"It's fucking hypothetical," I snap. Fucking Five. "Do you want me to handle this or not?"

Five opens his hands, as if to say, *Handle away.*

"Pax," I say, trying to be calm. "Look, man. You gotta just come to terms with this. You have to drop this idea of…" God, I can't even say the words. What kind of guy dates his friend's baby sister?

"I can't," Pax says, suddenly sober and serious. "I can't. I fucking fell for her, man. I fucking fell for her. She's my fucking soulmate. That's it," he says. "That's the end of the discussion. I love her."

"How could you possibly love her? How long have you been dating, for fuck's sake?"

Paxton sneers at me. "You don't understand," he says. "And you, of all people, *should.*"

I deserve that. I fell in love with Ellie in the span of a week. Sure, it took us a while to get our shit together, but we basically had a few weeks of serious dating before I proposed.

And now look at us. House—farm, really—dog, planning a wedding.

Pax goes back to his drinks and while the blender is whirring and he's dumping salt onto a small dish for his margarita, Five and I exchange looks.

We can't afford to have this kind of discontent between the Misters right now, Five's look says.

I got this, my look says back.

Then Pax is done making his drinks and he takes them both, one in each hand, and slumps down on the living room couch. Scout jumps up next to him, settling with her head on his lap like he's got her full support and sympathy.

"Maybe I should start from the beginning?" Pax says, slurping once from his margarita, then next from his mint julep.

"Maybe you should," I say, as Five and I follow him into the living room and take seats in opposite-facing chairs. "But you need to know, Pax, there is no way you can have this relationship right now. Not while all this shit is happening. Not when people are out to get us again. Because we need everyone to be cool. Your love life needs to take a back seat to Mister business."

Pax sighs, like we might finally be getting through to him. Sighs like he just might walk out of here tonight and take my advice.

"One day," he says. "You're like… doing great." He looks up at me with glassy eyes. They are bloodshot. Lids sagging like he's been up forever. Like he forgot what sleep is and hasn't rested in lifetimes. "You know who you are. What you're doing. Where you're going. And then a girl named Cinderella sends your whole world spinning. She's got blonde hair, and blue eyes, and a body a nineteen-fifties starlet would kill for."

He stops talking to smile at me. I smile back. I've never seen Pax like this.

"And she starts talking about motorcycles, and guns, and bands you have wanted to listen to again for a decade or more. She wears black leather whenever possible. On her feet, on her back, in her hair. She likes strawberry ice cream and books by Stephen King. Her fingers have silver rings on them. She likes anything with a feather on it. A hat, a hair clip, earrings. And she surfs, you guys. Like, for real. She surfs. And she fucking cooks. Tacos and spaghetti. Food I love now but never ate in the Limitless Farms dining room back in the bluegrass."

10

Pax sighs and slumps even further down into the couch cushions.

"She's like a happily ever after, you know? She's like a till death do us part."

I just stare at him. Blink.

"I get it," Five says, picking some lint off his suit. "I get it, Pax. I do. The Shrike girls are pretty hard to ignore."

"Yeah," Pax agrees. "How the fuck am I going to ignore *this*?" He pounds a fist into his heart. "And she's not going to fade away, you guys. She's not a fade-away kind of girl. She's going to fight. You have no idea how much fight that girl has. I mean, like I said, one day I was great. Just doing my thing. And then… and then this perfect fucking princess walked into my life."

CHAPTER TWO

PAXTON

EIGHT WEEKS AGO

Malibu Colony is a haven for somebodies. My house rents out for two hundred thousand dollars a month in the summer. But I didn't rent it out this year. I'm enjoying it. I'm enjoying the gate that keeps the world away a mile down the road. I'm enjoying the movie stars who jog on the sand when the tide is low. I'm enjoying the breeze, and the sunsets, and the salty mist that finds its way onto my face while I'm drinking a beer and watching the Rams play a pre-game.

This place is my castle. My home. My world.

And no one knows about it but me.

Not my father, who hasn't bothered to call me in more than a decade. Not my friends, who have no idea what I'm doing nine days out of ten. Not even my mother, who only visits me in the Del Mar house because if she's going to set foot in the state that birthed my bastard of a father, she wants to hear the horses run as she drinks on the terrace.

It's big, and modern, and has six lounge chairs lined up in front of the glass terrace wall that separates me from the Pacific Ocean. It's got a rooftop terrace with a fire pit. And a lap pool surrounded by tall palms that make music when the wind catches the long, slender fronds in just the right way.

There are solar lights along the polished concrete walkway that leads from the front of the lot on the street all the way back to the beach. And there are surfboards leaning up against the wall of the house next door. All I have to do is walk by, grab one, and slap that sucker down onto the foam.

And the light. Holy fucking shit, the light. You never know what color it will be. Maybe pink in the mornings, coming from the east—it shines in through the front bedrooms and lights up the whole upstairs. Or deep red, or orange, or yellow in the evenings when the world moves west towards the night.

It's like a fucking fairy tale.

And the best thing of all is the constant roar of the monster outside. The power the ocean commands. It's like a general barking orders twenty-four hours a day. Orders like, *Hear me. See me. Know me.*

I don't take orders very well, but those kinds of orders I can handle.

Hear me. See me. Know me.

I can relate to that.

People know me as Mr. Mysterious. The tall one. The dark one. The scary one. But only one person on this earth understands Paxton Vance. And she is tucked away on the breeding farm she bred me on. She hears me. She sees me. She knows me.

My mother is the only woman I trust.

I have heard it all, seen it all, known it all when it comes to people.

And none of it is good.

People are bad. That is the lesson she taught me early using my own father as an example.

People are bad.

You keep your head down, you do your job, and you go to bed alone for as long as you can stand it. Those are the truths of my world.

And she was right, wasn't she? Three years out of the protective environment of private education and rolling hills covered in gourmet grass and I was looking straight down the barrel of a very dirty reality of prison, public shame, and regrets.

The front door buzzer rings out into the house, so I set my beer down on the coaster protecting the glass-top end table and shuffle my bare feet past the dining room, down the stairs into the courtyard, past the lap pool and the palm trees, up the stairs into the front house, and cover the distance to the door at a jog.

Don't want her to think I'm not home.

I smile at that.

Don't want her to think I stood her up.

I chuckle at that.

Don't want to keep her waiting.

I get to the door, stop and look at myself in the hall mirror—tanned golden brown, muscles making the perfect outline, hair tousled and messy from surfing this morning—and open it up.

"Hey," I say.

"Mr. Brown," she says, with a wink. "Nice to finally see you again." She holds a large paper sack with a receipt stapled to it out for me to take.

I grab it, then move aside. "Come in, let me find my wallet." I make a half turn, then turn back. "Hey, you've never seen the house, have you?"

"Nope," she says, blushing a little.

We've been flirting all summer. A little wink here. A coy smile there. I have no idea who she is other than the take-out girl from Buster's Surf Subs. I don't even know her name. All I know is that she drives a classic powder-blue VW Bug and she smells delicious every time I see her.

"Well, look around if you want. Go find the view. I'll just be a second. I think my wallet is upstairs on the beach side."

I jog away, knowing full well she is checking out my ass, my tightly muscled back, the curve of my shoulders.

The ladies can't help it. I'm quite a specimen.

I don't ever leave the Colony in anything other than a suit or tactical gear. But when I answer the door for take-out girl, I am nothing but a half-naked surf bum.

"OK," she says, a little excitement in her voice.

I know where my wallet is. It *is* upstairs on the beach side. I know that because I put it there on purpose.

Take-out girl has been coming here all summer to drop off my food. I order from Buster's at least once a week. More, if I'm home. Work has been pretty busy recently, so I've missed her the past two weeks.

Time to make up for it.

I pass the pool, take the stairs three at a time back into the beach-side house, then hook a left up more stairs where the master bedroom is.

My wallet is on the bed.

I walk over to it, pick it up, and I'm just about to go out onto the terrace to wait for her to find the ocean so I can look down at her from above when she says, "Wow. Look at that fucking view."

I whirl around.

Now… I planned how this might go. And while I did place the wallet on the bed on purpose, it wasn't done with the presumption that she'd follow me up here. I figured she'd linger in the hallway for a minute, get a glimpse of the pool on the other side of the guest house, then wander down that way, admiring the palm trees as she looked up at the sky. Then make her way towards the living room and kitchen where the money shot lives.

Once you see the waves crashing twenty feet away, your feet have no choice. You move towards that call of *hear me, see me, know me.*

Her feet do indeed travel and cross the required distance. As she brushes past me, I catch her scent. It's something sweet. Almost innocent. Strawberries, maybe. A milkshake. A bakery.

Sugar, I realize. She smells like sugar.

It's so opposite of everything she appears to be. She's got a black biker jacket on, cut to the shape of a woman. It's been cool the past few days, some afternoon rain, but it's not cold enough for this jacket. It hangs off her shoulder a little, giving me a glimpse of honey-bronze skin and the thin strap of her tank top, which has tiny silver spikes as accents. The jacket has patches sewn on it. Colorful ones, mostly with skulls and motorcycles. But only pictures, no writing on them. And it has zippers. They jingle, along with the zippers

11

on her black leather boots. Not Doc Martens. Something flashier than that. Some kind of cross between a biker and a cowboy boot. Her tanned legs are bare and long. Her thighs disappear under a short black and white tartan skirt that reminds me of an inappropriate school-girl uniform.

When she reaches for the top of the glass railing, a million little silver bracelets slip out from under her cuff and sing to me.

She sighs. Long and soft. "God, I love the ocean. I grew up in the mountains, mostly. On a farm." She laughs—loudly—and turns away from the water, leans back against the railing. Like she's posing for a photo.

She's so damn pretty, she could be a model.

"You're so lucky."

"Yeah?" I ask, wanting very badly to tuck a stray piece of jet-black hair behind her ear so I can see her face better. Her makeup matches her outfit. Dark, dramatic eyes. Eyelashes so long, I'm not sure how she sees past them. And full, glossy pink lips.

The pink lips throw me a little. It's like her scent. Something counter to what she appears.

"What's your name?" I ask.

"Cinderella," she says.

And maybe, coming from anyone else, at any other time, that might come off as ridiculous. But now, right here in this moment, it seems… inevitable.

"Of course it is," I say, walking towards her. She has to tilt her head up as I approach because I'm tall and she is just average height for a woman. Her neck is long and graceful, like a ballerina's.

How many other things can she possibly be? All wrapped up into this one unique package?

"Why am I lucky?" I ask, leaning on the railing, trying my best not to let her know how interested I am.

She draws in a deep breath and turns with me. We study the beginnings of a sunset for a moment. "This place, right?"

"I like it," I say. "But it's just a place."

"Yeah, but not everyone gets to have all this, you know."

"Where do you live?" I ask, turning my head to look at her. "It can't be that far away. No one drives into Malibu to work as a take-out girl."

"I was sharing a house with some friends for the summer."

"Summer's just about over," I say.

"Yeah." She sighs. "I know. I'm leaving tomorrow."

"Oh," I say, surprised at the level of regret I feel. "Where to? Back to school? You go to college? UCLA?"

"No. I'm done with college."

"Oh," I say again. "You look young."

"I know." She laughs. "I'm twenty-three. Just turned."

"Where *did* you go to college?"

"UCLA," she says. "You guessed right."

And I don't know why, but I know it's a lie. "What did you major in?"

"Mechanical engineering."

I spit out a laugh.

"What?" she says, turning to face me. But even though her protest comes off slightly offended, her eyes come off totally playful. "I don't look like an engineer?"

"Not even a little bit, sugar."

13

She tries to hold in a grin, fails, and turns her head away. "Well, I am," she says firmly.

"Then why the take-out job? Shouldn't you be working for some firm or something?"

"I'm not ready to settle down yet."

"No?"

"No."

"Where will you go tomorrow?" I ask.

She looks at me. Dead straight in the eyes. And says, "I'm moving in here with you."

CHAPTER THREE
CINDY

Paxton Vance, AKA Mr. Brown to me, doesn't laugh and I know I've played every card right these past several weeks. I knew he was interested the very first time I came to deliver him food. Two sandwiches. One foot-long roast beef with extra mayo, lettuce, and tomato. One foot-long grilled chicken with avocado and ranch. Both on white. He always gets the same thing.

He drives a current-year black Audi A7, which surprises me since it's luxury, but not up to what his standard should be. He bought this house cash six years ago, which would make him just a little bit older than me at the time, and he paid fourteen million for it.

He's a Leo, which is complementary to my Gemini. And his birthday just passed three weeks ago. He was out of town for it and didn't celebrate with a foot-long.

He likes to cook and last night he grilled sea bass on the rooftop deck, then ate alone as he watched the sun set.

"With me?" he says, unfazed.

"I think I'd like to get to know you better, Mr. Mysterious." Which is a lie. One of several I just told him. I know everything about him already. I've been studying him for years, just biding my time. Malibu was the perfect place to make my move though, so I waited. He usually rents the house out in the summer. "Better than I already do, anyway," I say, winking at him.

"Oh, fuck," he says. "Who the hell are you?" His tone has changed from fun and flirty to dead-ass serious.

"Don't get crazy, Paxton," I say, using my secret coy smile on him. He draws in a breath like he wants to say something, but changes his mind and stays quiet. "I'm not here to mess with you. I'm just here to meet you."

"So you did," he says, in that low growly voice. "Now what?"

"Now…" I shrug. "We begin."

"What are we beginning?" he asks.

"A beautiful relationship." And then, before he can laugh, I play the next card. "Working relationship, Mr. Vance. Working."

"I don't need an engineer, sweetheart. So I'm not sure what exactly we'll be working on."

"Oh, silly. That was a lie." I laugh. "Just to fill the space. A placeholder. I wasn't sure if this conversation would go the way I planned, so—"

"The way you planned?"

"—so I wanted to keep things neutral just in case."

"In case what?" His voice rises slightly, but not much. I know Paxton Vance well enough from spying to know he doesn't fly off the handle or overreact. His style is calm. Cool. Completely at ease.

"Just in case we didn't get this far into the conversation. You're going to hire me, Pax. I know that. You don't realize it yet, but you will."

"I'll ask again, just for the sake of the game," Pax says in that serious *I don't fuck around* voice. "What will I hire you to do? Bring me food?"

I don't even miss a beat. "I'll be your assistant, of course. You need help. I've been watching you—"

"Watching me?"

Oh, oh, oh—is that a little freakout I hear coming? Maybe? Possibly? Will Mr. Mysterious really lose control so easily?

"I think you better leave, Cinderella. Or whatever your real name is."

"That's my real name, all right. My mom had a thing for Disney princesses. She named me and my sisters after them. And since I'm the youngest, and no parent in their right mind wants to name their kid Cinderella, I got stuck with it. Oh, how I wish I was born first. My oldest sister, Aurora,got the normal name."

"Disney?" He bellows out a laugh so loud, some dog-walking guy down on the beach looks up at us.

"Pax," I say, taking his hand. He looks down at our newly entwined fingers, startled. "I'm good at what I do, I promise. You need me. You really do."

"Your occupation is? Stalker?" Another laugh. This is going well.

"Private investigator with firearms permit. My daddy taught me to shoot, so you don't have to worry about me and weapons. I can do it all. Handguns—even a .45—shotgun, high-powered rifle. I have my own Kevlar and I've been doing mixed martial arts since I was nine."

"Where... how... the fuck did you get a license? You're a baby."

"Shhhiiit," I say. "I started working for Daniel Stow when I was eighteen. I logged my four thousand hours by the time I was twenty. I graduated from high school when I was

17

sixteen. So by the time I moved to California for college, I had two years of undergrad done. I, sir, have a master's degree in criminology, law, and society from UC Irvine."

"I thought you were an engineer."

"And you believed me!" I say, excited. "See how good I am!"

"And you did not work for Daniel Stow. I know Daniel Stow. Hate that motherfucker too."

"I know. He talks about you all the time. Which is where I got the idea to meet you. He hates you back, in case you're wondering."

That's another lie. Not the hate part—I think everyone hates this guy but me—the idea part. But no need to bombard poor Mr. Mysterious with the truth at this point. I've got him eating out of my hand.

"What does he say about me?" Paxton says, an angry look crossing his face.

"Oh, the usual," I say, waving a hand, like that's neither here nor there. "Unstable, mean… *guilty*. But I was intrigued. And the more I learned about you, Pax, the more intrigued I became. So I started following you."

"Jesus fucking Christ. I'm gonna need a restraining order." He grabs that dark, wavy hair for a second with both fists, like he's losing his mind.

"You need me. I know you need me. I'm good. So…" I beam a smile at him. "I'm your new assistant."

He's got me by the arm and he's dragging me back into the house.

"Where are we going?" I ask as I try not to trip down the stairs.

"You're leaving."

"I'm not leaving! I just got here!"

"Your boss at the sandwich shop is looking for you. You gotta go. And I'm never calling there for takeout again."

"I don't have a boss!" I yell. "I own the shop!"

"What?" At least he stops. We're all the way down by the pool now. And shit. I had that master bedroom right in the palm of my hand two seconds ago and now look. All the way back downstairs. "You own it? How the fuck—"

"Paxton," I say sternly. "I'm going to need you to focus. OK? Listen. To. Me."

"Who the fuck—"

"I'm Cinderella Vaughn." God, another lie. But it has to be done. He cannot know I'm his best friend's baby sister, now can he? That would pretty much ruin everything. "I'm a licensed private investigator with a firearms permit. And I'm your new partner."

"You said assistant!"

"We can start there. Sure."

"No," he says. "You're leaving, I'm forgetting this whole thing, and—"

I yank my arm from his grip and cross my arms over my chest. "I'm not leaving. We're in business together now."

"Is this how you weaseled your way into Daniel's business too?"

"Weaseled?" I sigh. God, he's just not getting it. "I'm not *weaseling*. And God, no, I never fucked Daniel. Gross. He's old enough to be my grandfather."

"Fucked?"

"Paxton, do you always have to ask so many questions? Why are you so clueless? We are soulmates. Get it? This is fate slapping your face. I'm fate."

19

"You're crazy." He laughs.

"No," I say firmly. "My methods are unorthodox, yes. But so are yours. So you see, we're perfect for each other."

I smile, my speech complete. Not exactly how I rehearsed it, but close enough.

"The house with the friends?" he asks.

I hold my thumb and pointer fingers close together. "Teeny, tiny lie."

"Leaving tomorrow?"

"Lie. I own that house."

"How the fuck do you own a beach house in Malibu? And a sandwich shop?"

"My mommy and daddy are rich. Isn't that how you got your money?" Why is he wasting time on this trivial bullshit? He should be dragging me back up into that bedroom so he can fuck me against the window.

"No," he growls.

"Yes," I say back. "Your father is Charlie Vance. Your mother is Mariel Hawthorne. They have billions more dollars than my family."

"I earn my money, Cinderella."

Oh, God. I have dreamed about him saying my name like that. "I like to earn mine too!" I squeal. "See how much we have in common?"

"You're crazy," he says, pointing a finger at me.

"I lick my lips and imagine myself sucking on it."

"You just said that out loud."

"I did?" I laugh. "Oh, well, I have a habit of that. Speaking my thoughts out loud. It's weird at first, but you'll get used to it. See, when you're named after a fictional character you get all sorts of ideas about who you are. So when I was a kid

I used to imagine myself as a character in a book and everything I did, I sort of narrated. I was practicing for telling stories in the future."

"Lies, you mean?"

"No, no, no, listen. Stories. Like… I'd be walking around the farm in the winter and I'd be all, 'Her boots made a crunching noise as she passed over the snow.' I narrated my life. I'd be all, 'Her father's motorcycle sounded like the thunder of wings and the pounding of hooves.' We had a lot of bikes at our house. And horses. So don't judge my similes."

"Am I dreaming right now? Am I having a stroke?"

"No," I exclaim. "This is real, Pax. That's what's so great about it. This is all real. We did it," I say, sighing with relief.

"Did *what?*"

"Found each other. Now we'll be together forever."

CHAPTER FOUR

PAXTON

She's nuts. I grab her arm again, tugging her along with me—ever careful not to be too rough, lest I get slapped with a rape charge again—and stop at the front door.

"I understand," she says. "I get it. It's weird coming face to face with your soulmate. So I'm going to give you some time—"

"Great," I mumble, throwing the door open. "See ya around, sugar. Watch out for falling tiaras or dropped shoes or…" Fuck it. I got nothing for this.

I slam it closed and engage the chain lock. I haven't used that thing in… ever. The house is wired up from top to bottom, courtesy of an alarm company Oliver recommended. And thank God for motion detectors. Because I'm making sure everything is armed tonight, boy.

Fuck.

I take a deep breath and realize she left my sandwiches here and I forgot to pay her.

Oh, well. She's the boss, right? She can't get fired. Besides, she owes me those two sandwiches as far as I'm concerned.

Crazy fucking girl.

I grab the paper sack and walk back to the beach side of the house, taking a seat on the terrace.

I eat, trying to get the weird girl out of my mind. Why today? After so long without a girl, why do I have to get horny and decide I'd like to fuck today?

Well, I picked the wrong girl. And isn't that the story of my life? Jesus. Has there ever been a good one?

No.

No. I am a crazy bitch magnet. Every single one of them has been certifiable.

I tried to tell myself I'm just one of those charismatic men, the kind who attract followers and whatnot. Charming and handsome. I can't help that a majority of women find me irresistible.

It's why I played that game in the first place, right?

Well, isn't that sweet. Does everything have to come back to *her?* That fucking bitch who tried to ruin my life?

Forget about it, Pax. Just eat your dinner, take a shower, and think about surfing tomorrow morning.

So I do.

And I don't even wonder if the food is poisoned until I'm scarfing down the last bite of the chicken avocado ranch.

Isn't that the preferred method of killing enemies in fairy tales?

It wasn't. Poisoned, I mean. Because I feel fine when I wake up at dawn and grab a cup of coffee before I hit the waves. I pull my spring suit up my body and slip my arms in, flexing my muscles a little to get comfortable, then get my favorite board from the side of the house and jog down the sand. It's not exactly cold this morning, maybe sixties. But it's clear that summer is just about over and all the tourists have gone home because there are only about half a dozen guys out waiting on waves.

I run into the surf, drop onto the board, and start paddling.

I don't talk to anyone, but I know all their faces. The middle-aged dude who lives a few houses down. He's a year-round guy. Lived here when I moved in, and I've never said more than ten words to him at a time, so I have no idea what he does, other than surf every morning and leave his rooftop terrace hatch unlocked—even when he's not home. Finding that out was a happy accident when I was drunk one night and decided I could jump from roof to roof. I got tired at his house and discovered he doesn't lock his hatch. He's got a hot wife, too. Probably some model from days gone by, because she's attractive in that beachy California kind of way even though she's got to be pushing fifty.

The two teen actors. I only know they're actors because I did background checks on those hoodlums last year. They have a house in Burbank—not too far from Mr. Corporate, now that I think about it—and don't live here full-time.

Then there's the three twenty-somethings who wear suits during the day, just like me, and all drive cliché cars, just like mine. They live next to old dude with hot wife. They share that house and throw a lot of parties. I had to check them out too because the police came once and that is the kind of shit I need to know about.

But that was last year and since then, no more problems.

They all nod at me when I turn around and sit up on my board to take a look around and admire my house.

I love this place. It's more home than home.

25

And that's when I spot another surfer. Even though it's barely dawn and the morning haze is cluttering up the visibility, I know who the newcomer is immediately.

Her.

Bakery girl. I wonder if she smells like sugar covered in ocean salt water?

Her dark hair is pulled back into a long ponytail and her spring suit is white with black stripes on the arms.

She paddles straight for me.

I look around, weigh all my options and decide not to make a big deal about it when I've got six witnesses who probably wonder on a regular basis who I am and why I'm so mysterious.

No way. If this bitch thinks I'll put on a show for the locals, she's got another thing coming.

"Good morning," she yells—so fucking loud—when she gets over the breakers.

I glance at the other guys, notice they're noticing us, and take a deep breath when one of them paddles closer.

"Hey," he says, once he knows I can hear him. "Do you know that chick?"

"Why?" I growl.

"I've seen her around the neighborhood. Fucking fine, man. You dating her?"

"I don't do dates." I snort.

"Good," he says, turning himself around in the water. "Because I'm hitting that shit right the fuck now, bro. This was just a courtesy call."

I narrow my eyes at his back as he paddles to his friends. He's one of the party-house guys.

26

"She's all yours," I call after him. He doesn't answer. Asshole.

"Pax!" the sugar princess yells.

I have to take a deep breath and count to ten so I don't bark, *Shut the fuck up.* I paddle towards her so she won't announce my goddamned name to all these strangers again and when we're about twenty feet apart, I say, "Keep your voice down."

"Sorry," she says, sitting up on her board and swiping the long strands of black hair out of her eyes. "Forgot. You've got that whole Mr. Mysterious thing going on."

"Jesus fuck. Will you shut up?"

"They can't hear me," she says, waving a hand over towards the party-house guys. "I saw him talking to you and I didn't hear a thing. What did he say, anyway? You both looked over at me after."

"He says he wants to fuck you."

"Oh." She laughs. "Did you tell him I'm taken?"

"No," I growl. "I don't give a shit who you fuck. I don't even know you."

"Yet."

"Not *yet*, princess. I'm not going to know you *ever*. In fact, I know too much about you already. Don't tell me any more details because I'm not interested."

"You sure about that?" she says, looking over her shoulder at an incoming wave. "And don't call me princess." She frowns for a moment before turning it back into a smile. "My oldest sister claimed that nickname."

"Aurora?" I laugh, trying to decide if I should take this wave just to get away from her. But party guy number one

27

looks like he's getting ready, and it's cutting away from me, so I don't.

"You remembered!" Sugar says. "*Yes*. See, we're gonna get along so well, you and I. So, so well."

"Look, Cinderella." I have to shake my head at her name. I can't even take this conversation seriously calling her that. "I'm a private kind of guy, as you *know*." I stress that last word, just to make sure she understands I'm pissed off about this bullshit. "So you're gonna go your way and I'm gonna go my way, and we're both gonna forget any of this ever happened. I'm not interested."

But just as the last of my words are coming out of my mouth, she starts furiously paddling, her attention on an incoming wave. The swell lifts me, carries me forward a little, and then I bob back down. But Cinderella is already up, weaving back and forth, riding it out.

She's good. Better than I thought she'd be. I kinda figured she was just playing out here. Trying to get my attention, but no. The girl surfs.

And owns a sandwich shop. And a house. In Malibu.

I don't know. Something about this is all kinds of wrong. All the little red flags are waving at me. All the little alarm bells are going off.

Hmmm.

She ditches the wave near the beach, and she's getting ready to paddle back when the party-house guy who wants to make a move surfs right up next to her and falls into the water. When he comes up, they are both laughing. Talking. Smiling.

Oh, is that how she's gonna play this? Get me jealous?

I don't do jealous.

They paddle back together and she hangs out with all three party guys after that, completely ignoring me.

I catch a few waves, then head back to the house.

Games, man.

I can play with the best of them. But I just don't do it anymore.

CHAPTER FIVE

CINDY

Paxton Vance was born Paxton Nathaniel Vance to Mariel Hawthorne and Charles Vance thirty-one years ago. His parents never married, but his mother did give him his father's last name—against his father's wishes.

After all the snooping I've done on him over the years, that one little tidbit says more about Paxton's family life than anything else. More than the non-existent child support payments, more than the lack of summer vacations with the paternal side of the family, more than the occasional visits Charles Vance took back to Kentucky every few years.

Why did his father even bother, I wonder? It was clear from the beginning he was never interested in his unexpected progeny. Charles Vance has a huge family. Seven brothers and sisters, although four of them are only half-siblings. His own father was a known serial philanderer. So it's almost fate that he had the same inclination.

But unlike Paxton's father, his grandfather could afford the bastard children he spawned. A hit movie in the late Seventies secured his place in Hollywood history. He had several greater roles after that, until the early two thousands, when he was just too old to pull off that bad-boy leading man character anymore.

Since then he's been quiet, out of the public eye, and from what I can gather, a full-fledged alcoholic. Just like his son, Charles.

Mariel Hawthorne, on the other hand, has never been a casual relationship kind of woman. Which is why it never made sense that she allowed known deadbeat playboy Charles to seduce her in her early twenties.

I got her school records—Mariel was an overachiever at the very best all-girls' boarding school in New England—and every teacher made remarks on her private nature, standoffish attitude, and serious goal-setting.

Her family comes from a long line of Kentucky thoroughbred breeders. They don't train them, they just buy and breed them. And Mariel seemed determined to keep her father's legacy as a producer of some of the most famous racehorses in American history alive.

Limitless Farms, under the management of Mariel, has produced eleven Breeders' Cup winners and nine Kentucky Derby winners, just to name a few. Last year at the spring sale, she bought four mares and six yearling colts with purer bloodlines than the Queen of England. She spent eleven million dollars at that sale.

But she also sold ten pregnant brood mares and six fillies and she came out ahead more than ten million.

Her net worth places her among the very richest and powerful women in the world, if not history.

And ninety-nine point nine-nine percent of the population of people on this planet has no idea who she is. She is not a one-percenter. She is so much richer than any hipster label can describe.

And she got it all from horses.

I checked. That woman is as clean as Charles Vance is dirty. Limitless Farms prides itself on its one-hundred-percent transparency policy. Publishing her yearly earnings even though it is not a publicly traded firm.

I'm not sure what to make of that, honestly. Why would such a private woman publish her net worth so openly? Every sale and purchase is public. She goes to the spring and fall auctions at Keeneland as herself. She does not hire someone to appraise the horses and bid for her via internet or phone. She sits her ass in that pavilion and raises her numbered paddle like everyone else. And she meets with prospective buyers in person. I know, I got a meeting with her at the on-site stables at Belmont last year, feigning interest in a breeding contract.

She's quick though. She took one look at me—I was using a false name of course—and deduced I was a nobody not worth her time. And although she was pleasant and smiled the entire time, she was very clear that her services were out of my budget.

But those were some of the most interesting five minutes of my life.

That is Paxton's mother.

Someone he cares very deeply for. In fact, I don't think it would be presumptuous of me to say that Mariel Hawthorne is the most influential person in my Paxton's life.

He's a mama's boy.

God, that is so damn cute. I want to squeeze him, it's so cute.

It also explains a lot about his behavior over the past ten years. His demeanor, as well.

Imagine being twenty-one-year-old Paxton Vance. Senior year at Brown University. Majoring in business and at the top of his class. And having to make that phone call home to explain that he is one of the infamous Mister Browns.

I don't like imagining that conversation actually. I don't think it involved tears, or anything so dramatic as that. I don't think it was filled with screaming or accusations. Or even apologies.

I think it involved the words, "I will fix this. I will make it right."

Fix it.

The words are in my thoughts before I even realize their implication.

That's what he does now. For money. He fixes things. He hides the dirt, sweeps it under the rug, and makes everything go away.

But his own problem has never been fixed. Never cleaned up. And he hates the fact that he has put that smudge on his mother's pristine family name.

When people hire me to find things, the very first thing I do is find a motive for the contract. Why do they need me? What are they after?

Most of the time I get hired to spy on a spouse. One party thinks the other is cheating. They want answers, they want confirmation, they want proof.

So when I decided to spy on Paxton, I needed to assign myself a motivation. Why do I need to know about him? Why does he intrigue me?

It was my brother, Oliver, who got me interested in Pax. They weren't friends when they were accused. Not even close. Oli was a first-year, fresh out of pledge week, and had only been living in the house for two weeks when the accusation happened.

He didn't tell *me*, of course. No one told me anything. I'm the baby of the family. Five years younger than Oliver and fifteen years younger than my oldest sister Aurora—Rory, as we call her.

But I was the only one still living at home when it all happened. Oliver came back to the farm, called my parents into the office, and closed the door. I had that office wired for years by that time. My father and his secret life have always intrigued me. And even though I learned absolutely nothing about my father and his past with that wire-tap, I did learn the truth about Oliver and some of what happened that night at Brown.

I watched the news relentlessly over the next several months. People showed up—people like Ford Aston, and his son, Five. Ford ducked out of this little problem at Five's insistence, but then Five and Oliver went away, came back, went away again. I snooped into every public record I could find about each of the Misters, and when I came up with Paxton Vance's biography, well… color me obsessed.

My older sister Ariel is a computer genius. She and Oliver got interested in computer coding watching Five Aston develop apps when he was a teenager. Five made a ton of them, and a ton of money, before he left home in the middle of ninth grade to attend Oxford.

Five is the real genius in my family. Ariel and Oliver are just his protégées. I got lucky because I'm the baby. Everyone ignores the baby. So I watched what Ariel and

Oliver were doing and did my best to keep up until I talked Ariel into teaching me more when I was thirteen.

And even though I wish I could've wire-tapped the Aston residence to get the full story behind Five and his infamous father, Ford, I never needed a wire-tap to understand the full extent of what Five does with his spare time. Because I grew up watching it with my own eyes.

Hacking.

Oliver and Ariel got into some trouble when they were teens. Ariel is just a few years older than Oli, so they were fast and tight all growing up. They had a match-making business when Ariel was in high school and one of their teenage clients was threatening to expose the whole scheme.

Until Ariel called in Five.

Then it all went away.

He's kind of a fixer too. And I have wondered more than once if Mr. Mysterious is working for Five.

But I don't think so. There is no evidence of that. Five is a work-alone kind of guy, unless he needs Oliver's help.

So back when the Misters were accused of rape ten years ago, Five asked Ariel and Oliver to hack into all the Mister records to see what they were dealing with, and I found the files on Ariel's computer that Christmas when she left her laptop open while she was taking a shower.

I saw everything, but it was Mr. Mysterious who captured my full attention.

Mysterious didn't even cover how to describe him back then. It wouldn't come out that he was the son of Charles Vance for another few weeks. And by that time I knew everything Ariel did about him.

His story was the stuff movies are made of. Fairy tales and conspiracy theories.

But I was only thirteen. I was ill-equipped to do my own snooping. And that's part of the reason I went down this path of private investigator.

I needed more information than Ariel had. I needed to know everything about this man.

And now I do.

Almost.

I'm so close. I know all about his family. His mother and his father. Their wins and losses. I know about his business. I know what he does, who he does it for. I know so much more than anyone else in this world. Maybe even more than his own mother.

But I don't know all of it. That one crucial piece of information is missing.

What happened that night?

What was Paxton's role in that accusation?

I need this. I need it like I need water and air. Like I need *him*.

Five was quick to shut them all up. So their stories were all secret from day one. But I knew some of Oliver's story and even though I found no proof, there has to be a connection between Oliver and Mr. Mysterious beyond the charge. Some how, some way, their stories conjoin and that's why they have been tight friends ever since.

At least… that's what I think. I'm not sure, but I think I'm right.

Why else would a loner like Pax seek out my brother as a BFF? There's a three-year age difference, which is no big deal now, but back then, seniors didn't hang out with freshmen. I can't figure it out. These elusive details are still missing.

But not for long.

I'm going to get to the bottom of this if it's the last thing I do. I'm going to get to the bottom of it and I'm going to do that by being the most important person in Paxton's life. His best friend. His lover. His confidante.

And no amount of pushing me away, or feigned disinterest, or logical reasoning will deter me.

I will figure out his secret. I will figure out what happened that night. I will find all the evidence, I will put all the puzzle pieces together, and I will give him a gift to seal the deal.

I will make it right for all of the Misters.

But most of all, I will be the person who gives Paxton Vance all the information he needs to call home and tell his mother that it is done. It is fixed. His name, and by extension, hers, is cleared.

I will save him. Because he really *needs* saving. He needs to stop this fixing he's been doing. He needs to stop dealing with the low-life Hollywood scum. Stop erasing their mistakes in some desperate, unconscious attempt to try to erase his own.

Mr. Mysterious' business is about to come to a screeching halt and he will thank me later.

Even if he hates me for it now.

CHAPTER SIX

PAXTON

For a mystery girl, Cinderella sure does get around the town of Malibu. After the not-so-chance meeting in the surf, she was everywhere. At the carwash last Tuesday when I pulled in to get my car detailed. She was laughing and talking with Raul, the owner, like they were old friends. *I'm* his old friend, not her.

The next day she was in Big Kahuna's Surf shop picking out a new bikini when I took my board in to get a fin repaired. I know Big pretty well, but he's not in the shop much doing repairs, so he came in special for me. And did he greet me like the friend I am? No. That old bum only had eyes for my sugar-smelling stalker.

The day after that it was the dentist—and my hygienist talked with her from the next room the entire time. I heard all about her dates with party guy. Then the doctor came in and proceed to flirt with her for seven minutes as I waited (not so patiently) for my check-up. Then, yesterday, she was back in the ocean with me. Paddling around in her new bathing suit, ass cheeks practically hanging out.

She was with the party guys, not me, this time.

And as much as I'd like to say it didn't bother me, it bothered me.

"Yeah," I say into my phone. "I'd like a foot-long chicken avocado ranch and a foot-long roast beef classic."

"Your address?"

Cinderella didn't answer the phone. "16 Colony Road."

"Be about thirty minutes."

"Thanks," I say, then end the call.

Yup. I'm gonna have it out with her as soon as she gets here with my sandwiches.

I open up my laptop to see if I can find any dirt on her while I wait, when my calendar pops up.

I'm just about to click it closed and open up my browser when I notice something.

Detailing appointment on Tuesday.

Surf shop appointment on Wednesday.

Dentist appointment on Thursday.

Did she hack my calendar?

I snort out a laugh. Then another. "Nah," I say. "No way."

But the more I think about it the more it makes sense. Cinderella Vaughn hacked my ass. She's been following me around town.

I close my laptop and pace. I pour another drink and check my watch. She'll be here with my food in five minutes.

I go to the front house and peer through the upstairs window and wait. But instead of the powder-blue VW bug, a small white pick-up with the Buster's logo on the side pulls up.

And it's not Cinderella who gets out with my sandwiches.

I jump down the guest house stairs three at a time and land with a thump just as the doorbell rings. I unlock it and pull it open with a rush.

The kid on the other side jumps back a step, then laughs. "Shit, dude. Scared the fuck out of me."

He looks like he's about seventeen, needs a good dermatologist, and could use about twenty more pounds on his six-foot frame.

He starts rummaging in his pocket for the takeout ticket and says, "That'll be fifteen—"

"Where's Cinderella?"

"Huh?" he asks, holding out my receipt.

"Your boss?"

"My boss?" He laughs again, more nervous this time. "You mean that weird hot chick? She's at a party tonight." He nods his head off to my right. "Down the street that way."

"Party guy's house," I say, but not to him. Just to myself.

"What?" Skinny Kid looks confused.

"Nothing," I say, pulling a twenty out of my pocket. "Keep the change." I thrust the bill into his empty hand, take my bag of food, and slam the door.

That little sneaky, flirty bitch.

I jog past the pool, drop the sandwiches on a side table, take the steps in the main house three at a time, and go all the way up to the rooftop deck.

The music has been playing in the background for about an hour. Nothing too loud or thumpy, so I've mostly ignored it. But now that I'm up here, it's pissing me off. There are at least two dozen people crowded onto the party guys' roof deck. They have a double lot—assholes—so their deck is twice the size of mine.

And there she is. Not wearing the leather jacket. No. Wearing nothing but that same bikini she had on yesterday.

41

Has she been hanging out with these guys all fucking week? After she hacked into my calendar and then stalked me all over Malibu?

Oh, hell no.

These houses down here on the beach are exactly six feet apart. So I jump over to my neighbor's rooftop, walk the ten paces it takes to get to the edge and jump again. There are people on the roof of the third house between me and party guys, and they see me coming, hands up in the air, arms flailing with protests, but I ignore them, keep walking, and jump onto old dude's house before they even realize what's happening.

"I'm calling the police!" someone yells from behind me.

They're renters. So I know they don't know who I am or where I came from. But I do know that the Malibu PD will be here within five minutes if they do call, so I jump one more time and knock over a guy who drops two drinks as he falls.

Amateur.

I push my way through the crowd of partiers, protests coming from all directions now, and stand right in front of little Miss Sugar Cookie.

"Pax," she says, huge, satisfied smile on her face.

She did this to make me jealous. She fucking stalked my ass all week to keep me interested, then accepted an invite to the party house knowing full well I always order food on Friday night if I'm home, and tonight she wouldn't be the one to deliver it.

"I didn't think you'd come." She turns. "You guys," she says, calling for the surfers I've spent the last two months ignoring out in the ocean. "Look, he came!"

"Hey, man," the tall one who asked me if he could nail Cinderella last week says. It comes out amicably enough, but I see the way his eyes are squinting. He probably hasn't gotten far with her yet. She's playing a game, after all. And she's clearly interested in me, so not gonna fuck another dude while she's winning. So that look says, *Stay the fuck away*.

I shoot the same look right back as I take Cinderella's hand and start leading her towards the stairs.

"Hey," party guy says, standing up real fast. "What the fuck do you think you're doing?"

I look at Cinderella, who smiles, then over my shoulder at party guy. He looks like he finds the idea of a fight interesting. "Taking her home."

"She's not going home, asshole. You are. She's here with me."

I shrug and look down at Cinderella. She smiles again. "Um, hey, Matthew... I hope you didn't get the wrong idea this week. I love hanging out with you. It's been a lot of fun. But I'm dating Pax."

"Since when?" Matthew asks. Those eyes of his are practically slits right now.

Cinderella opens her mouth to say something, but I clamp a hand over it to shut her up. She doesn't need to make this any worse than it is. "None of your fucking business," I answer. "And if I were you, I'd drop it. Just walk away, kid. Just walk away. Because she's playing games with both of us and even though I don't like to be played like that, I do like to win. And this right here is me winning."

He throws a punch. I knew he would.

People are screaming, bodies are shifting. His fist hits me square in the jaw, but it's weak. I don't even feel it. The sirens are blurping down below on the private road, the lights are flashing, and then all hell breaks loose.

I still have a hold of Cinderella's hand, so I tug her towards the edge of the roof. She jumps with me like a motherfucking badass. And we both land on the opposite house at the same time with a thud.

The tourists the next house over are screaming for the cops. Pointing at us. But there is so much hell breaking loose right now, I'm pretty sure all that goes unnoticed. Cinderella has Old Dude's roof terrace hatch open and we jump down into the narrow stairs that lead into a master bedroom and head straight for another set of stairs that brings us down to beach level. No one is here tonight. The place is dark, so we slip out the front and onto the beach, holding hands in the shadows created by the thin line of orange light spreading out on the Pacific Ocean like a carpet.

We walk slowly, but breathing hard, as we casually make our way back down the beach to my house. It's high tide right now, so we are squished up against the front of all the other houses, practically walking underneath the stilts that keep the ocean out of their living rooms. No one calls for us to stop.

I open the glass gate that leads to my beachfront patio, let Cinderella enter before me, then close it up as we leave the party behind.

She flops on the couch. Huge smile on her face. And then pulls her knees up to her chest, squeezing her tits together so they practically fall out of her itty-bitty bikini top. A long, happy sigh comes out from between her perfectly plumped lips. "I knew you'd miss me." She turns her head slightly, looks at me from the corner of her eye. "Eventually."

"Eventually," I huff.

"Ah. I see you got your food." She gets up, grabs the bag of sandwiches off the end table near the stairs, then flops back down. "I'm starving. I'll take the roast beef."

I stare at her for a moment. Consider my options.

Kick her out. Not gonna happen.

Fuck her right now, then send her on her way, satisfied that she's out of my system. Unlikely to pan out the way I imagine.

So we eat dinner. She talks, scarfs that sandwich down like a champ, and I listen to a story about how party-guy Matthew tried to hit on her all week as she laughs.

"I don't find that funny," I say, finishing off my sandwich.

"I know," she says. "You're the jealous type. I was just making sure you've still got a pulse, since you're so quiet."

"Hmm," I say, looking down at my phone to check the security cameras in front of the house on my personal app. "Looks like the cops are gone, so I think that's your cue."

"You're kicking me out? Really?"

"I'm not into you, kid."

"Kid? Please. Come on. I'm twenty-three."

"I'm thirty-one. I'm pretty sure we're not after the same thing. Especially after that freak admission that we're soulmates. There is no happily ever after in my future, I assure you."

"Why? Because you don't deserve one?"

"Shit. You're gonna psychoanalyze me? How about we start with you? You're a crazy stalker. And I'm not interested in your fetish obsession with Mr. Mysterious. I'm just not interested."

She licks mayonnaise off her fingers, crumples up the sandwich paper and stuffs it back into the brown bag. "I think you are. I think you're intrigued with my story."

"Your *lies*, you mean."

"Hey, look, if you're given the name Cinderella at birth you make the most of it. So I like to act my stories out. What's the harm?"

"You're gonna go to prison for hacking."

"You're pressing charges?" She laughs, like this is way more crazy than her behavior.

"I could."

"You won't." She gets up, grabs the paper from my sandwich, stuffs it inside the brown bag, then walks into the kitchen and throws it away.

"What do you want?"

"A night with you."

"Sex?" I laugh so loud, she startles. "You're stalking me so I'll fuck you?"

She shrugs, and my eyes track those huge tits as she does that. "Is that such a bad idea?"

Both her hands go behind her back. Her fingers fumble around for a second, and the bikini top falls forward, slim strings hanging down each side of her breasts. She reaches around behind her neck and a few moments later, the top drops to the floor.

I watch her silently, then get up, walk to the stairs and go up. I turn in the hallway to see what she does next.

She climbs the steps towards me. Slowly. Like she's afraid I might spook and she'll have to chase me down.

But I don't spook.

This is what I wanted, right? Since the first time I saw her at my door with the brown paper bag.

When she reaches the top of the stairs she starts untying the strings of her bottoms. One hand on each hip until they fall to the floor.

And she just stands there. Naked for me. Some spotlight from outside filtering in just enough for me to see the dark outline of her nipples and the seductive curve of her hips.

"What do you want to do now, Mr. Mysterious? Keep playing the game? Or give in and win?"

I picture my mouth on those nipples, my palms wrapped around the swell of her breasts. She bites her lip like she's nervous, but catches herself and stands still. Not moving. No hesitation, or shyness, or uncertainty.

"He looks at me like I'm sustenance."

"What?"

"His face nothing but confusion and lust."

"Seriously? It's story time again?"

"He wants me, I know he does. He sees all of me right now, but it's not enough."

"Stop it," I say. "You hacked into my fucking calendar."

"I'm a tad obsessed with you, sorry."

"What do you want?"

47

"The same thing you do."

"To fuck you senseless and then leave town and forget it ever happened?"

She shrugs. "If that's what you want. But I have so many better ideas."

"Like what?"

"Don't you think we should wait until afterward to talk about it?"

"After what?"

"After you fuck me senseless and we fall asleep in each other's arms."

"If I fuck you senseless you won't like what comes after."

"I'm a big girl, Mr. Vance. I know what I'm getting into."

"I don't think you do."

"Are we gonna stand here talking all night?" She slips a hand between her legs, her fingers moving in small circles over her clit. "Or would you like to see how ready I am to take this to the next level?"

My dick grows despite all the warning bells going off in my mind. And my hand finds my thick shaft through my shorts, automatically fisting it as she watches.

"Let me help you with that," she says, walking forward until she's right in front of me. Her head turns up and I catch the blue of her eyes in that elusive light from somewhere outside. She covers my hand with hers, and then her fingers are unbuttoning my shorts and pulling out my cock.

She smiles as she drops to her knees and I can't stop my hands from fisting her hair and giving it a tug.

Moans from both of us as she takes me in her mouth. My head falls back, hers tilts up. Eyes on me, and only me.

I want to drown in those eyes. They are the ocean outside. They are the power of the waves and the sting of the salt.

"I hope we don't regret this in the morning," I manage to mumble.

She leans back, letting my cock fall from her mouth, her eyes never leaving mine. "I hope we do."

CHAPTER SEVEN
CINDY

"What's that mean?" Paxton asks.

"Shh," I say, putting his hard cock back in my mouth. I lick his tip and then run my tongue up and down his shaft until all thoughts about tomorrow are safely tucked away in some unknown, forgotten place.

He moans and gives my tangled hair in his fist a firm yank, signaling for me to stand.

"Tired of me already, Detective?"

"Detective?" He stares hard at me, those dark eyes of his pure steel. I know what he is. I know what he does. I know what he's done. But I don't care. The way he's looking at me right now wipes all those things away. Besides, I'm no stranger to the underworld. I'm not some innocent girl. It might appear that way on the outside, what with my presumably perfect life on the Shrike Ranch outside Fort Collins, Colorado. My childhood was filled with riding lessons and ballet. I won the St Joseph's spelling bee four years in a row. I was an honor roll student the moment I stepped into high school.

But none of those things are who I am now. They are just where I came from. And seeing me from the outside is nothing like knowing me on the inside.

"Detective," I say again. "You like find things out about people, right? It fits you. Like it fits me."

Paxton is still looking at me with that cold glare. Like he loves and hates me at the same time. "You're not staying the night."

I shrug. "Why would I?"

"I'm just trying to be crystal clear with you... Cinderella. And before this goes any further, I'm gonna need a background check."

"What?" I laugh, my hand still absently pumping his cock.

"Background check, Sugar." He repeats it with more conviction. "You can suck my cock while I run a background check on you. And if you decline, there's the fucking door, sweetheart."

I make a pouty face. It's real too. "You don't trust me."

"Not even a little."

"You think I'm hiding something."

"We're all hiding something. So it's no big deal. I just want to know what that something is going forward."

I place my lips on the tip of his cock, pucker them, and give him a sweet kiss. "Go ahead then. Check me out. I'm real."

He places both hands on my shoulders and steps away. I slide down onto my butt and watch him walk down the stairs and then come back a minute later with a laptop. He beckons me with a finger and passes me in the hallway, takes a seat on the bed, opens his legs, and places the open laptop off to his right side.

"You can stay and watch if you want. If you're confident I won't find anything interesting. You can suck my dick while I run your name and we'll just pretend like this little interlude never happened once I'm finished." He stops, training that glare on me once more. "But if you think I'll find something, even," he says, holding his thumb and pointer finger a minuscule distance apart, "something very small, then I'd advise you to leave now. Because I don't do business with liars."

"So this *is* business?" I smile.

He doesn't. "Everything is business."

I think about this for a moment. What will he say when he really does find out the truth? But I decide that's a problem for another day. He's not going to find anything right now. Not running the name Cinderella Vaughn. I always knew he'd check. I've planned for this moment very thoroughly. He'll find everything he's looking for… and I will stay Cinderella Vaughn in his mind until he gets suspicious and puts all my lies together.

But by that time he'll be hopelessly in love with me. So it won't matter who I really am.

He will fight for us.

"I'll stay," I say, crossing the distance between us and taking a seat between his legs. His cock has softened slightly, but when I wrap my hands around him again, the tip of my tongue doing a seductive dance across the tip of his head, it jumps back to attention.

He starts typing as I try to relax and enjoy the moment.

I have Mr. Mysterious in the palm of my hand. I have his dick in my mouth and once this little expected formality is over, I'll be in his bed.

I don't ever expect to leave that bed. Figuratively speaking. Once Mr. Paxton Vance gets a taste of me, he will never want anyone else.

"Where did you grow up?" he asks, pulling me back from my future.

"Colorado," I say. I can't lie about that. There are many Vaughns in this world, but the Vaughn identity I've attached this name to all over the internet happens to be with my cousins. And they live in Colorado.

"Hmmm," Pax says.

"Hmmm," I moan back, making my throat vibrate as I suck on his cock.

"Jesus," he says, leaning back a little, making his dick fall out of my mouth.

"You don't like it?" I ask, blinking up at him innocently.

"Just give me a second." He goes back to typing. "I have a few friends in Fort Collins. You ever heard of Shrike Bikes?"

"No," I lie. "Should I have?"

"Before your time, maybe," Pax says, absently.

I *am* Shrike Bikes. Baby Shrike, that's me. It's just too funny not to laugh. But I hold it in because the moment is precarious.

"You went to Catholic school?" A snort comes out with the question.

"My parents are very traditional."

"Says here your father owns a tattoo shop. Doesn't sound very traditional to me."

Jesus Christ. He got that info fast. "Haven't you ever heard of those Jesus bikers?"

"Your dad's a Jesus biker?" Pax looks down his nose at me, like I'm totally full of shit.

"Call him up and ask him," I say coolly.

"Hmmm," Pax says, looking back at his screen.

I'm sure if he's found a picture of my Uncle Vic he won't be doing anything as stupid as calling him on the phone. He's a scary motherfucker. All tatted up from back in the day. Still part owner of Sick Boyz Inc., my mother's family-run tattoo shop.

Pax closes the laptop and sets it on the night stand.

"Satisfied?" I ask sweetly.

"No, princess—"

"Don't call me princess. I told you, that nickname belongs to my older sister."

"Aurora?"

"We call her…" I stop myself just in time from saying Rory, which he will surely recognize from his visits to my parents' farm with Oliver over the past few years, and realize I fell into a trap. He has my sister's name. My *real* sister. And of course, none of my cousins are named Aurora.

"Is the third degree over then?" I ask, hoping to God he won't open that laptop back up and go looking for an Aurora Vaughn. That would be bad. Very, very bad. Because Rory's middle name actually *is* Vaughn and she will pop right up, only her last name will be Shrike and my whole plan will go—

"What do they call you then? At home?"

"Sugar," I say, breathing deeply to stop my panic. "They call me Sugar… just like you did." They call me Baby Shrike. But I can't tell him that, now can I? Fuck. How did I get here? I literally had his dick in my mouth and now I'm about to blow my own damn cover with this stupid mistake.

"Sugar what?" Pax asks. "You sounded like there was something else at the end of Sugar. Sugar what?"

"Sugar…" And before I can stop myself, I blurt out… *"Cookie."*

"Cookie?" He laughs.

Oh, fuck. I need to stop talking.

"Yeah," he says, threading his fingers through my long black hair. "Yeah, I can see it, actually. You smell like a fucking bakery. Sugar Cookie it is, then." He leans down to kiss me on the lips.

I look up at him, my eyes filled with… relief, I'm sure. And I'm sure he can tell. I'm absolutely sure he's going to call me on this. I'm positive that he's been digging in Oliver's family history and somewhere along the line he's heard of Cinderella, even though I haven't let my parents call me my given name since I was twelve.

"Sugar Cookie," Paxton says, whispering into my mouth.

"Yes," I squeak out, all sorts of lies flooding my mind as I try to pick just the right one to keep this ruse going.

"My cock is getting cold," he breathes. "I think you better wrap your sweet little mouth around it and keep it warm."

I exhale long and soft as he guides my head back to his waiting dick. And then I relax, take him in my palms, and lick him like he's the best thing I've ever tasted.

His hands leave my hair and my eyes track them as he lifts his shirt over his head and tosses it aside. The muscles in his chest are cut angles, hard and deep enough to cast shadows in the dim light leaking through from outside. My eyes trace the curve of his shoulders as I take him in, my tongue pressing against his long, thick shaft. He closes his eyes for a moment, but opens them back up almost immediately.

"Fuck," he says. "You're damn sweet and pretty, Cinderella. I bet you explode, don't you? I bet you come like a superstar."

My fingers are between my legs, rubbing little circles against the sensitive folds of my pussy.

"I bet you scream, too. Don't you?"

"Mmmmmm," I moan against his skin. But before I even stop humming, he's pulled me up and thrown me face first down on the bed. I squeal with equal parts delight and shock.

Fuck it. Maybe I did mess up, but fuck it. I'm going to enjoy my first time with Paxton Vance. I've been working towards this night for years. I've been fantasizing about him since I was thirteen years old. Everything I've done since I first laid eyes on him in that newspaper article was with this moment in mind.

I don't care what he finds out tomorrow. I don't care if he's pissed off. He will never be able to walk away from me. He will never forget this night.

Paxton Vance will be thinking about the day Cindy Shrike walked into his life 'till death do us part. No matter what I do, no matter what 'I finds out, we are meant to be together.

Now I just need to convince him of that little fact.

"I like it on top," I say.

"Too bad, Sugar. I like you face down so I can play with your asshole while I fuck you from behind. But maybe later I'll let you ride me. If you're good. If you scream for me. If you come at just the right time."

And then he thrusts inside me. So hard, I slide forward on the bed. So deep I gasp with the sharp pain. He rests his chest on my back and whispers in my ear. "Your pussy will get used to my size soon enough, Cinderella. But don't worry, I'll go easy on you tonight since we're on the maiden voyage."

CHAPTER EIGHT

PAXTON

Cinderella's lips pull back in a smile as she looks at me over her shoulder. Her hips thrust backwards, urging me to take her, to keep going. I grab her hair and pull as I ease away, lifting my weight off her back. Her perfectly tanned skin is already dotted with little beads of sweat.

"Don't go too easy on me, Pax. I'm not as fragile as you think. And your cock is the perfect size. You won't hear me complain about that."

"You little slut," I say, letting go of her hair so I can grab her hips. I slam her ass back into my cock, our skin-on-skin contact echoing off the ceiling like a series of slaps as I pound her hard, then harder. She moans, her hands reaching up to grab the white cotton duvet, and then they become fists. Like she's desperate to hold onto something.

I let go of one hip, reaching under her to find her pussy, and begin to strum. Her moans get louder and louder as I increase the friction on her sensitive spot. And just as her back is arching, I stop.

"No, you asshole!" she whines.

But there's no need for her to worry about me leaving her hanging. I flip her over on her back, spread her legs wide, and crawl between them. My hands flatten against the folds of her pussy, pulling them slightly apart... just enough for me to slip my tongue inside and lick.

Her spine arches and her back comes off the bed. I hold her in place at her hips with both hands, fighting her, not letting her escape my swiftly flicking tongue.

"Oh, shit!" she cries. "Shit!" She writhes under the pressure of my punishing lips. Her legs begin to kick, catching a shoulder and a kidney in quick succession.

"Oh, my God! Oh, my God!"

"Be still," I murmur into her wet folds.

"I can't, Pax. Oh, my God. Just make me—"

She screams. Her kicking goes wild, knocking me in the head. I'd laugh, because it's so fucking cute. But her hands clamp down on my shoulders and—

"Aww, fuck!" I yell, as her nails draw blood. "Jesus."

She stills, hands over her heart as she breathes and pants her way through the lingering contractions of her orgasm. Each time a wave hits her, she lifts her hips up and I take the opportunity to kiss her swollen clit.

"I have never—"

"Shh," I say. "I'm not interested in what you have and have not done with anyone but me. Now, be a good little cookie and climb on top, Cinderella. It's time to go to the ball."

She's still breathing heavy as she wiggles herself upright, using my outstretched hand to steady herself. Then she slides her leg over top of me and plants her hands firmly on my chest. My cock is throbbing with anticipation. She has her relief from the build-up, but I've barely started.

"Just lie forward," I say, pulling her face into my neck. "I'll do the rest."

She does as she's told. I like this side of her. The obedient side.

Her mouth seeks out the skin just below my ear and she kisses me like we've been lovers for eternity. I close my eyes for a moment and enjoy this new feeling. There's something very intimate and sexy in that little move.

Her kiss becomes a nip, becomes a bite, and it's on.

I wrap my arms around her back, holding her so tightly to my chest, she's gasping for air, and I pound her from below. My balls slapping up against her ass, her huge breasts smashed against my chest. We are slick with lust, and carnal desire, and the sweet sweat you only get from lovemaking.

I come inside her—forgetting everything I know about safe sex, and unwanted babies—because in that moment I am gone, man. I am in some erotic fucking heaven of my own creation with this little bombshell of a girl who weaseled her way into my life with sandwiches, and jingling boots, and that stupid little powder-blue VW bug.

I am gone.

Later, when she is sleeping beside me and I am looking down on her hot twenty-something body... I realize something.

She's a natural blonde.

My hand slips between her legs, eliciting a sweet moan from her lips as I play with her pussy. And I can't stop myself. I can't stop even if I want to, and I don't. I help myself to more, and more and more as I dip my face between her legs and wonder—as she begins to writhe again—what

61

she might look like if all that jet-black dye was washed out of her hair.

"Huh," I laugh to myself, hours later, when the sun is coming up and my semi-waking dreams are filled with visions of a blonde princess wearing a blue dress.

"What?" she asks lazily, angling her body into the curve of mine like we were made this way.

"You're definitely the bombshell version of a Disney princess."

I feel her smile against my shoulder.

And then it all fades away.

I stumble out of bed, searching for my ringing phone. Cinderella is still sleeping, but all the movement and the damn ringing makes her turn over and expose her breasts to me.

Jesus fuck. They are spectacular. Tight nipples in the middle of dark pink circles of peaked skin. They fall slightly to the side, but they are so big they don't lose their shape, but instead make perfect mounds on top of her chest.

My mouth wants nothing more than to take them in and suck until she's begging me to fuck her again.

The ringing stops, and the silence jolts me back to reality until a sharp ding signals a voicemail.

I place my head in my hands, rub my hands down my scratchy face, then get up and walk to the bathroom to take a piss. When I'm done, my phone is ringing again and I manage to tab the accept button in time to save myself another voicemail as I pull on a pair of cut-off sweats.

"Yeah," I groan.

"Mr. Vance," the voice on the line says.

"Who is this?" Usually I'm good with voices. I can remember a voice forever. But I'm distracted right now, and I don't feel like racking my brain when a simple question gets the job done just as easily.

"Liam Henry. I hired you to help my son a few years back."

Steven Henry. Yeah, I remember that stupid little fuck. "What can I do for you, Mr. Henry?"

"I think the better question is, what can I do for you?"

"OK," I say, walking down the stairs to take this conversation to the kitchen. "Shoot. Tell me. I'm all fucking ears, man."

"Hmmm," Henry says, like he hates my guts but has to talk to me because he needs something. I don't take that personally. I expect everyone to hate my guts. It sucks being nice to an asshole like me. Especially when I hold all your dirty little secrets. "I think this calls for a personal meeting. How soon can you be in Miami?"

I think of my little bombshell upstairs and smile. "A week? Maybe two if I lose interest in what I'm doing here. But I have to be honest, Henry, that's not looking good."

"This is a job, Mr. Vance. Are you, or are you not, a professional?"

"A very busy one at the moment. If we have this out over the phone I'll get your problem sorted twice as fast. How about that?"

"No," he says sternly. "In person."

"OK, well, it's gonna be a week, maybe two—"

"I'll come to you."

"Fantastic. How about Monday at—"

"How about today at six PM?"

"What time is it now?"

"Noon."

I sigh. Well, I can fuck her once more, then we can take a shower and fuck again, then take a nap. "I guess that'll work. Where—"

"I'll be at your house."

I get the hang-up beeps and the line goes dead. So I just stare at it for a few seconds and then toss it over onto the couch as I go searching for the coffee I most definitely need.

"Who was that?" my delectable little bakery girl asks, coming down the stairs rubbing sleep from her eyes. She's wearing a half-buttoned dress shirt she must've pulled out of my closet.

Her legs, man. I know I've seen them in skirts, and shorts, and bikini bottoms plenty of times. But coming out from under that dress shirt. Fuck. Sexy doesn't even cover how that shit looks.

"Just work," I say, filling the coffee pot with water.

"You're leaving me today for work?" Cinderella pouts. "On Saturday?"

"Nah," I say, smiling. But with my back to her, so she can't see. I feel like I have a girlfriend all of a sudden. And it doesn't feel like a bad thing. "He's coming here tonight. So unless you've gotta work, we can spend the whole day together."

"I don't have to work," she says.

I start the coffee maker and turn to face her. Fuck. She is fun to look at. "So what's the story with that? The sub shop? You bought it"—it's crazy, but everything about her is crazy—"to stalk me?"

Another shrug. "Is it creepy?"

"Depends, I guess. Why are you so interested? Are you some *femme fatale* out to screw me up? Or…" God, the smile on my face.

"Or?" she prods.

"Or the distraction I've been waiting for." I exhale. Unsure what those words mean. Knowing full well what those words mean.

Cinderella walks towards me, her mouth not smiling, not frowning. Just flat. And my honesty feels like a mistake all of a sudden. "What does that mean?" she asks, taking my hand in hers and placing my palm against her cheek. She's warm and her cheeks are flushed pink. Her lips gently brush my fingertips and that little red flag that I tried to put away last night is flying again. "What kind of distraction do you need?"

What's wrong with me?

That's a loaded question.

"I'm just…" I can't stop looking at her mouth. I want to kiss it. And even though I don't consider myself to be an impulsive person, I do kiss it. I lean down, take her face in both hands, and it's the gentlest, the softest, the sincerest kiss I've ever had. "Tired," I say, practically whispering. "I'm tired of thinking about things. Of fixing things. I'm tired of all of it. I bought these two islands in the Exuma Cays and I've been fixing them up, you know? One is sorta shitty. Just a small house and I haven't done much to it. But the other one is perfect. I remodeled it all. Kitchen, bathrooms, everything."

"Two islands…" she says, letting her sentence drop off. Then, "Why do you need *two*?"

"I…" But it's such an important question. The answer is so telling, it makes me stop.

"Pax?" she asks. "Why do you need two islands?"

And even though I've never articulated the answer, I know the answer. "The backup plan, right? I always have a backup plan. I bought the little one first but then I realized it wasn't what I needed. Too small, too insignificant. Too easily washed away in a big storm. So I got another one nearby."

"Just in case?"

I bump my forehead into hers and nod. "Just in case."

"It sounds a little like running away," she whispers.

"Call it whatever you want, I guess. I just like to have options."

"Running from the past? Do you really need to run?"

I think about this for a second. Yes and no. "No, I don't. But I want to. I want to leave everything—everyone—behind. Stop working and just do nothing for a while. Sit on a beach. Catch fish off a boat in the middle of nowhere. No cell phone, no email, no problems."

"It doesn't sound very fun. The leaving everyone behind part. You have friends and family. Wouldn't you miss them?"

"No," I say, pulling away, stepping back. "Not really. They wouldn't miss me either, so who cares."

"Hmmm," Cinderella says, side-stepping me and walking over to the coffee pot. She reaches up and opens a cupboard, pulling out a coffee mug like she's helped herself to coffee in my house a million times.

It reminds me of... *me*. In Nolan's houses. The way I help myself to his things when I'm there. The way I know all his houses intimately, even the ones I have no right to claim. Because I use them whenever he's not there. He has almost as many houses as me, and you can only stay in one at a time.

She's been in here before. In my house. Without me.

This should be the last straw. This should be the part where I freak the fuck out and drag her to the front door, slamming it in her face after pushing her outside. This should be the part where I grab my things and walk away, leaving her behind.

She's lying about a lot of things. I'm not sure anything she told me was the truth, if I'm being honest with myself. In my line of work, you gotta rely on instinct and every instinct I have about Cinderella Vaughn is screaming lies... lies... lies. And all it would take is one more search. One more thorough search when I don't have her looking over my shoulder or sucking my dick to distraction, and I'd figure out what the lies were.

So what's stopping me from getting that truth?

This is the part I'm suddenly having problems with. It's like... it's almost like... I'd rather not know. Maybe ignorance is bliss? Maybe having access to whatever you need, whenever you need it, isn't all it's cracked up to be?

I watch her pour her coffee. But then she turns, without adding sugar or milk, and hands it to me.

67

"Here," she says. "Let's sit and be still together for a little bit. I'd like to hear more about your escape plans, if that's OK. Just in case you bolt and I have to go after you."

I take the mug and set it on the island countertop. "If I… do *bolt*, you'll never find me."

"So I guess you better not do that, Mr. Mysterious. Or you might miss out on the chance of a lifetime."

I smile and turn the questions to her. "What about you? You don't come off as the most grounded person."

"Oh, God." She laughs, reaching for the teapot and filling it with water. She sets it on the stove and turns up the flame, then turns to face me. Leans her hands on the counter behind her. Smiles. "No one has ever dared to call me grounded. I'm as flighty as they come. And not in the ditzy blonde way, either." She stops, looks away quickly, then catches her mistake and looks me in the eyes again. Recovered. She *is* a natural blonde. That is something she's hiding for sure.

"Is that the reason the carpet doesn't match the drapes?" I ask, taking a sip of my black coffee as I try to hide my smile.

"I didn't think you noticed."

"It's my job to notice, Sugar."

She draws in a breath through her teeth at the nickname. "I think we might be the two most secretive people on the planet right now, Mr. Brown."

"Hmm," I say, wanting to wince at the name, but deserving it. It was the one I gave to the sub shop, after all.

"Do we want to share these secrets?" I ask.

She shakes her head slowly. "I don't think so. Not yet."

"So we're going to ignore all the red flags and warning bells?"

"Do you have a better idea?"

How did I get sucked into this conversation? Why am I still participating in it? What is happening? Inside I'm screaming, waving my arms around like that robot on that old-ass TV show. Warning, warning, warning. But outside I'm as cool as they come. "Not really," I say.

"Well, me either. I'm sure they're gonna come out eventually. And by that time we'll have it all figured out."

"Will we?"

She nods. "We will."

When the teapot whistles she makes herself a cup and we go out to the beach patio and lie next to each other on top of a giant double lounge chair and take in what's left of the summer sun. She's still wearing nothing but my dress shirt and her bikini bottoms. I'm still wearing nothing but my cut-off sweat shorts. And the beach is filled with people, and kids, and games of volleyball and surfers.

But we pay no attention to any of it.

CHAPTER NINE
CINDY

It's an afternoon of silence and whatever the word is for non-silence. It's not that we're quiet, because nothing about us is quiet. And it's not like we don't talk, because we never seem to stop talking. But we're silent in all the ways that matter. The past is closed up and put away. The future isn't even here yet, so there is no reasonable way for it to interfere.

He calms me though. Tethers me to the ground like one of the weights draping over the side of those giant hot air balloons. All my wanderlust tendencies seem to disappear under his scrutiny. He looks at me like he knows me. But of course, he doesn't, since I've told so many lies, even I'm having trouble knowing who I am.

We go inside after a few hours of meaningless conversation and have sex on the kitchen counter. It's slower this time. I sit there, my legs wrapped around his middle as he kisses my neck and makes me come.

We take a shower and he fucks me again, this time pressed up against the cold tile wall. Afterward, we nibble on crackers and cheese and a plate of cucumbers he sliced, since his fridge doesn't have much in the way of food. And I can see him watching the clock, wanting me to leave before his business arrives, and not wanting to tell me to leave so he can do business.

So I woman up and do the right thing.

"I'm going to go home and get cleaned up." All I have in the way of clothing is the bikini I came here in, so I'm putting the top back on in the master bedroom when I make this announcement.

"Where will you go after that?" he asks.

"Where will *you* go?"

I get a shrug. "I'm not sure yet. I might need to leave for this job."

"I'd hope you'd take me with you, since, you know, I work for you now."

We both smile at that.

"The detective smiles," I say. "Like the thought escaped him. But now that it's back, it was like it never left."

"That's weird, you know. Narrating shit like that. Making us into some kind of story."

"I don't care."

"I think that's why I like you."

"The careless part?" I ask, wondering how we got this way overnight. Wondering if it's a good or bad sign that we fell into each other's arms like old friends or old lovers.

"Yeah," he says, leaning against the wall in front of the stairs that lead down to the living room. "No," he corrects. "Not careless. Careful, but uncaring."

"We are two of the most unsolvable riddles ever, Mr. Vance."

"I think I like that about us, Miss Vaughn."

"Well," I say. "I know where to find you."

"Do you?"

I nod. "I do. Thanks for a great time, Pax. I'll see you later."

I go down the steps and I'm just about to turn towards the pool and walk to the front house when he calls out after me.

"Cinderella?"

"Cindy," I say, stopping to look up at him. "You can just call me Cindy."

"Cindy." He smiles. "You didn't turn into a pumpkin last night."

"No," I say, feeling sad and happy at the same time. "I might have on someone else's ball gown at the moment. But I'm real. I swear."

I turn away feeling off. I walk a few houses down to where I parked my car last night, the hot concrete stinging my bare feet, and get in. I sit there for a few seconds, ignoring the fact that I came here to party with one guy and went home with another. I don't feel bad about it. Not at all. I came to Malibu for one thing and one thing only and that was Mr. Mysterious.

I got him.

But now what? What to do with him is the only thing on my mind.

I start the car and drive up to the front gates of Malibu Colony and ten minutes later I'm five miles up PCH and turning into the beach-side campground. I pull into the parking spot next to my camper and sit there for a minute, sweat rolling down my back in the stifling heat of the late afternoon, and watch the minutes tick off on the dashboard clock.

I get out, eventually, and make my way inside. I grab a pair of jeans and a t-shirt, slip my feet into the sneakers I use to... well, *sneak*, and drive back to Malibu Colony. There's no parking on the street, so I take up my usual spot by Buster's and jog down into the Colony by way of the public beach access path. I'm three doors down from Paxton's house, sitting on the street-side porch of the place we used to escape the party last night, when a silver Mercedes parks in front of Pax's house and an older gentleman gets out, looks around with either nervousness or caution, buttons his dark gray suit coat, walks up to the door, and rings the bell.

A few seconds later he steps out of view and I start walking in that direction.

"Hey," a voice calls from behind me.

Shit. I turn and smile at one of the party guys. I can't keep their names straight. Tyler, or Matthew, or Thomas. One of them is calling after me.

"Oh, hey," I say, forcing my feet not to shuffle in impatience. I'm missing part of that meeting right now. I need to get rid of this guy.

"What happened—"

"Are you having another party tonight?" I interrupt. "Because last night was a bust."

"Sorry about that," he says, a sheepish smile on his face. "Yeah, sure. We have parties every weekend. Are you coming back?"

"Definitely," I say.

"Are you dating that guy again?"

"I told you before..." Matthew. I think he's Matthew. "We've been dating forever. We're just one of those on-and-off kind of couples."

"So you're on now?"

Fucking men and their stupid jealous gene. "No. He took me to his place last night when the cops came, but I left immediately and forgot… my earrings. The nice ones. I need them back. That's all. What time should I come by tonight? For the party?"

He looks like he has more questions. Maybe he's even observant and knows I wasn't wearing earrings last night. But my question stops that line of thought and refocuses it on something unrelated to the mysterious man down the street.

"How about nine?"

"How about I'll see you then?"

He nods towards Pax's house. "Want me to go get those earrings for you? So you don't have to bother?"

"I got it, thanks." I give him a little wave as his buddies start calling his name from inside their house.

Go back inside, I pray. And my luck holds, because when I get to Pax's front door, he's gone.

A few weeks ago I broke in and stole Paxton's house keys, had a copy made, and then returned them. Since then I've been making frequent visits. I slip the key in the door as quietly as I can, but I'm confident they are on the beach side of the house, so way out of earshot. And then I sneak inside.

I tiptoe inside the foyer and softly down the steps that lead to the pool.

"I don't think so," Pax says from the living room. I freeze, and realize I've missed something. Shit. Probably something important.

"Why not?" the visitor asks.

"Because I just don't think he's like that. He's not that kind of guy."

"I don't think you know one single grain of truth about that *guy's* life."

I slink past the tall palm trees, then back into a corner just on the other side of the entrance to the beach side of the house.

"So you've said," Pax replies. There's a clinking of ice in glasses, like they're having drinks. "So you've hinted over the years. But you know what, Liam? You never do anything more than hint."

"I've never had reason to." He pauses. "Until now."

"And what's changed?"

"He's been… doing things out of character."

"Like what?"

"Like…" But the pause this time is extended.

"Like?" Pax urges.

"Like not paying his debts."

"He owes you something? Since when?"

"He's owed me his whole life, Vance. Like I said. You have no idea who he is. Did it ever occur to you that he might've been the guilty one?"

A laugh from Pax. "No."

"No?"

"Never. I always thought Nolan was guilty. He acted guilty as hell. Weston never acted guilty. Little things like rape charges don't bother powerful people like Weston Conrad, but even so, he's not the guilty one."

Mr. Corporate. They're talking about Mr. Corporate.

"Then who? You?"

More ice clinking inside glasses. A pause. Then, "Say that again, old man, and I'll do something about it."

A half snort, half laugh from this Liam guy. Like he finds that notion ridiculous. "No need. I don't think it was you. Your mother didn't raise you that way."

What the fuck is going on here?

They definitely know each other. But what is this about?

"No," Paxton says. "She didn't."

"But," Liam says, "you're one half Charles Vance as well." And then laughter. Like uproarious laughter.

I get a chill up my spine.

"He didn't raise me, as you well know."

"No. He never raised any of them, did he?"

"You wanna tell me why you're here?" Pax says, his voice dangerous now. Like he's out of patience.

Yes, please. I'm dying to know.

"I told you," Liam says. "I need Weston Conrad… taken care of."

Pax is silent for so long, I chance a peek around the corner of the wall.

Shit. I slink back immediately. He was looking *right* at me. I peek again and he smiles. Liam's back is to me, so he doesn't see what Paxton is looking at. "What exactly does that entail?"

"You just… make him disappear."

"And how do you propose I do that?"

"Try bait, Mr. Mysterious. I hear it's your favorite method." Liam stands and I ease back into my corner. "So do we have a deal? Will ten million dollars erase this ridiculous blood bond you have with the rest of your accomplices?"

Accomplices? What?

"I'll think about it. I just got a call not twenty minutes ago from someone else, so I can't do anything until that's over. They paid in advance."

"Well, I'm not paying you in advance."

"Then I'll be in touch. And let you know when I'm free."

"Don't keep me waiting too long," Liam says. "If you say no, I'll just find someone else to do it."

And then there's the sound of expensive shoes on the hardwood floors. They come towards me. I freeze, not even half hidden behind the thin trunk of a plan tree, holding my breath, my eyes tracking them as they pass.

Pax doesn't look at me—neither does Liam—and they continue past the pool and up the stairs into the street side of the house.

I bolt out of the corner and go up into the beach-side living room, hoping that Liam guy didn't decide to look over his shoulder at the wrong moment.

"So you're spying on me?"

I whirl around, surprised Pax is back here so fast. He must've practically shoved that guy out the door. "What the hell was that about?" I have so many questions. My obsession with Paxton never had anything to do with my brother, Oliver. But they were talking about the Misters. Something to do with Mr. Corporate. And if there's one Mister involved, that means all the Misters are involved. Including my brother. "You were talking about Mr. Corporate."

"No," Pax says. "I'm talking about what you're doing sneaking into my *house*, listening in on my private *business*. I've hurt people very badly for far less serious transgressions, Cindy."

"We're partners—"

"We're fuck buddies."

"Huh," I say, disgusted at his characterization of last night. "OK. Fine. We're fuck buddies *and* partners."

"I didn't hire you, Miss Vaughn. I've been humoring you. I think it's cute. And I wanted to fuck you. Or… I did. Until you stuck your nose into things that don't smell good. None of this is your business."

I stay silent. Reconsider my options. Pax is not one of those guys who allows himself to be manipulated very easily. One inkling that he's being played and he either walks away or starts playing the game with me. There is no in between with him from what I can see. He does this with every casual relationship I've watched him in.

They are all one-night stands or players in his game.

Which am I?

I could tell him the truth—I'm Oliver's baby sister—and everything would be fine. I'd be in, no questions asked. Someone he'd probably confide in. Trust immediately.

But I'm not here because of Oliver. I'm here for him. And if I told him who I was, there'd be no chance of ever becoming his girlfriend. Ever.

So I play the only card I have.

"How about we settle this with… a game?"

CHAPTER TEN

PAXTON

I tense up at the offer. I stare hard at her. And all the things I should've been wondering about last night are suddenly the only things that matter.

"Who the *fuck* are you?" I ask.

"I've been watching you," she says softly

"Who. The fuck—"

"For a very long time." Her voice is laced with sweetness. But for some reason it reminds me of poison.

"—are you?"

"I know more than you think." This time it's a tease.

"I might consider that a threat. People who threaten me generally end up dead. You think you're some kind of spy, Sugar? You come in here bragging of your firearms permit, calling yourself a private investigator. Well, look here, cookie, you have no idea what you're doing. You're just some small piece of entertainment that makes a lot of noise and puts on a nice show. Some kind of diversion. And you know what I do with diversions?" I take a few steps closer. She steps back, bumping into the kitchen island. "I—"

But the phone rings. The fucking landline, which is hanging on the wall of the kitchen right next to Cinderella.

Before I even know what's happening, she's got the handset up to her ear, saying, "Hello?"

I freeze. She stares at me. "Yes, he's here. Who may I ask is calling?" She bites her lip, eyes never leaving mine. She holds out the phone. "It's your mother."

I cover the distance between us in two long strides, snatch the phone from her, cup my hand tightly over the transmitter end, and growl, "You better take this opportunity to run the fuck away, Cinderella. Because it's the only chance you're gonna get."

I turn my back to her, place the phone against my ear, and say, "Hey, what's up?" as I walk out the back door to the patio and look across the ocean at the low-hanging sun.

"You have a girlfriend?"

"No." I laugh. "*No.*"

"Paxton, girls don't answer your home phone. Who is she?"

Why now, for fuck's sake? I don't hear from her in months and now, right now, this is the moment she decides to call? "Is there something I can do for you, Mother?"

"You didn't answer my question."

"And I'm not going to. What's up?"

She sighs on the other end of the phone. "Something very interesting was just delivered to the house."

My whole body goes tense. "What was it?"

"I don't think we should talk over the phone, Paxton. I'll come see you," she says, a lightness in her voice that shouldn't be there. "We'll talk then. And go to the races. I haven't been to Del Mar in ages."

Fuck.

"The Debutante Stakes is next weekend. There is a Limitless filly running who I'd like to see. I have a car scheduled. I have other meetings with potential clients so we'll meet in the barn. Shall we say… fiveish on Saturday?"

"Mother." I sigh, pinching the bridge of my nose. "I really don't have time for this right now. I just got a call from Nolan and I have to do some digging for him."

"You don't even like Nolan."

"I know." I try to massage the headache out of my temple with my fingertips. "But it's weird and I can't ignore it. So I need to go help him out because West isn't around and he's part of the problem. I can't ignore them, you know that."

"Well, I'm advising you not to ignore this either. As I said, Paxton, I have something to show you. You will want to see this. Now put that girl back on the phone. I need to ask her something."

"You don't, believe me." I stare straight in Cindy's eyes as she waits, a pinched look on her face. I turn my back to her. "And she's already gone, anyway. Just leave it, Mother."

"Call her back inside, Paxton. I have a question for her. And you know full well I will not take no for an answer. So you might as well just give in to me and get it over with."

I huff out some air and turn around and find Cinderella leaning up against the open patio door. Arms crossed. Frowning. I walk over, cupping my hand over the transmit end of the phone again. "Don't say *anything*," I whisper, as I hand her the phone.

She looks surprised, but takes the phone and places it to her ear out of instinct. "Hello?" A pause. "Cindy," she says, looking at me. "Yes, I do." Then, "Yes, that's true. How did you know?"

I shake my head at her, then drag a finger across my throat in a *cut it off* motion.

But Cindy is smiling. "I love them." More smiles. "I'd *love* to."

I pull the phone out of her hand and put it up to my ear. "No. Whatever you just asked her, it's no. I'll see you next weekend—"

"Paxton?"

"*What?*"

"You need to bring her along."

"Why?" What the fuck is happening? I mean, Jesus Christ. I spend ten years doing the most questionable shit to dig scumbag offspring out of scandal and none of that was half as frustrating as Cindy and my mother right now in this moment.

"I'll explain on Saturday. See you then."

I get a dial tone, so I walk back inside and place the handset back on the base in the kitchen. "What did she ask you?"

"She asked if I like horses. Well, first she asked me my name. And I said Cindy because Cinderella, right?" She rolls her eyes. "And then she asked if I liked horses. Which is a yes, of course. I always had ponies growing up. And then she said, 'You love the races, don't you?' And of course, I said yes again." Cindy looks up at me. "She invited me to Del Mar next weekend to watch a race. So I get to meet her. She said if you didn't bring me with you, I should just pick up my ticket at will call and show up in the Turf Club at five."

"Is that right?" My head begins to pound.

"That's right." Cindy shrugs.

"So you're going?"

"Oh, hell the fuck yes, I'm going."

"What if we play that game tonight?" I ask, grinning, but it's one of those evil grins. "And you lose."

She swallows hard, then lifts her head up and squares her shoulders. "I'm a winner, Mr. Mysterious. You should get used to that fact. And I'll play that game with you if you want. But it's got nothing to do with your mother, whom I *will* be meeting next weekend. Even if I have to drive myself."

I don't think she knows what the game is. I think she's been researching me. Came upon some clue from back in the day. I'm not sure how it got out, but she's an investigator, right? Her job is to find dirt on people.

But my job is to cover it up. It's like an ironic little paradox.

I walk over to her. Right up next to her. She's not small, but I tower over her. She looks up with those giant blue eyes and I remember something.

"You're blonde."

"What?" It comes out as a whisper.

"The carpet doesn't match the drapes, sugar. You're blonde. You've got blue eyes and the face of a fairytale princess. Why do you dye your hair black and wear all that shit on your face?"

"Excuse me?" She narrows her eyes at me.

I narrow mine right back. "You heard me," I say, grabbing her shoulder and pulling her in closer. Our faces are less than an inch apart. If anger wasn't coursing through my blood right now, it might appear I was gonna kiss her.

I am not going to *kiss* her.

85

"You wear that makeup to hide. You dye your hair to hide. These clothes," I say, pinching the fabric of her vintage Metallica t-shirt between my fingers, "are your disguise. You're a sweet little liar, aren't you? Tell me, Cindy. Which of the many things you told me since we've met are lies and which are actually true?"

I'm going to *threaten* her.

"Let go," she says, placing both hands firmly on my chest and pushing me back. My feet don't even move. I am a wall as far as she's concerned. A mountain. Made of stone. Immovable. Insurmountable. Unconquerable.

"Let go? I thought we were fate, sugar? I thought we were partners?" I growl those words out like she's the enemy.

She straightens her back and levels her gaze at me. "I'm not afraid of you."

"You should be," I say, leaning so close to her face our noses touch. I stare into her eyes. "Find your own fucking way to Del Mar, bitch. But if you know what's good for you, you'll stay the fuck away from me and my family."

CHAPTER ELEVEN

CINDY

Paxton disappears after that. For almost the whole week. He told his mother that Nolan called and asked him to do something. Is that where he went? Or is he already working for that Liam guy? I know the Nolan he's referring to is Mr. Romantic. And the job with Liam was about Mr. Corporate. What I don't know is how much of this involves my brother, Mr. Match.

I case his house all week. I don't bother going back to Buster's and hoping for a delivery call. That driver I was bribing to let me know about Paxton's sandwich orders was fired, so I can't weasel any more information out of that little deal.

I go into his house every night, careful to disarm the security system so there's no alert, just to check and see if he's home. But he's not. And there are no messages on that landline phone. There isn't even an answering machine.

So I wait in my trailer down PCH. And I hang out in the waves with the surfers in front of his house, hoping he'll surprise me and come out there like he usually does when he's in town.

But he never comes, so he's not in town.

Where is he? What is he doing? The week drags on so slowly, it makes me want to scream into my pillow at night. And by the time Saturday morning rolls around, I'm aching for him. Just a look at him. I get up early and plan my outfit, wondering what Mariel Hawthorne is really like once you get to know her, and then make the four-hour drive down to San Diego county in weekend traffic.

I have never been to Del Mar racetrack, but I have been to Belmont that one time I was stalking Paxton's mother. She said meet her in the Turf Club, so that's where I head once I get inside.

They have a dress code, so I am appropriately attired as I hand over my ticket for inspection and smile at the man guarding the door.

"Right down that way, miss." The usher points to a section of tables.

"Thank you," I say, smiling sweetly. I have no intention of going to my seat. I head to the bar and order a mint julep.

"It's not the Derby, ma'am," the bartender says with a wink.

"I just like them." I shrug.

"Coming up." He steps away to make my drink and I turn around, come face to face with Paxton, and hold my hand over my chest, startled.

"Jesus, Pax. You don't have to sneak up on me."

He grins like he's got a secret.

And he looks… fuck hot. I've seen him in suits. I mean, he wears them all the time. Usually with one of those red power ties. But they are usually black and formal.

Today he's wearing a light gray suit with a coral tie and matching pocket square.

I have to take a deep breath as I stare up into his eyes, trying my best not to overly appreciate him.

"One mint julep," the bartender says behind me.

"I'll have bourbon," Pax says, eyes never leaving mine as he reaches behind me for my drink.

"Yes, sir," the bartender says.

"These things will kill you," Pax says, looking me up and down with far less self-control than I exhibited as he hands me my drink. What a possessive little move with the drink. It makes me flutter a little. "What the fuck did you do to your hair?" he asks.

I shrug. "You didn't seem to like the dark." I paid three hundred dollars that I didn't really have for a salon in Malibu to get my natural color back. But I like the result. It's been dark for years now and I've missed my natural look. "So this is me."

His fingers find their way into my thick head of golden locks, rubbing them between his fingers. "That's quite a trick."

"It was time." I sigh, then take a sip of my drink. "I haven't been blonde since I left home at eighteen."

"Why not?"

"Bourbon," the bartender says, still behind me.

Pax reaches into his pocket, pulls out his wallet, then puts two twenties on the bar as he takes his drink.

"Change?" the bartender asks.

"Keep it," Pax says with the smooth assurance of a man with money. "Have you seen my mother? I'm going to assume you know what she looks like, seeing as how you're a private investigator. *With* firearms permit," he adds, taking a long sip of his whiskey.

"I just got here. You?"

89

"Same." He takes another drink. "Let's go find her then." He takes my unoccupied hand and places it on his forearm, leading me away.

"Why are you being so nice?" I ask, suddenly very, *very* nervous.

"Don't mistake cautious for nice, Cinderella. My mother wants to talk to me. She wanted you to be included. And I can't help but think there's a reason for that."

"Like what?" I ask. We step down a few stairs into the main dining room. There is an unobstructed view of the finish line directly ahead, and Pax leads me all the way down to the front to a group of empty tables. "Where have you been all week?"

"Busy."

"Doing what? You told your mother you had to do something for your friend Nolan. He's Mr. Romantic, right? Don't you think it's odd that you get a call from Mr. Romantic and then that Liam guy shows up asking you to *take care* of Mr. Corporate for him?"

But Pax ignores me, takes out his phone, and sends a text. He gets a ping back before he can redirect his attention to me. "She's in the barn." And then under his breath, "Of course. Come on. We'll meet her down there. The race she's interested in is later tonight. She'll hang out there until post time if I don't pull her away."

"Are you going to answer me?" I ask, stopping so he has to stop too.

"What do you want me to say?"

"Where have you been all week?"

He downs the rest of his drink and then sets his empty glass on a shelf the bettors use to pore over their racing forms. I decide to do the same, slamming my glass down a little harder than I should.

"I was on the East Coast. With Nolan. Some pretty weird fucking shit went down."

"Like what?"

He looks me in the eyes. "I don't know if I should trust you or not. I don't know why I haven't kicked you aside yet. But…" He sighs, like he's really got a lot on his mind. Like he's tired and just needs a moment to catch his breath. "Tell me why you're here, Cindy."

I get the feeling he needs this answer. "Something happened, didn't it? With your friend."

"Why are you here?"

"I just like you," I say. It comes out soft. If he seems tired, then I must seem defeated. Because that's kinda how I feel. Why am I stalking him? Do I really know anymore?

"Are you…" But he stops. Looks away.

"Am I what?" But he stays silent. "I'm not here to hurt you. No one hired me, if that's what you're after. I swear, I'm just a girl who saw your picture on the news and got obsessed. OK? And yeah, it's weird, and wrong, and creepy. But I'm really not any of those things. I swear it. I'm just a girl who likes a guy."

He looks at me. Finally. "That's it?" he asks. And somewhere in that small, almost insignificant question, I find vulnerability. "That's all this is? Just a girl who likes a guy?"

I shrug. "That's it."

"OK," he says, giving in. And even though I should feel a little relief that he doesn't push me harder about the truth, I don't feel relief. I want to tell him. I want him to know me. I want to know him. Not in the stalker way. That's nothing but information. And the sex didn't give me much insight. Not the way we did it, as fuck buddies. "Maybe we can talk about it later then?"

"Yeah," I say. "I'd really like to talk about it later."

And then I realize that could mean two things. I'd really like to talk about it later because I don't want to talk about it. Or I'd really like to talk about it later because now isn't the time, but I'm dying to talk about it.

I don't have a chance to ask him which way he took it, because he turns away and leads me through the crowd of people.

To the barn we go. It's a longish walk, past crowds of well-dressed people holding drinks, laughing and talking easily. Pax smiles at a lot of them. Some call his name, saying hello. He's polite, but never stops walking. He's one of those men who always seem preoccupied with life. Always have something on their mind.

People notice this. People feel… not jealous, really. But outside of him, I can just tell by the way everyone watches us, they want to know more. Like me, I realize. He has this magnetism that draws you in, but he also has this *stay the fuck away from me* vibe that prevents an invasion of privacy.

It's paradoxical, I realize. He's a walking paradox.

He leads me down several levels until we are on the floor with the bettors. We make our way out into the paddock area, where a dozen or so good-looking thoroughbreds are prancing, eager as their jockeys are lifted up on their backs and trainers lean into whisper last-minute advice.

Paxton pulls two ID badges from his suit coat pocket and shows them to a security guard. The guard smiles, nods, waves us through.

And then… "Wow," I say, my eyes darting everywhere at once. Things were busy out front, but the bustle back here in the barns is something else altogether. Horses walking on the coolers, being led by grooms, standing beautifully, like kings and queens, in their open-air stall doors.

This place drips with money.

"Never been to the back side?" Paxton asks.

"I have," I say, before realizing the only other time was at Belmont, when I was stalking his mother. Dear God. What if she recognizes me? "But it wasn't like *this*."

"This is a stakes race. It's kind of a big deal, even if it's only for two-year-old fillies. They want to see the girls who might go far next year and this is one of the races that count. The best young ladies in Southern California are in this race."

"Oh," I say. "I'm not really up on racing."

"Well," he says, staring down at me as I gaze up. "You look the part."

I smile, possibly blush, and then shake my head a little.

"That's a nice dress. Were you stalking me this morning?"

"What?"

"The dress?"

"What about it?"

"You match my tie."

"Oh." I laugh. "No." And it's the truth. "I just picked something out of my trailer this morning."

93

"Mmmm-hmm." But he doesn't believe me. And then he says, "Trailer?"

We both spot his mother at the same time and thankfully that question has the opportunity to go unanswered. Paxton's stride lengthens slightly as he makes his way towards her. She is petting a pale yellow horse with flaxen mane as she laughs and talks with a man.

"Mother," Paxton says, once we're close enough so he won't have to say the word too loud.

"Paxton," his mother says, tsking her tongue. "Well, look at this lovely vision you brought with you. Cindy?" she asks, holding out her hand.

"Yes," I say, nervously allowing her fingertips to grasp mine.

"Well." She looks up at the man she was talking to with a smile. "This is a very good omen."

"You brought us good luck, Pax," the man says.

Pax is looking at me, then the horse. We both get it at the same time. I look like the filly, thanks to my impulsive hair change.

"Oh, my dear," Mrs. Hawthorne says, redirecting her attention back to me. "You are adorable."

The filly is nuzzling me, so my hand reaches up out of habit to stroke her nose.

"Is this your rising star?" Paxton asks, nodding towards the horse.

"Yes." His mother beams. "Did you know she's full sister to Aladdin's Prince Charming, last year's Triple Crown winner?"

"No," Pax says. His eyes squint at the horse with more scrutiny. "I didn't. Last year's Triple Crown winner was one of ours?"

"How could you not know that?" his mother says, her voice high. "Paxton Hawthorne Vance—"

"I don't keep up with the horses, Mother. You know that."

She lets out a long breath, then turns to the man. "William, will you excuse us? We have some family business to discuss."

"Sure thing, Mariel. You know where to find me."

He walks off, Mariel's gaze lingering on him for a little longer than necessary.

"William Barker?" Paxton asks, leaning down to whisper in his mother's ear. "Really?"

"What's wrong with William? We've been friends for twenty years."

"You're dating a trainer? What happened to, *I will never date another horseman for as long as*—"

"Oh, pssssshhhh," his mother says. "I say all kinds of things in the heat of the moment. William is one of the good ones. And he saw beyond this filly's pretty looks and found her potential. I have to respect that, don't I?"

I can't help but feel a connection to the beautiful horse. People have a hard time seeing beyond my looks too. Which is why I dyed my hair dark in the first place. I bet if that filly had the means, she'd make herself bay, or black, or brown just to be taken seriously.

"You want to tell me why we're here?" Pax says, impatient.

I'd like to know that as well. Family business should not include a newly acquired fuck buddy.

And then she pulls something out of her small clutch purse. Paxton steps away, my hand falling from his arm as he tries to make his retreat. It takes me a moment to figure out what has him so rattled, and then I see what his mother is holding in her hand.

A silver envelope.

"What the fuck is that?" Pax says it too loud. I look around and people are staring.

"Paxton," his mother whispers. "Your language."

"Where did you get that?" Pax snatches the envelope out of her hands and opens the flap, takes out a silver card, glances at it. "What is this?"

"Are you done now?" his mother asks.

"Mother," Pax says, rage filtering into the single word. "I need to know where you got this. It's very important."

I know the significance of the silver envelopes. Well, not entirely. But I know that a silver envelope was part of the evidence against my brother and his friends back when they were accused of raping that girl in college. I overheard my parents talking about it one night, just after he was accused.

"Um," I say, unsure what to do. Clearly this is not a moment for an almost stranger to witness. "I think I'll wait in the clubhouse."

"Cinderella," his mother coos, her eyes lingering on Paxton a moment before turning to meet mine. "Since you've decided to play a part in this, I think it's best you stay."

"How did you—"

96

"Know your *real* name?" She smirks at me. And the way she stressed the word really has me worried for a moment.

Does she know who I am? Does she know who my brother is? If she outs me right now, I can kiss anything I have with Paxton Vance goodbye. Once he knows—

"I have eyes, darling. We've met before, remember?"

"You've been stalking my *mother*?" Pax asks.

"Oh, calm down, Paxton. She's a horsewoman. Didn't she tell you?"

"I did," I say quickly. "He knows I grew up on a farm."

Mariel keeps her gaze trained on Pax. "She comes from quite a family."

"Tattoo artists, I hear," Pax says.

"Yes," Mariel says. "Some of them *are* tattoo artists."

I catch the threat in the way she says some of them, but Paxton is looking at the envelope again. "Did she send you this?" Then he whirls towards me.

"Don't be silly, Paxton. This is mine. From a very long time ago."

"You are cordially invited—" Pax starts reading, but Mariel takes the card from his hand and presses it to her bosom, looking very nervous, losing a bit of her perfected composure.

"Do not ever read it aloud in public," she whispers. "It's not something you read in public."

"Why? What the fu—" He stops the curse word, barely, then takes a deep breath to compose himself. "Tell me what this means. Things are happening again, Mother. I just got back from a very messed-up week on the East Coast with

97

Nolan. And it involved a a certain silver envelope. I need to know what the hell this means."

"And you will," she says, then looks around. All three of us look around, actually, acutely aware that there are a lot of people back here in the barns. "But not here. William has offered up his office for us to talk. Let's go there."

She leads us through the shed row of stalls, past dozens of beautiful horses, their heads reaching for us, looking for treats as we pass them, and then stops in front of an open door to waves us in.

Pax throws up his hands. "After you," he says. Like manners were bred into him like the joy of running was bred into these horses, and he can't possibly enter a room before a lady, even if he wanted to.

The office smells like money, if money smelled like the track, and everything is covered in a thin layer of dust the way barn offices often are. Paxton grabs two fleece saddle pads, places one on the chair behind the desk and motions to his mother to sit there, then places the other on a chair for me.

We both sit, our dresses safe from dust, as Paxton closes the door and turns the lock. "Now," he says, coming back to stand between us. "We're gonna talk about this." He looks at me. "And no one is leaving until I know everything."

CHAPTER TWELVE

PAXTON

I have to admit, seeing Cindy as a blonde has definitely had the effect she was going for. I'm not a sucker for blondes—I like girls of all flavors equally. But, Je-*sus*. Bombshell is the only word to describe this woman as a blonde.

Nope, her tits aren't any bigger today than they were yesterday. In fact, she's not even showing any cleavage right now. That dress is the perfect combination of tailored, sophisticated, and sexy without being trashy. But she is so strikingly beautiful, it's hard not to stare.

And the color. I have to scratch my chin as I think about the coincidence of the color. We look like a couple. A powerful, beautiful, coordinated couple.

A team.

"Read it out loud," my mother says, handing Cindy the silver envelope and card.

"Wait," I say, putting up a hand. "She doesn't really need to be here. I get it, you've got my attention."

"What are you talking about?" Cindy asks, ready to read like she was asked.

"Paxton," my mother says, using that feigned voice of reason I remember all too well from my childhood. "Shut up and listen for once."

I glare at her.

She glares back.

Do I not intimidate *anyone* anymore? There was a time when—

"'You are cordially invited,'" Cindy starts. She squints her eyes. "Some of the lettering has worn off."

"Let me see," I say, making a swipe for the card.

Cindy slaps my hand. "You can't see it any better than me. Just give me a second."

I look at my mother and roll my eyes. She indulges me with half a smile. "It's old, Paxton. The engraving has worn thin. Be calm."

Be calm.

I take a deep breath just as Cindy continues.

"'You are cordially invited to Pledge'—that's a capital letter. Not sure if it's important or not, but..." Cindy looks at me. "Just giving you the facts. 'To Pledge Silver.' Also capitalized." She stops and frowns. "I don't get it. What's Pledge Silver?"

"Sounds like a furniture polish," I say.

"Right?" Cindy laughs. Her whole face is different with the new hair. Fresh, and innocent, and fair. She's not wearing the dark eye makeup today either. In fact, I'm sure she's wearing makeup, but it's hard to tell. She looks... natural.

"Are the two of you in kindergarten?" my mother quips. "This is very serious and you won't be laughing when we get to the end of this day, I'll tell you that right now."

I want to share another smile, but Cindy goes back to reading, properly chastised.

"'The Event'—what's with the capital letters?" Cindy looks at my mother for an explanation. "It's important, right? They are proper nouns?"

"Cynthia," my mother says, getting her name wrong—on purpose, I can only assume—having a hard time with the Disney aspect of it. "We will discuss the hidden meanings once you finish. If," she stresses, "you can manage that?"

I wait for Cinderella to correct her about her name, but she doesn't. She takes in a silent, but deep, breath, and keeps going.

"'The Event will start the Game of your life. You will pledge allegiance to the party, place your pieces on the board, and take your chances with your partner as you storm the world with your prowess.'" Cindy frowns. "I think they overdid it with the P words."

"They can be dramatic, I agree. Keep going," my mother says.

"The rest is just dates and times. The thirty-first of October." Cindy frowns again. "Halloween. Weird. At midnight. Creepy." She stops reading and hands me the card. "There's no year, but that card looks... vintage."

I look it over, but that's it. That's all that's on it. "What is this?" I hold it up and look at my mother.

"An invitation, of course."

"To what? Some fraternity?"

"No," Cindy says. "Some kind of Skull and Bones stuff, right?"

"Secret society?"

My mother remains silent as we work through things.

"It's meant to like... scare people," Cindy says. "Or make them feel special, right?"

My mother absorbs our guesses and expectant looks, folds her hands on the dirty desk, unmindful of the dust all around her. "Something like that. Yes."

"It's yours?"

She shrugs in my direction, noncommittal. "No, not really mine."

"Well, where did you get it?" I feel a headache coming.

"A friend."

"Mother," I say, anger and fatigue getting the best of me. "What the fuck is going on? And don't"—I point at her getting ready to point at me—"scold me about language. Weird shit is happening again. Do you understand what I'm saying?" I roll my eyes in the direction of Cindy, just to make sure she knows not to say anything too *specific* in front of her. But my mother waves her hand at me, like she's unconcerned.

"This is why I've called you both here today."

"Both? What are you talking about? Cindy has nothing to do with this."

"Perhaps," my mother says, smiling at the beautiful girl who just happened to drop into my life. "We can always hope, anyway. Can't we?"

Cindy's eyes go big. "I don't know what you're talking about."

"No, dear. You wouldn't."

I want to ask so many questions, but I know my mother better than anyone. She's being cryptic, and when she gets in one of those cryptic moods, there's no getting her to say more than she feels necessary. So instead, I huff out a long breath of air and sit in the chair next to Cindy, resigned to the fact that Mariel Hawthorne is in charge here.

"The letter came from the Silver Society. Have either of you… heard of it?"

"No," I say, my patience just about done. "But I've certainly seen those envelopes before."

"And the invitation?" my mother asks, cocking one eyebrow at me.

"No." I shrug. "It wasn't an invitation."

"What was it?"

I have never told her this. Never told anyone this. Nolan got a glimpse of my evidence back in his house on Martha's Vineyard, but it was only a glimpse. He has no clue what I was up to that night back in college.

"Was it a game, Paxton?"

How to explain to your mother that you were playing *that* game, *that* night? And how to explain that the two cannot possibly be related, even though they must be? They must be related. Silver envelopes have followed me my whole life. I asked Perfect about it just yesterday, while all that shit on Martha's Vineyard was being wrapped up. He denied having seen any silver envelopes. But he called me back later last night and told me about the scavenger hunt he sent Ellie on. He used silver envelopes. Did that count?

Hell the fuck yes, it counts. Why the fuck would he use silver envelopes?

He didn't have an answer. Said they were nice. Sophisticated and elegant.

And then Nolan. I asked him too. And he said he sees them everywhere. Even back in school, he said he got an invitation to a party but he threw it away and never went.

Was this *his* invitation?

I get up so fast, my chair scrapes across the dusty barn wood floor. "I need to call Delaney."

"No, you do not, Paxton." My mother is calm and cool. Unfazed. Collected. "Whatever is going on with him is not related to you."

"He said he got an invitation back in school and it came in a silver envelope."

"Nothing," my mother repeats, "to do with *you*. And you haven't answered my question. In what capacity did you use—or see—silver envelopes back in school?"

"I've never seen one," Cindy says. "Do I need to be here for this? I have no clue what you're talking about."

"I'll deal with you later, Cynthia." Cindy winces at the name. "But for now, please be still and let Paxton answer."

I exhale again. Long and loud. "It was a game. I was playing a game that night."

"This game have a name?" my mother asks.

Cindy shifts uncomfortably in her seat. When I look over at her, she bites her lip.

"Ransom," I say. "It was called Ransom."

"Were you playing with *that girl*?"

I nod. Slowly. Guiltily. "I was."

"What did you do to her?"

"Nothing she didn't ask me to do."

"Was anyone else playing?"

I nod.

"The other Misters?" Cindy asks, leaning forward in her chair.

I shake my head.

"Who?" my mother demands.

"The other girls from some new house. First-years, I think. I don't remember their name."

My mother takes out her phone, taps the screen, studies it. "Kappa Delta?"

"No."

"Alpha Chi Omega?"

"No," I say. "I told you, they were new. They weren't Greek."

It's my mother's turn to let out a long breath of air. "Well," she says softly. "OK. I don't know who they could be then. How did the game end?"

"With me in jail, obviously." So pissed off. I look over at Cindy. She won't even meet my eyes.

"No, Paxton. You didn't go to jail that night. How did *that* night end?"

"I don't know, with... fuck. I don't really remember. It's been ten years and it's all kind of a blur these days. I just remember waking up with people shouting at me. Jesus fuck, who cares? The only thing that mattered was I ended up in *jail*."

"You don't think your little game had anything to do with those charges?"

"Do you?" She stares at me with that cold, hard look I remember growing up. "Yeah, of course I think it's related. How the fuck could it *not* be related? It was called Ransom, for fuck's sake."

"*Language*, Paxton," my mother practically growls.

"Did you kidnap her?" Cindy asks.

"Stay out of this," I say, irritated.

"Sorry," Cindy says, putting both hands up like she's surrendering.

"Did you kidnap her, Paxton?" my mother asks, her question devoid of emotion.

"It's called Ransom. So yeah, I fucking took her. Like I was *supposed* to."

"What did you do with her?" Cindy again.

Jesus fuck. "Does she really need to be here?"

"She really does. What did you do with that girl, Paxton?"

"I fucked her. OK? I tied her up, made my ransom demand, and then we fucked. We laughed and we fucked. I didn't even know Perfect had taken her out that night. I didn't know anything about what Romantic was doing with her. I didn't know shit, other than I was playing *the game*."

Long, loud exhale from both women as they sink back into their seats.

"Did you use a silver envelope?" my mother asks. "For this ransom demand?"

I feel very guilty right now. Very. Fucking. Guilty. "It was part of the game. They sent me the envelope and the card. They said make the ransom demand by cutting out letters from magazines. So I did. It was a *game*." They both stare at me. "I didn't *rape* her."

CHAPTER THIRTEEN

CINDY

God, I feel awful being here for this. I shouldn't be here for this. I stand up, walk the two paces that separates my chair from Paxton's, and place my hand on his shoulder. "I don't think you raped her, Pax."

He looks up at me, eyes angry and red and hurt. "Who gives a fuck what you think?"

I recoil, stepping back on my heels. I'm just about to rip him a new one when he looks at his mother and he... deflates.

That's whose opinion he gives a fuck about, I realize. Hers.

He's right. I don't matter. None of this is about me. He was the one accused of raping a girl ten years ago and he was the one who had to explain things to his mother after that happened. I can see they love each other. I can see they are very close. He respects her. She is tough and there is so much dignity spilling out of her blue blood, she practically smells like class.

"Thank you," Mariel says. "for telling me the truth after all these years. And I'd like to say, Paxton, that never once— not even for a moment—did I ever think you were guilty of that crime."

"So what?" Paxton yells. "The only thing that matters was the accusation, right? It's enough, isn't it? To ruin a guy. To take away all his chances. All his plans. Erase his future. Do you think I'd be doing what I do now if I had graduated from Brown?"

"That isn't what matters—"

Pax slams his fist on the desk, scattering dust into the air. "It does matter, goddammit. It *is* what matters. I shouldn't have had to make that fucking call. I shouldn't have had to explain myself. I shouldn't have had to do any of that. It was a fucking game. She was laughing. It was a joke. And those fucking bitches—"

"Who?" Mariel asks, standing up from her chair, both hands flat on the dirty desk as she leans forward. "Who were they? I need names, Paxton. I need *names*."

Holy fuck. "I need to go," I say, standing up and walking quickly towards the door. I unlock it, pull it open, and walk out before either of them can trap me there with their commands.

I'm somewhere on the backstretch of the Del Mar Racetrack. It's dark now, we've been talking long enough for that to happen. The lights are on in the barns and there are a million people bustling around. Grooms and horses, trainers and owners. Just so many people it's hard to reconcile the back room talk with the celebratory fun going on out here.

"Cindy," Pax yells behind me. "Stop," he says.

I keep walking, thankful I wore chunky-heeled shoes for this trip into the barn, because there is dust everywhere and the only thing between me and the filth are these platform sandals. I feel like I'm choking on it. Like this dirt represents all the disgusting things that happened to the Misters ten years ago. To my brother, I realize. Oliver was part of that. He made that same phone call. He had to explain himself

108

too. He had to look my mother in the eyes and say, "They're gonna say I raped her, Mom. And I just need you to be brave and tune it all out."

And my parents had to call the lawyers, and Ronin. Fucking Ronin. And then Ford showed up, and Five. And...

"Cindy," Pax says, his hand on my shoulder.

I realize I'm crying. Not like some little dribble, either. But a full-on waterfall of tears are streaming down my face.

"What's wrong?" he asks. "Why are you crying? I'm sorry. I didn't mean to yell, I swear. And my mother can get a little intense. She's sorry too. Stop," he says, gripping my shoulder tightly now, making me halt. "Talk to me. What's wrong?"

But I can't even tell him, can I? Not without giving away who I am. And I'm not going to do that. I don't think there's a future for us after all. I think what's happening here is me getting a big ol' dose of reality. Of adulting. Or... coming to terms with a fantasy that will never be anything more than some teenager's crush on a man she never really knew.

I never understood. But I do now. I understand what that accusation did to them. To Oliver, who hasn't had a real relationship with a woman since. To my mother and father, who already had so much sadness to deal with over the years, and who had to put on their brave faces and say, "No! Our son did not do this." And probably all my sisters as well. I was too young, I realize. Too fucking young and stupid to comprehend what that word really *meant*.

Rape.

"I need to go home," I say quietly, unable to look him in the face.

"You can't drive home tonight. It's far, Cindy. Almost four hours away."

No. Home is more than a thousand miles away and that's where I want to be right now. With Oliver. And my sisters. I want to see my brother and sisters and my mom and dad. And give them all a huge hug. Say, "I'm sorry this happened. I'm fucking sorry I didn't understand. And most of all, I'm sorry I ran away chasing some phantom man named Paxton Vance."

I should've been concerned with Oliver. Why wasn't I focused on what really matters? Him. His innocence. His reputation and good name. Especially after all the bullshit they went through when I was little

Oliver. My sweet, sweet brother. My *only* brother.

I should be looking for who set *him* up. I should give up on Paxton Vance and concentrate on the only Mister who matters. Match.

"Cindy?" Pax has been talking this entire time. I am wiping my tears away, trying not to draw too much attention to myself. But it's dark where we're standing. On the edge of the barn and the paddock area. There are a ton of people. Trainers, jockeys, owners all dressed up in their special clothes as they drink champagne and laugh and hope for their horses to come back winners.

"I'll take you home," Pax says, finally understanding that I'm not going to talk to him anymore. "But my mother will be very disappointed if we don't at least stay for the race. It's up next, then the day is over and I'll take you home if you want."

I nod, still silent, and let him lead me through the paddock, down the aisle towards the stands, and then back up into the clubhouse.

This time when we get to the Turf Club, every table is full except the five Paxton leads me towards. We stop at the one centered between two more empty tables on either side and Pax sighs, reading my mind. "These are reserved for groups of twenty. My mother hates crowds, so she buys all four seats at each of the five tables and then watches the race alone."

I feel like I'm maybe under control again. My face is dry, the tears have stopped. "I guess she won't be here alone tonight, will she?"

Pax smiles. I think it might be the first real smile I've ever seen from him. It's not a grin, like the ones he used on me in Malibu. Or a smirk, his default setting. Just small, and warm, and kind. "No," he says. "She won't be alone tonight."

The golden filly's name is Aladdin's Cinderella. Full sister to Aladdin's Prince Charming, last year's Triple Crown winner. The first such winner in almost thirty years, I figure out through conversation. When Mariel and her friend, William, start shouting her name as they come down the homestretch, Pax shoots me a weird look.

And when the race is over and Pax leans in to kiss his mother, saying, "Congratulations, Mother. You did it again. She won," Mariel Hawthorne looks straight at me and deadpans, "Of course she did."

I think about those words as Pax and I walk to his car. He is insisting on taking me home. Saying he will take care of my car, but there is no way in hell I'm driving home alone tonight. I think about all the things those words could've meant but only come up with one that makes sense.

Of course she did.

Like it was ordained.

CHAPTER FOURTEEN

PAXTON

"Hey," Cindy says in a low voice. "Where are we going? The 5 freeway is right there."

"I've got a house here in Del Mar. We're staying there tonight."

"You have a house in Del Mar?" I can't tell for sure in the low light of the street lamps, but when I glance over at Cindy, she appears confused.

She's definitely been spying on me. Looking me up. I'm sure she's got all my public assets catalogued in that head of hers. And this house in Del Mar isn't one of them. For good reason. Reasons like this.

"Yeah, right at the top of the hill, actually." I pull into the driveway that leads to the gated community in the cliffs above the Del Mar Racetrack and flash my ID at the guards when the window rolls down.

They know me.

"Hey, Pax. Twice in one week, huh? Maybe you should just move down here?"

"Maybe I should," I tell the guard. "Just the night though. Going back up to LA in the morning."

"Day at the races? Win anything?"

"Just this girl."

Cindy huffs out an objection, but the guard and I just chuckle.

"She looks like a keeper," he says.

"We'll see. Have a good night."

"You too," the guard says, winking.

"That was rude," Cindy says once my window is up. "Keeping me?"

"He said it, not me. What do you want me to do? Get out of the car and beat the shit out of him for insulting you?"

She crosses her arms and turns her head.

"I can," I snarl. "If you want. And I won't even think twice about it. Just say the word."

She's silent, but I don't give a fuck what she thinks about that offer. She needs to understand who I am. What I am. What I do. She needs to be afraid of me.

"You don't scare me," she finally says, like she's reading my mind.

Whatever. She's been weird since that night she followed me up to my bedroom. Everything about her is off. I'm giving it one night, I decided. One night to crack her secrets, then I'm tossing her back. Plenty of fish in that sea out there.

I wind my way up the streets of the high-end neighborhood leading to my house—well, technically, it's Mr. Romantic's house now. I sold it to him a few years back. But he and I both know this is still my place.

I sort of consider all of Nolan's houses mine, I realize. I use that monstrosity out on Martha's Vineyard for business every time I'm on the East Coast. Which isn't that often, I admit. But it's nice to have a place to crash when I'm there.

The palm trees in front of the house are all lit up—everything is on a timer here—and Cindy says, "Whoa. This is kinda nice."

"Not used to nice things, Miss Vaughn?"

She says nothing.

"It is nice. This was the first house I bought out of college. For my mother, really. She was cruising the real estate listings and texted this one to me, gushing about how nice it would be to live next to the track. Well, to live in luxury next to the track. So I bought it."

"For your mother?"

"For me. But her too. So she can stay here when she wants."

"Is she staying here tonight?"

"Nah. She wouldn't stay when I have a girl with me."

"I'm not with you, you know."

"I know." I stop the car in front of the door and turn it off. "Let's go. I'm tired."

Cindy gets out of the car and follows me up to the entry, leaning on the stucco wall as I key in the code to unlock the door.

The alarm pad beeps and flashes red at me.

I smile over at Cindy, key in the numbers again. Get a longer beep and more emphatic flashing lights.

"Problems?" Cindy asks.

Fucking Nolan. He must have changed the code after I admitted to pinching his house back east whenever I wanted. Asshole. After everything I just did for him, this is how he repays me?

I huff out a breath of air, ready to punch in the numbers in again, but Cindy's hand on my arm makes me stop and look at her. "If you get it wrong three times they'll call the cops." She nods her head to the sign in front of the lit-up palm tree. "I know that company. They don't mess around."

We stare at each other.

"This isn't your house."

"It's mine."

"So why don't you know the code?"

"I share it with another Mister. Like we share the jet."

"Hmmm," she says, like she knows I'm lying. "Shall we get a hotel? Or take our chances with jail?"

"We're not going to jail. Don't be dramatic."

"So call him up and ask him for the code."

I hesitate.

"Problem?"

"He's not home."

"He has a cell phone, right?"

I look behind me, wonder if any of the boutique hotels here in Del Mar will have openings, but then look back at Cindy when she pulls a cord out of her purse and hooks it up to her phone.

"They have ports in them." She smiles at me, plugging the other end into the bottom of the security pad. "Backdoor access, so to speak."

"Well, that's not very secure."

"No one knows about it."

"Except you?" I laugh.

"I know someone high up in this company. An old friend."

"Really." Hmmm. "A friend of a friend of mine *owns* this company."

"What's his name?" she asks with a smirk. "Maybe he's my contact."

116

She's fishing for more information. I bet she already knows that one of Match's sisters owns this security company and she's trying to get me to cough up more information.

"It's a woman," I say. "Can you get it to open or not?"

Her thumbs are already flying across the keypad of her phone and a few seconds later, there's a cheery ping and the pad flashes green as the locks disengage.

She reaches forward and opens the glass doors, pushing them inward. Then waves a hand. "After you."

"I insist," I say, faking a smile and stepping back to make her enter first. "Who says chivalry is dead?"

She enters, I follow, and flick on the lights to the living room from the master panel near the door.

"Well, this is quite nice. Is that the track down there?" She's at the terrace doors, already sliding them open, and the sea breeze blows her hair softly around her shoulders.

Who *is this girl?*

I walk over to the bar, calling out, "Drink?" as I go.

"Sure."

I grab two crystal tumblers from a shelf, then reach for the booze. "Bourbon?" I ask. "There's no way in hell we've got powdered sugar for a mint julep."

"Bourbon straight?"

"Rocks?" I suggest.

"No. That's gross. How about a margarita?"

"Margarita?" I practically snort. "What kind of drink is that?"

"A fun one," she says, frowning.

117

I'm twisting the cap of the bottle when I stop and take her in again. The light is low in here and it bathes her in a softness that makes me wonder again. Who is this girl?

"Want me to make them?"

"What?"

"The margaritas. It's that or nothing for me."

"I can make them," I say. "Blended?"

"Of course."

Of course. "Lemon or triple sec?" I ask.

"Strawberry," she says back.

I laugh. "We don't have strawberry."

She shrugs. "Then forget it. I'm not thirsty."

"We don't drink because we're *thirsty*."

"Then why are we drinking?"

"Because I really fucking need one."

"Too much talk about silver envelopes today?"

"Who are you?"

She shrugs. "Cinderella, that's who."

I can't stop looking at her. She's so fucking... mysterious. I almost laugh when that word pops into my head.

A hand goes to my chin as I consider what to do. Then I walk towards the door, pulling my keys out of my pocket.

"Where are you going?"

"To get you some fucking strawberries."

"Don't forget the salt," she yells after me. "And some powdered sugar!"

I try to slam the door closed on my way out of the house, but Nolan put a soft close mechanism on the hinges so the glass won't break by accident, and it's about as anticlimactic as this whole fucking day.

I rev the engine of my Audi, then back out of the driveway, screeching my tires.

CHAPTER FIFTEEN
CINDY

I stay out on the terrace, even after Pax comes back and starts blending up the drinks. He says nothing, just gets to work. And ten minutes later, after many 'fucks,' and 'shits,' and 'goddammits,' he casts a shadow over me when he blocks the lights from behind.

"Your drink, my lady."

I smile, but tuck it away before I turn to face him. I take the drink and sip. "Mmm. That's nice."

"It's weak as fuck," he says, grimacing as he swallows. "And sweet."

"I like sweet drinks."

"Sugar," he says.

"Hmm?" I ask, looking up at him

"You smell like sugar. These stupid drinks you like must leak through your pores."

"Could be worse." I take another sip, then a gulp.

"Well," he says, holding his margarita glass out when I come up for air. "Cheers."

"To the end of a very confusing day."

"I'll drink to that."

"Should we talk about it?" I ask, not really wanting to talk about any of it.

"What's to talk about?"

"Right."

We both turn to the sound of the crashing waves down below, then lean our forearms on the terrace railing, drinks in hand.

"This is pretty. I bet Nolan Delaney comes here a lot."

I catch a small chuckle from him. "How'd you know it was his?"

"Are we talking about it?" I ask, looking up at him.

"No. But Nolan doesn't come here much. I really did buy this place for my mom. But I needed money to buy those islands, so I sold it to Nolan." Then he adds, "With the understanding that he'd keep it safe for me. So it really is still mine."

"Except for the deed and all that good junk." But I'm still thinking about those islands.

"Why are you here?" he asks.

"You brought me here," I say.

"No. I mean, why are you *here?* In my life."

"I don't really know, Paxton. I'm asking myself that very same question."

"You've been stalking me," he says. "For a long time, from the looks of it."

"Yes." I sigh. "Obviously."

"And now you don't like what you see."

"I'm just questioning a lot of things tonight, that's all."

"About me? Or why you've bothered?"

"So we're talking about it?" I ask again. "Because once we start this, Pax, we won't be able to stop."

He's silent for a moment. I finish my drink and hold the empty glass in my hands, twirling it around as I look out over the ocean. There's a nice moon tonight. Not full, not dark, not crescent, just enough to see the beach and the track down below.

"You want to go to bed?"

"With you?" I ask, a tingle running up my body at the thought. He's so fucking handsome in this gray suit. His tie is loose around his neck, probably from the frustration of my drink demands, because it was tight before he left for the store. I bite my lip as he stares at me, that tingle turning into something more urgent as I stare back.

"Why not? We could make it fun. Turn this day around. End it on a high note."

I have dreamed about sex with Mr. Mysterious for years. Since I was a kid, actually. And I know we've fucked three times already, but that was different. That was the other me. This is the real me. And now that my plans are all falling into place, it feels… fake. Like I forced this.

"I wouldn't want to force you," I say, that word stuck in my mind.

He laughs. Maybe a real one. "You're the most striking girl I've ever dated. You're not forcing me to do anything."

He has no idea how well-planned this relationship was. "Are we dating?" I ask, suddenly sad.

I know he's looking at me. And I know I'm being weird. I also know that I should make a decision right now and then never look back. Either stay here, sleep with him, and tell him the truth tomorrow—since we've decided not to talk about it tonight—or walk out and never look back.

I'm on the verge of option two when I feel his hand slip around my waist. "Whatever it is that's bothering you, can it wait until tomorrow? Or is it urgent?"

123

I like the feel of his hand over the thin fabric of my dress. It's large, and warm, and when he pulls me closer, I feel weak with want.

"That was a lot of information to take in. From your mother. Don't you think?" I chance a look up at him and regret it immediately. He's somber. I don't think I've ever seen him somber.

"Are we talking about it?" he whispers. "I don't mind talking about it. If that's what you want."

I lean up and kiss him. Softly. Right on the mouth. He doesn't kiss me back and when I open my eyes, he's looking at me. He takes the drink from my hand, sets both glasses down on a nearby table and then wraps his arms around me and holds me close. His lips are on my neck, and that urgent feeling I had turns into unquenchable desire.

He holds my face, turning me towards him, and then his lips find mine and we are kissing again, only this time it's him leading the way. It starts slow, his hands dropping back to my waist. My hands reaching up for his shoulders. His kiss remains soft. Such a contradiction between the man on the outside I've come to know and the one I stalked all these years

But I don't know him, do I? Not one bit.

He frightens me a little. His perfectly planned childhood, his unplanned past, and his unorthodox present. Like he's drifting through life, just waiting for something to happen as he takes bad opportunity after bad opportunity and tries to make something good out of them.

"Let's go to bed," Pax says again.

I don't challenge him in any way this time. I don't care what the meaning is behind his words.

He takes my hand, leading me back into the house and towards the stairs, taking those two at a time so my much shorter legs have to struggle to keep up. A shoe falls off my foot halfway up, the other follows a second later. The floor is cool and feels good as I follow him across a long catwalk that overlooks the living room and into a dark bedroom.

He doesn't turn on the lights and he wastes no time touching me. His fingertips are lifting up my dress, feather-light touches across the bare skin of my outer thigh. Kissing me, fisting my hair, finding the wetness between my legs as the tingle becomes urge, becomes starvation and hunger for more.

"Take off my clothes," he says. "Start with the tie."

It's already loose, so it slips over his head.

"And don't hurry. We're not in a hurry."

I've come to expect passion to equal fast, and hard, and out of control. But this is nothing like that and yet… it is passionate.

I tug on his shirt, lifting it out of his pants. My hand grazes against the thick bulge hidden away in there, making him bite my lip just a little. Just enough to get my attention.

Oh, he has my attention all right.

I don't want to think about tomorrow. Maybe tomorrow won't even come?

"Need help?" he asks, whispering the words into my mouth.

I say nothing, just continue to fumble with the buttons of his shirt until I finally get them all undone and I drag the expensive fabric over the curve of his shoulders and let it drop to the floor.

His hands are dealing with the thin straps of my dress. They slide down, over my shoulders, his mouth momentarily distracted by my skin as he kisses and nips. My arms fall straight down my sides as he slips the top of my dress down to my waist, cups my breasts in his palms, pushing them up towards my chin, squeezing them until I let out a, "Ohhhhmmmmm," sound.

"If you talk. If you say one word," he says, "I will lose control and this will not be anything like I've imagined it."

I want to ask him how he's imagined it.

But why ask when I can be patient and see for myself?

He bends down, taking the skirt of my dress with him, and the silky fabric whooshes to the floor, making a small breeze against my ankles.

He stands, kissing me and nipping me. "Pants, Cindy."

My fist is around his cock, squeezing him the way he was squeezing me just seconds ago. He's warm, and hard, and ready for me.

"Pants," he says again.

The button flips undone. Then the zipper is open and my hand finds the flesh of his cock. Warm and thick.

Pressure on my shoulders as he guides me backwards. I bump into the bed and sit automatically. He drops to his knees in front of my face, giving me one more kiss before pushing me back into the soft comforter.

I sigh, arms above my head at his silent urging. His mouth is on my ribs, his tongue tracing across my stomach, his kisses dropping lower and lower and lower until he's licking me through my panties. His fingers find their way underneath the fabric, pushing into me, making me gasp with pleasure and surprise.

I say nothing as his mouth works on the delicate fold of skin that will make me come in a matter of seconds if he doesn't back down. Two fingers inside me. Stretching and searching for that spot…

"Ohhhhmmmmmmmm," I say again.

"Shhh." He vibrates the request against my clit and my hands fly to his biceps, fingernails digging in, my legs rising up and open to give him more access. He stands, kicks off his shoes, drops his pants and then leans over me.

"I'm gonna fuck you for real now."

CHAPTER SIXTEEN

PAXTON

I grab her ankles and spread her legs wide, easing over the top of her—my chest to her breasts, my cock positioned at her entrance. She's so fucking wet. I wrap my fist around my dick and flick her clit a few times. Her whole body arches in response.

"You like that," I whisper, continuing the motion.

She says nothing, her eyes squeezed tight, biting her lip, fingernails digging into my skin.

I plunge inside her and she goes soft. Our hips move together for a moment, kinda slow. Kinda easy. But then I lean down into her neck and bite her earlobe, going faster and faster as she responds to this new direction. Her tits bounce against me, legs wrapped around my body, knees pressed against my hips.

And she smells like sugar.

Everything about her is sweet. The little moans she's making. The scent of her hair. Her pink lips and those perfect nipples. I lean in and bite her lip. Her eyes open and I start pumping her harder. Slapping against the inside of her thighs. Everything is wet, and hot, and time just needs to stand still so this never has to end.

"I'm gonna come," she whispers.

"Not yet—"

"Ohhhhhmmmmm. Shit. Oh, fuck, yes! Fuck me! Fuck me!"

"OK." I laugh, enjoying her little show. "Yeah, OK. Come, sugar. Come all over me."

Her hands are suddenly in my hair. Twisting and pulling like she's holding on to me. Never gonna let me go.

"Pax," she moans out. She's still fucking coming. I feel wave after wave after wave of contractions against my dick as I slow down.

"No," she says. "Harder! Harder, harder, harder…"

I speed back up. Pounding her now. She is gushing with come. My dick slides in and out of her pussy. I stand back up, grab hold of her hip bones, and watch the curve of my cock enter, and almost exit, her opening. The lips of her pussy wrap around my shaft like a glove. Like we are puzzle pieces fitting together.

And then her fingers are there. Pushing against her clit. Rubbing as she continues to moan. I slap her hand away. "I don't need help."

She laughs, eyes closed again. "Something is wrong with me. I'm so fucking horny right now. I just came—twice—and I need more." Her eyes fly open and she stares at me. "Flip me over."

Nobody tells me that twice. I step back and flip her whole body over, push her knees up, press her head down onto the comforter and tongue her wet pussy, flicking against her clit.

"I forgot to tell you—"

"Are we talking about this?" I ask, still trying to lick her.

"I'm a squirter."

"What?"

"Shit!" She wiggles away from me, kicking out and squirming her way across the bed.

"What the fuck are you doing?"

"I don't want to ruin this bed! I'm telling you, I'm a squirter and this will be pretty messy if we keep going."

I grab her by the ankles and pull her back to me, then reach under, lift her up, and hoist her over my shoulder.

"What are you doing?" she squeals.

"Taking this to the shower."

I walk across the room, flip the light on in the master bath, take her into the massive shower, and set her down on the marble bench. "Don't move," I say, my eyes never leaving hers as I reach around and feel for the steam switch on the wall, flick it on, and then look hungrily at my girl as the mist wafts around us in floating tendrils. "Squirter, huh?"

She bites her lip to stifle a laugh.

"And you know this how?" I should shut the fuck up. I don't want to know how she knows. But I can't help it.

She shakes her head and giggles.

"Cindy."

"When I masturbate, it just—it gets—overwhelming and then... you know. That happens. And the way you were touching me in there. It felt like..."

"Masturbation?" I say with a cock-eyed smile. "Nice recovery." I drop to my knees, push her back so she's resting against the wall, and do it exactly the way I was. Quickly flicking my dick against her clit. She grabs on to the edge of the stone bench this time, her knees pulling up automatically.

"Like this?" I ask, never taking my eyes off her.

And then she's out of control. Her moans turn into gasps, turn into screams. I cup my hand over her mouth automatically, momentarily startled as she writhes, and kicks, and yes—squirts.

I don't think anything has ever turned me on so much in my entire life.

I take her hands, pulling her up to standing. She wobbles, like she's not under control yet. So I reach under her thighs, lift her up, press her against the wall, and pound her hard until there's no way I'm stopping. I pound her until there is nothing on my mind but coming inside her. She squeezes my hips with her thighs, so tight. So focused. My hands come up to her face, glistening from the steam, and I kiss her, and fuck her until she comes again and there is only one thing left to do.

Finish.

"Fuck… yes…" That was perfect.

She collapses against my chest, spent and tired. I walk backwards until I find the bench, and then sit down with her in my lap. Her face is buried in my neck. We are sweaty, and hot, and breathing in the steam like the air we are sucking is lifesaving.

I rest my head back against the wall, close my eyes, and let go. Maybe for the first time in my life I just let it all go. The past. The jobs. The future. It's gone. Wiped away in the aftermath of lust.

After a few minutes of stillness, she eases backward, gets up, turns the steam off, and then starts the shower. She makes the water cool, then grabs my hand and pulls me to my feet.

We wash each other. Hair, body, soul.

And then we dry each other off and I lead her out to the bedroom. Collapsing onto the soft comforter, not even bothering to get underneath it. I just grab her and never let go. Pull her into my chest, wrap my hands around her breasts, and… sleep.

I wake up to sun beaming down on my face, reaching for Cindy. Finding her gone. What did I expect? I swing my legs over the side of the bed, rub the stubble on my jaw with both hands, and then stand up and take a piss in the bathroom.

That was the best sex I've ever had and I know—I just fucking know—it's only the beginning if I get to see her again after we talk about it.

I pull on some boxer briefs and walk towards the stairs, surprised when I cross the catwalk and see her—back to me—cooking at the stove in the open kitchen down below.

I don't say anything. I don't even know if I have words for what this is. What I'm doing. But I stop at the top of the stairs when I see the shoe. Left there last night as I brought her up here.

It's fitting, right? Cinderella leaves a shoe on the stairs and then Prince Charming has to go looking for her with only that one shoe as his clue.

The other shoe is further down. And it's a good sign, I think. That we are not that story. She didn't disappear. I don't have to go searching for her. We can spend the day together. No one to stop us. Start something new. No rules, or expectations, or baggage to drag us down.

Well, that's a fairy tale too, I guess. Because I've got baggage, man. I've got a huge amount of baggage and there's no fairy godmother coming to make it all better.

"What are you doing?" I ask, reaching the bottom of the steps.

"Cooking," she chirps, flipping something over in a pan. This is the Cindy I know. Happy, cheerful, easygoing.

"Where'd you get food?" I say, coming up behind her and wrapping my arms around her body so I can squeeze her tits and kiss her neck. She's wearing an apron, of all things. It's yellow, like her hair. With cookies on it. And a tank top and shorts.

Sugar. Goddammit if she doesn't smell like sugar. Even after staying in someone else's house, taking a shower with their scented soaps and shampoos, and frying bacon in a pan.

"I borrowed your car and went to the store."

"You... left?" I ask.

"I came back." She says it like she might not've.

"Where'd you get these clothes?" She's wearing my dress shirt and a pair of man's shorts that must be Nolan's. Which means she's been snooping around the house while I was sleeping. "What time did you wake up?"

"What?" She feigns ignorance.

I feign with her. Are we talking about this yet? Who she is? Where she came from? How she knows all these things and why she's been watching me?

If we talk about that, well, then we'll have to talk about my mother. The Silver Pledge—whatever the fuck that is. Those envelopes, the note, the game. "Smells good," I say. I can play along. I don't even mind playing along.

"What time do you have to be in the office today?"

How'd she know I have to be in the office today?

Forget it. We're not talking about it.

"What time is it?" I ask.

"Eleven thirty."

"Shit," I say, threading my fingers through my hair. "I have a client today."

"I know. Mr. Walker's son went missing two weeks ago. It's out of character and no leads so far. The police aren't interested, so he came to you."

We really should start talking about this. But instead of starting that conversation, I say, "Do you want to help me find him? I could use a good assistant."

She looks over her shoulder, gives me a sidelong smirk. "You don't even have to ask. I'm already on it. I pulled up his phone records and even though there doesn't seem to be a pattern, there is. A number he calls every Tuesday evening. He's called it without fail for over a year, but he only calls once a week, so it's not an easy pattern to see when you look at all the hundreds of other calls and texts he sends. He's a chatty guy. But I found it. So we can start there if you want."

I pull her hair aside, giving myself better access to her neck. And I kiss her again. She sighs, leans against me just slightly. Just enough to let me know we don't really need to talk about it. Denial is our friend today.

She squirms out of my embrace and grabs two plates sitting on the counter. She scoops up some scrambled eggs from another pan, then the bacon, loading up each plate as the toast pops up. "Butter that for me, will you?"

The butter is sitting out on the counter already, soft. So I grab the toast and butter it up, dropping the slices on the plates just as she whisks them away to the dining table in front of the big picture window that overlooks the racetrack.

"I made mimosas, too. You like mimosas, right?" She smiles at me.

I hate champagne. But I smile back and say, "Almost as much as I like margaritas and mint juleps."

"I hope you're hungry," she says, smiling into her glass as she takes a drink.

"I'm gonna fuck you on my desk this afternoon."

She almost spits out her mimosa.

"And then at my house tonight."

"OK."

"And we're never talking about it."

She swallows hard and nods. "OK." It's softer than the last OK, filled with relief and maybe even some regret. But then she forces another smile, lifts her glass and says, "To new beginnings."

"I'll drink to that."

I do believe I will come to love this drink. And all the girly things this sweet-smelling Cinderella has brought into my life. If only for the fact that they symbolize something.

Not a beginning. But an end.

Fuck those silver envelopes. Fuck that rape charge. Fuck everything but what happens from this day forward.

It's over.

I *am* Prince Charming in this story, and I decree the bullshit to be over.

CHAPTER SEVENTEEN
CINDY

Everything is smooth sailing for almost a week. We find that jerk of a son for Mr. Walker. He was on a drug binge. We looked up that one number later that day and traced it to a phone booth—who knew they still have those things?—outside the Derryman's Pub in Santa Monica. Some high-end dealer uses that thing as an office. So we followed him and... well, all sorts of boring drama unfolded. But the point is, we cracked that case in three days.

Since then, Mr. Walker has referred us to many of his "private" friends, as he likes to call them. Just little things. One guy thought his wife was cheating. One woman thought her husband was cheating. And it occurs to me now that the very nature of Paxton Vance's business has begun to change.

It's like... It's like he's not a fixer anymore. He really is my fictional detective.

We never do talk about it. Even though it feels—to me, anyway—that there's this big question mark hanging over us, we don't talk about any of it. Not his mother, not the day at the races, not my past, not how conveniently I left my life in Malibu behind and moved in with him. Not any of it.

The phone rings and I pick it up. "Mr. Vance's office. How can I help you?"

"What?"

Oh, shit. I do not need more than one word to tell me who is on the other end of this phone.

My brother, Oliver.

I clear my throat. "Mr. Vance's office," I repeat, using a fake high voice. "How can I help you?"

"Since when does he have a fucking secretary?"

"Assistant," I say, still using my high voice.

"Is he there or not?"

Hmmm. I never knew my brother was such a dick. "No, I'm sorry, sir. He's out of the office for the... week."

I smile and wave at Pax through the closed glass door to his office, then shake my head, stick out my tongue like this is nothing but a stupid sales call, and he laughs, looking back down at his paperwork.

"The fucking *week*? When exactly will he be back? I tried his cell, but he's not picking up. Why isn't he picking up?"

He's not picking up because he left his cell at home today by accident. Jesus Christ, what if Oliver comes here? No. No. He's all the way over in Colorado. This is no big deal. "He's... in the Exuma Cays, Mr..."

"Shrike," Oliver says, thoroughly annoyed with me now. It's not my fault Pax is off gallivanting. Well, if he *was* off gallivanting, it wouldn't be my fault. And Oliver doesn't know he's not. So... *dick*.

"Mr. Shrike, Mr. Vance is gone for the whole week and won't be back until next Monday. He's on a break. No tech out there."

"Since when? I know damn well he's got internet and TV on that fucking island."

Shit. *Think, Cindy*. "He's on that other island." Yeah. That *other* island. He's got two, he told me that.

"Since when does he have two—never mind. Let him know I called if he calls in. And tell him to hit me back, pronto."

The phone goes dead and I just stare at it for a second.

"Who was that?" Pax asks from his open door.

"Um…" Shit. How much did he hear? "I have no idea. Some rude salesman asking about copy machines."

"Copy machines?"

I have to control my eye roll at myself. Copy machines? *Who the fuck sells copy machines anymore, Cinderella?* People just use printers in an office this size.

Pax narrows his eyes at me. Suspicion, I realize.

"He was handsome in a rugged sort of way."

The narrow eyes widen. A smile.

"A real man's man with his rolled-up sleeves and loose tie."

"Is this how you see me?" Paxton asks.

"Smart enough to get into Ivy League schools. Wise enough to get by without them."

"Shit," he whispers under his breath.

"And the first time I walked into his office, desperate for help—"

"Oh, I get it. This is some nineteen-forties detective noir?"

"—all I could think about was how long it would take him to bend me over his desk—"

Now he laughs, but stifles it with a closed fist in front of his mouth.

"—hike up my skirt, and take me from behind." I stop to smile with him. God, he's cute. "Hoping, when he finally did

139

that, he wouldn't see the run in my stockings. The broken buckle on my shoe—"

"Downtrodden dame," Pax says. "Nice touch."

"—the cheap scent of my perfume."

"Sugar, baby. Like you stepped out of a bakery every time I see you. There's nothing cheap about smelling sweet."

I have him now. That phone call is long forgotten. But… it's fun. So I keep going with my little narration. "And he'd just lose himself in my lust."

"Lust, huh?"

I take a deep breath. Happy. Happier than I've ever been, I think. "You're fun, you know that?"

"*You're* fun," he says, coming close enough to grab my waist and twirl me around. "Is this how the story starts, then? You're a dame looking for help from the down-and-out unorthodox detective?"

I go up on my tiptoes and kiss him, our mouths fitting together in that perfect puzzle-piece way they do. His hands slip from my hips to my ass, and he gives my cheeks a squeeze before hiking up my skirt, exposing my bare skin to the cool office air.

"I won't be able to find that run in your stocking, sugar. Because you're not wearing anything but this thong."

"I'm not really a stocking kind of girl, but I can be if it turns you on."

"Should I pick up a trench coat?"

I laugh, then lean into his neck and just sigh.

"What?" he asks, nuzzling my hair.

"I like you."

"Well." He kisses my earlobe. "That's perfect. Because I like you too."

"You don't think I'm weird, even though I can be a little over the top?"

"You?" He pulls back in mock surprise. "No."

"I know, right?" We smile at each other. Why did I start the story again? Oh, yeah. Phone call. What phone call?

"You're definitely unique, Miss Sugar."

"Miss Sugar," I huff.

"And impulsive. And quite the little liar."

"What?" Shit. What does he know?

"I own the sub shop," he says, faking a high voice. "I was checking on you in there." He nods his head to his office.

"Dammit. I was gonna tell you."

"I don't care."

"I lied about the sub shop. I was bribing the delivery driver so I could meet you once I noticed you were ordering takeout."

"So where do you live? Where do you keep the clothes you keep going home for?"

"With you. Now." I smile, not sure how this will go since this is kind of the start of talking about it. "But I was living out of a backpack in a trailer at the campground up PCH."

"Not a trust-fund baby?"

"Oh, I am." I laugh. "But my father likes to parcel that shit out a little at a time. There's all kinds of restrictions on it. I didn't even get a monthly allowance for college. Every semester he took a trip out to my school to pay my tuition in person. I got a little bit when I turned eighteen. Just enough to buy a car and live in the dorms. Then I got a little bit more at graduation. But I used it for grad school. You see the pattern, I'm sure."

"So you're broke?"

"Does it matter?"

"No," Pax says. "No, I'm just asking if you're broke."

"Not broke. I am an investigator. I have jobs I get off my brother's website."

Holy motherfucking shit. *What the hell is wrong with you, Cindy Shrike? Cinderella Vaughn has no brother.* I scramble to recover from my mistake.

"Well, I'm doing your jobs now," I say. "So I'm not working on anything myself. But I get by. I'm not broke."

"The trust fund is over?"

Whew. He didn't notice. "Do you get a trust fund?" I ask, following his lead.

"Me? Ha." He laughs. "No. My mother is a dig-yourself-out-of-your-own-hole kind of woman. But I don't need a trust fund. I made smart decisions back in the day."

He's got this weird smirk on his face. Like he's pulling something over on the whole world. "What? Did you steal it or something?"

"Steal it? Why would I steal it? That's a weird question. You remind me of Match, you know that?"

Oh, fuck. I was totally safe about the call and now we're right back where I started. "Who?" I ask innocently.

"Oliver Shrike? Mr. Match? One of the five who was accused? It's funny, when he and I had our first money conversation, he asked me the same thing. Said his father pulled some kind of con when he was younger and ever since he found that out, he was…"

I lose track of his words. I was there when Oliver found out the kind of stuff my dad used to do with his friends before any of us kids were born. It was crazy. Ariel was the one who dug up the dirt. Just a casual, *Let's see what kind of dirt we can find on Dad*, kind of thing. We never expected what we found.

"Cindy?"

"What?" Pax is looking at me expectantly. Like he's waiting for an answer. "Sorry. I just kind of spaced out for a minute thinking about your Mister friend."

"Hmmm."

What kind of hmmm was that? Suspicious? "I thought you were gonna fuck me on the desk."

"Is that right?" Pax says.

"We went from titillating fantasy to money. No one likes to talk about money, Pax. But sex," I say with a wink. "Now there's a fun subject." I lean back into his neck, trying my best to recapture the moment. But… it's gone.

Just then a knock on the door pulls us apart. I whirl around to see that man who came to visit Pax up in Malibu. Liam.

"What the hell are you doing here?" Pax says. "I told you, Liam. I'm not interested in your problem or your job."

"Who's this?" Liam's attention turns to me as I hastily finish straightening out my skirt.

"No one you need to remember," Pax says, turning to me. "Cindy, can you go grab me lunch from that sandwich shop down the street? Get my usual, please."

Is he kidding? Trying to get me out of here without this weirdo noticing me too much? Or blowing me off? "Sure," I say, not meeting his eyes as I pick up my purse and head towards the door.

"Let's talk in here," Paxton says. I chance one look back before I leave, but they disappear into his office.

CHAPTER EIGHTEEN
PAXTON

Liam is smiling like he's got a secret. It pisses me off that he came into my life uninvited for the second time. But I keep the temper in check as I close the door behind him, then walk around my desk and take a seat.

The polite thing to do when talking to an equal is to sit in one of the two chairs facing the desk, with the guest in the chair next to yours. But I sit behind the desk for a reason.

I'm the one in charge here, and I want him to know it.

Plus, his back is to the door and I can see straight through the glass to Cindy's desk. And I have the phone in front of me. "Let me just put this on 'do not disturb' in case Cindy comes back and wants to… disturb us."

Liam brushes a piece of lint off his navy blue suit coat, like he couldn't care less. "Pretty, that one. But a little slutty for a man of your breeding, don't you think? Her ass was hanging out her skirt when I came in."

"Why are you here?" I ask calmly, trying my best not to lean across this desk, grab Liam Henry by the tie, and choke this motherfucker to death.

"Mr. Corporate," he says, taking out a notepad from his suit coat pocket. "Do you know his real name?"

"Um." I laugh. "Weston Conrad. The guy I've known for ten years."

"And how well do you really think you know him?" Liam is smiling like he's got a secret.

"Look, if you've got something to say, then say it. Corporate and I aren't besties. We're not partners, or hell, even friends from my perspective. I don't give a fuck who he is. But you obviously think I should, so let's hear all your little secrets about him and hopefully that will explain away your bizarre stalking and I won't have to kill you over it."

Liam narrows his eyes, wondering if that's a threat, a joke, or a promise.

Damn, I hadn't realized how good it felt to be the bad guy since I've been hanging out with Cindy doing her cute little detective jobs. But I sort of miss these moments.

"Well, his name isn't Weston Conrad, for one. And for two, he stole something from me a very long time ago. Something I want back."

"I'll ask this again. And I'll try to be as concise as I can so you will stop wasting my time. What does this have to do with *me*?"

"I'd thought you'd like to know who set you up back in college. Forgive me," he says, standing up and buttoning his coat, "for interrupting the nooner you were about to have with your secretary."

"Sit *down*," I command.

"Oh, so you're interested all of a sudden?" But Liam unbuttons his suit coat and sits. Smiling like a cat with a canary.

"Corporate was accused too. It makes no sense that he was the one who set us up." But I have always had a problem with Corporate. I mean, I have always had a problem with Romantic too. But Corporate, he never did add up. Romantic has a pretty paper-trailed past leading from point A to point B in a nice straight line.

Corporate's past is like a dot-to-dot puzzle that I could never quite figure out. Match and Five and I worked on it relentlessly ten years ago when these charges came up. And even though Five has got to be one of the most talented hackers in modern day that I know of, we came up with very little before he went to boarding school as a teenager. Which means part of his past was hidden off the record for a reason.

"Well, he did set you up. He did. And I have all the proof and all the details and you will get every bit of it... once he's gone."

"Gone?" I ask. "You want me to *kill* him?" I laugh.

"I need him delivered to me alive so I can get this information out of him, but your run-of-the-mill accident will suffice once that business is taken care of."

"I'm not a professional killer, Liam. You know this." I have no problem killing people, but it's not what I do. I like people to think it is—keeps them scared. Distant. But I don't kill people for money, for fuck's sake. That's insane. My mother would never respect me if I was a paid assassin.

"You fix things. I need a fix."

"I only fix things if I have all the details."

He reaches into his pocket again, pulls out a neatly folded stack—kind of thick stack—of legal-sized papers. "And here's our problem," he says, grabbing the Mont Blanc pen off my desk and tapping it on the wood. "I have those details, and you can have them too, if you sign this non-disclosure agreement."

I laugh. Kinda loud. "First of all," I say, "I don't sign anything without a lawyer looking it over first. And second of all, I'm never signing that, no matter what. So if you'd like to pay for my services, it's going to be done with my own standard non-disclosure agreement or it won't be done at all."

"Fair enough," Liam says, folding the wad of legal papers back up and placing them back in his coat pocket. "I'll sign your agreement."

He's setting me up. I'm one hundred percent sure of it. But he does have my attention, so I get up, go to the file cabinet, and pull out the standard non-disclosure agreement I have with all my clients.

I slap the single piece of paper down on my desk in front of Liam and take my seat back behind it.

Liam signs.

I drag the paper over to my side, sign, then put the pen down and steeple my fingers under my chin. "Let's hear it."

"Weston Conrad isn't his real name. The Conrads aren't even his parents."

"Hmm," I say. "Go on."

"He's mixed up with a girl right now. Someone from his past. Do you remember her? Victoria Arias? They were dating when that charge came against the five of you."

"Kind of. Dark, right? Pretty? Wild?"

"Yes." Liam nods, smiling big. "I'd call her more than pretty, though. But yes. That's her. They broke up—"

"All the time," I say, recalling that little volatile relationship with ease, now that her name has been mentioned.

"But *she* is the reason you got in all that trouble, Paxton. Her. And *him*. They are the reason. And while I could really care less about Miss Arias—she has her own keeper who will take care of business on that end—I very much need Mr. Conrad to understand that I have not forgotten what he did to me."

"And you want me to teach him that lesson?"

"Just get him out of the country. That's all I ask. I have a team of people ready to take over once that happens. You won't even have to dirty your hands."

"Other than setting him up?"

"Correct."

"Why me?" But I know the answer before he says it.

"Because Conrad trusts you. Regardless of whether or not you are *besties*, as you put it. You're part of his inner circle."

"And he set me up. That makes zero sense."

"Oh, but it does. You just need more information. Information I will provide once he's out of the country."

I pick up my pen and tap the desk, thinking it over.

"I told you that first time I called. Your Mister friends are becoming a problem. That whole debacle with Allen and Perfect could've been a PR nightmare."

Mac.

"And now your Romantic friend is directing a lot of attention back to the five of you."

Nolan.

"Corporate needs to pay his dues. He owes me. And once I tell you the truth about him, you'll want your revenge as well."

West.

It's like a checklist, isn't it? One by one, we are all being drawn back in. "I'll think about it."

"You have one night, Mr. Vance. One night before I take things into my own hands and deal with the situation another way." He stands, buttons his coat jacket. Says, "You won't like that way, I assure you. So I'll expect a text this evening saying you'll accept my offer and an outline of how you will do as I ask. Use the same number I used that first time I called."

He walks out, closing my office door behind him.

I sit for a moment, then remember that Cindy came back and ducked under the desk, just as I pushed the intercom instead of the "do not disturb" button on the phone.

She stands up and looks at me through the glass doors of my office. I open the door and ask, "Did you catch all that?"

She nods. "What's going on?"

"I have no clue. But that shit that went down with Nolan last week was not cool, man. I might not like that asshole all that much, but he had nothing to do with anything that happened to us back in school. I know it for a fact. I saw his dirt and that's all it is. It's dirty as fuck, for sure. But it's got nothing to do with the rape charge."

"So it really was Weston Conrad who set you up?"

"I don't know. I don't *fucking* know."

"What are you gonna do?" She hesitates. "You're really going to work with that guy? Pax? He's unstable, clearly. He's fucking creepy."

"Yeah," I say, letting out a long breath. "Yeah, you're right. I'm gonna pretend to think about it for a few hours, then send him a text saying no."

150

She smiles. "Good. Good. I know this is the right answer. You need to stay away from him."

"Let's take the day off, huh? Go back home. Grill some steaks, make some stupid girly drinks, and just forget about Liam Henry."

Cindy smiles. "That's definitely the best idea I've heard all day."

I try not to be silent and introspective as we start the drive back up to Malibu, but I don't have to try too hard because Cindy is chatty enough. It kind of sucks that she's part of this. That I dragged her into something that's got nothing to do with her. Especially since Liam already saw her, so even if I wanted to keep her out of this whole mess, it wouldn't be easy to pull off now.

Girlfriends are dangerous.

Match knows this better than anyone. It's why he fucks them and leaves them as fast as he can.

Girlfriends are nothing but collateral damage waiting to happen.

CHAPTER NINETEEN

CINDY

"So what do you think?"

"Hmmm?" Pax says as he changes lanes. The traffic on the 405 is horrendous. And we are still a long way from Malibu.

"My detective story?"

"Oh," he says, braking hard as he tries to maneuver into the next lane.

"Where are you going?"

"We're taking PCH. I can't handle this shit anymore. I really need to think about moving."

"Moving where?"

"Huh?"

"God, are you even listening to me?"

Pax smiles and shoots me a wink. "Sorry. I'm just preoccupied with road rage at the moment." He swerves over, then again, and takes the off ramp at El Segundo. "I love your story. I can totally see you in one of those sexy pencil skirts with the thick-heeled pumps and your hair up in a forties do. You'd rock that shit, Sugar."

"Thanks," I say, blushing. "You'd rock a trench coat and fedora too. So I got the idea when I was seven and my parents took this murder mystery train up in the mountains."

"Mountains? I thought you lived on a farm? Your dad's place comes up as Severance, Colorado."

Shit. Why am I so stupid?

"Well, yeah," I say, recovering quickly. "But you know, the mountains aren't too far away. We'd go there sometimes."

"Don't they have one of those murder mystery trains in Canon City? I think I remember Match telling me about it once. That's pretty far from Severance, right?"

Damn, he's really up on his Colorado geography. "That's the one," I say, nervously swallowing. Does he know more than I think he does? Is he testing me to see if I'll lie? And did I ever tell him I was from Severance? Nope. I'm pretty sure I didn't.

He was checking up on you again this afternoon, Cindy. Duh! You're doing good pretending this Liam shit didn't rattle your world. Keep going...

"Asshole," Pax says, flipping the finger to some guy who cuts him off. "I'm definitely getting out of California first chance I get. Sorry," he says, looking at me. "Go on. The murder mystery train?"

"Yeah," I say, dropping my suspicions. I think he's just distracted with driving. I'm being paranoid. "So they were all in costume, you know?"

"Yeah, I can totally picture it. How old were you? Did you have blonde pigtails?"

I smile, remembering that day. It was my parents' anniversary. But if Oliver was talking about it once, he might've mentioned that. So I don't bring it up. "I was young, I don't remember how old. But I was obsessed with Humphrey Bogart movies after that."

"Ha," Pax says. "Oliver likes those too. Must be a Colorado thing."

I don't move. He knows. He has to know.

"Are we talking about it?" I ask.

"What? Why? Do you *want* to talk about it?"

"Do you?"

"No," he says. "No. We're forgetting, remember?"

OK, yeah. I'm paranoid. "So anyway, I was obsessed with the old movies and I started dressing up and stuff. My mom's not into that kind of thing. Vintage class, and all that. She's more of a…" And my stupid ass is just about to say "bombshell," when I stop short. He will definitely know my mother as a bombshell. Oliver can't have left that out. My father calls her Bomb all the time. And I know Pax has been to our house at least twice. Both times while I was in college. So he never saw me there. But still. Once you see my mother, you form an opinion and you never forget it. "More Doris Day."

"Awww, you take after her, right? Sweet and shit?"

"Yup." I laugh, picturing anyone calling my mother sweet. Hell, anyone calling me sweet is just as funny. We are so alike. "Anyway, I got into it. We did *Death of a Salesman* in high school and I played the part of the Woman."

"The sexy tramp?"

"Yeah." I laugh. "I get it now, of course. But back then I just wanted to wear the clothes."

"Did you nail it?"

"Broke a leg. But really, it just fanned the flames of my obsession."

Pax gets quiet all of a sudden. Shit, what did I say?

"Me?" he asks, looking over for a second before returning his eyes to the highway. "Was I your Bogart?"

I glance past him, to the ocean, which is flying by as we travel north. "Maybe a little."

"We shouldn't talk about it."

"Right."

"We should just enjoy it."

"Yeah," I say softly.

"But I love your story. The real one and the fairy tale too."

I lean back into my seat, relaxing. OK, maybe he knows something? But he can't know I'm Oliver's sister. I just don't think he'd be so calm about that.

"We can play dress-up if you want," Pax says.

My smile is huge at that offer. "You'd dress up?" I laugh just picturing it. "In a trench coat and hat?"

"Sugar, if you put on some stockings and red lipstick— and maybe nothing else— I'll do anything you ask. You want a fantasy night, I'm there."

I lean over and place my hand on his dick.

He grins, changes lanes, and pulls off the highway.

"What are you doing?"

"That's a signal I don't ignore, Cinderella. You want sexy times? You get sexy times."

"It's not even dark out."

"Who cares? I got a boat at Marina Del Rey. Wanna see my boat?" He cups his hand over mine, making me squeeze his already thick cock.

I lean over and start kissing his neck. "Yeah, let's see the boat."

"Play with yourself while I drive," he says, not looking at me. "I want you wet and ready the minute we get there." And then he tips his sunglasses up and looks me in the eyes. "Do not squirt in my car."

I hold up three fingers. "Scout's honor." We laugh.

"But seriously," he says, staring over at me—laugh gone, smile gone. "Play with yourself while I drive. And start by taking those panties off, one leg at a time."

God, he is hot.

I kick off my sandals, place both feet on the dashboard, and then lift my hips up just enough to wiggle my panties down to my thighs.

He's watching from the corner of his eye.

"Keep your eyes on the road, Mr. Vance. I'm just feeling a little warm and need some relief. But this is none of your concern."

That smile is worth every bit of the cheesiness I feel right now.

"A nice woman," he says, giving me one more look as the panties make their way past my knees, slide down my calves, and stop at my ankles, "wouldn't need the kind of relief taking your panties off would provide."

"I'm not a nice woman, Detective. I'm a slut. I told you, I need help. And you blew me off back in your office because I have no money. Well, just because I can't pay you in money, Detective, doesn't mean I can't pay you at all."

His smile is so big. But he keeps his eyes on the road as he gets his laugh under control.

"Consider the show you're about to give me a down payment. Now turn your body so I can see you, and then open your slutty legs wide."

I do what he wants. I take off my seatbelt, angle myself with my back against the door, and then open my legs.

"Your skirt's in the way, Miss Sugar."

"That's Miss Sugar Cookie to you, Detective."

He's almost giggling and it makes me happy that I have the power to make *him* happy, even after that fucked-up visit from Liam Henry this afternoon.

"Pull your skirt up and play with yourself," he says in a low voice, then glances at me with heavy eyes. "This is the game I want to play right now."

"Don't worry," I whisper in a soothing tone. "I'm just getting started." I pull my skirt up and give him a good look. We stop at a light. I can see the marina a few blocks ahead off to the left. "Do you want me to do it like this?" I say. "Pushing my fingers inside myself."

"You little Disney whore." But he licks his lips. And I picture his mouth where my fingers are, licking and lapping against my pussy, and I have to close my eyes.

"I'm not a whore," I say in my best sultry dame-in-distress voice, then open my eyes again. "I forgot to tell you, I'm a virgin."

This time he does laugh. Loudly. "Are you?"

"Yes," I say. "So I might not want to do anything too fun today, Detective. I'm saving myself for Prince Charming."

The light turns green but Paxton watches me as my fingertips caress the wet folds between my legs until the car behind us honks.

He starts forward and then turns left, towards the marina. "Are you going to tease me, Miss Cookie?"

"Oh," I say, moaning a little. "I love teasing men. It's how I got into this situation in the first place."

"You pretended to be a whore? But when they found out you were a virgin, they—"

"Threatened my life," I pretend-sob. "You'll help me, won't you?"

"Tell me what kind of help you need, Miss Cookie."

"I just can't stop"—I pretend-sob again—"teasing. Help me stop. *Please.*"

He chuckles in a sexy you-have-no-idea-how-much-I-love-this-game kind of way. "I'll do my best, ma'am."

"Jesus fuck, are we there yet, Pax? I really do need you to lick my pussy."

But all I get in response is a sly smile.

Oh, shit. I have a feeling he's going to take my little fantasy farther than I expected.

CHAPTER TWENTY

PAXTON

I hold her hand as we walk through the marina towards the slip where I keep my boat. The place is busy. Crowded and bustling until we get away from the club house and onto the dock.

"This is nice. I love the water. One thing that I never got much of growing up."

"Yeah," I say. "It's perfect right now." I look down at her and smile. "Better than letting you tease me while I sit in traffic ready to murder someone."

She laughs a little as I put my hand on the small of her back, directing her to go right. "You know," she says, "just when I think I've got you figured out, you pull something like this on me."

"Like what?"

"A boat. Islands. Houses. All of it."

"Well, you can't have an island without a boat."

"It's on the wrong coast, though. You said your islands were in the Exuma Cays."

"Oh." I laugh. "I have a boat on that coast too. Besides, if you have two islands you really need two boats."

"Is that your rationale?"

"My story," I say. "And I'm sticking to it. But that brings us back to your story, Miss Cookie. After you."

I stop beside my boat and hold her hand as she steps up, then follow her on board. Her eyes are wide and excited. But

161

pretty soon they'll be heavy with lust. "I can help you with your little problem, but since you can't pay, I'll need something else from you."

She bites away the smile as I start to untie the boat. "Wait, we're *going* somewhere?"

"You want this whole marina to hear you scream, 'Fuck me, Detective. Fuck me harder?' OK by me, Sugar."

"Pax…"

"Of course we're going somewhere. What'd you think? I was bringing you here for a quickie? I don't do quickies. Not with girls I like."

A blush flushes her whole face pink for a moment. I bet her breasts are blushing too. "Detective," she says in a low voice. "This is all highly unorthodox."

"I solve the cases, Miss Cookie. Whether or not you like my methods is none of my concern. Now, for your own safety, I'm gonna need you to go down below, take off your clothes, and wait for me on the couch."

"For my own safety?" she asks.

"It's either that or take your chances with me ripping them off you."

Her mouth opens in an O of surprise, her hand covering it in a moment of shock. "Detective, that's inappropriate."

I finish untying the mooring of the boat and step in, making sure my hands rest on both of her hips as I gently move her aside. "And I'll tell you now, if you want my help, you have to follow my directions at all time."

"All times?" She tilts her head at me, eyebrow raised.

"All times. I'll give you till the count of five to get down below, or I'll rip your clothes off right here in front of the whole marina."

She puts a hand over one breast, simultaneously covering herself and indicating shock in one perfect gesture.

"One…"

She turns towards the stairs that lead to the salon, but I catch her muttering, "She was conflicted and yet her body was becoming warm with the anticipation of what was to come."

Can this girl get any cuter?

I smile big as I start the boat and back out of the slip, then make my way out of the marina towards the ocean at a painstakingly slow speed. All I think about is how she's waiting for me down below. Her naked body stretched out on the leather couch. Long blonde locks trailing over her breasts, trying to hide them. But there's not enough hair on her head to hide those voluptuous tits of hers. I love fucking her with her bra on. I love pulling it down under her huge mounds so the underwire practically raises them up to her chin.

God, I want to do filthy, *filthy* things with her mouth and her tits. Make her suck on them. Her little pink tongue darting out as it traces the line of her nipples.

When we finally get to open water, I set a heading and put it on autopilot. This boat is not as big as the yacht I have in West Palm Beach, but it's got everything I need for an afternoon of fantasy roleplaying with Miss Sugar Cookie down there.

I unbutton my shirt as I step down the stairs to the salon and the minute I see her—that golden body naked and waiting—blood fills up my cock until it's so hard, I have to resist the urge to grab it.

"I like to comply, Detective," Cindy purrs. "It's one of my favorite things."

Jesus. She looks like a fucking pin-up girl lying there. She's on her side, legs scissoring together like she's trying to stimulate herself. The little blonde landing strip of hair between her legs peeks out at me like an invitation. Her arms are strategically placed, squeezing her tits together to make them look even more perfect.

I finally get the buttons done on my shirt, take it off and throw it across the table as I pass, and then go to work on my pants.

"What will you make me do?" she asks, fake hint of fear in her voice.

"Anything I want," I say, pulling my cock out and fisting it, my hand moving up and down my thick shaft in slow strokes. "And what I want right now, Miss Cookie, is to make you suffer for teasing me back in the car. You're lucky I don't walk out of this case. Leave you to fend for yourself."

I hate to bite back the smile. Because my little sugar here can fend for herself just fine. But I like her damsel-in-distress playacting. It fucking turns me on.

"Suffer?" she asks in an overly dramatic protest. "But I didn't do anything you didn't *want*."

"It's too late now. You're here, we're heading west to nowhere in particular, and you've got my undivided attention."

"Please," she begs. "Please, don't walk out—"

"I won't, you little tease. But I'm going to teach you a lesson right now. A lesson you'll never want to forget." I reach her, pull her up to a sitting position, and then sit down on the couch.

"What should I do to make it better?" She places her hand over mine, which is still stroking my cock. "Tell me what you want."

"I want…" Goddamn. I want to fuck her is what I want. But this is way too much fun to rush things. "Get up," I say.

She stands up, bites her lip seductively, and stands there as I lie down on the couch where she just was.

"Now sit on top of me."

She straddles my thighs, positioning her pussy right over my cock, but I place a hand on her arm and say, "No, no, no. You wish my cock was going inside you, Miss Cookie."

"But Detective, I thought you—"

"You can stop thinking now. It's unnecessary. Scoot up and lean back."

Cindy scrunches her brows together, confused.

"You want to be a tease? Let's see who's the better tease."

"What are you doing?" she asks in her real voice.

"Let's play a game…" I say the words before I realize how she might take them. But she stops my worry with a smile. "Let's see who can hold out the longest."

"Oh, honey," she purrs. "I'm gonna win this game. What's my prize at the end?"

"You think so, huh? I'll tell you what. If you win, I'll sign that Malibu house over to you."

"What?" She's genuinely shocked. "Paxton, that's insane. Why?" She stutters for words. "What are you doing?"

"Why is it insane? I just want to make sure you're not sleeping in a trailer if you ever get tired of me."

"I don't need your house. And it's worth fourteen million dollars, that's why!"

"That was purchase price, Sugar. It's worth twenty-one million at the moment. And I know you don't need it now. You already live there with me. But it's a nice place, right? People get addicted to nice things and then sometimes they stay in situations just to keep those things. I want to make sure that never happens to us."

"I'm not taking your house, don't be ridiculous."

"Afraid you're gonna lose, Miss Cookie?"

"I'm not going to lose." She snorts. "In fact, I bet I win this little game in less than ten minutes."

"Well, if I win," I say, my voice a deep mixture of desire and arrogance, "then I want to meet your dad."

"What?" If I didn't know we were playing a game, I'd be convinced that shocked look is real. "Why?" She almost whispers it.

"You met my mother. I want to meet yours. And I have a feeling that Vic Vaughn doesn't let anyone meet his wife unless he gives them permission. Besides, that's what you do when you're serious, right? Meet the parents. Get permission. That's how my mother raised me, Cinderella. I can't help that I'm a traditional kind of guy."

"Pax—"

"Too chickenshit to play, Miss Sugar Cookie?"

"No," she protests. "No, that's not it. I'm just not sure—" She stops short.

But I know what she's going to say. *I'm just not sure we're that serious yet.* We are that serious. And even if she doesn't think so right now, she will realize it soon. "I want a meeting with your dad. And look, I know I'm a little rough around the edges, but I clean up well. I have manners, Cindy. I won't embarrass you."

She bites her lip. And damn, if she isn't the best little actress. I almost think she's really worried about this.

"Game on?" I ask, once again wincing at my choice of terminology.

She lets out a long sigh. "I won't lose. So in ten minutes I'm going to own your house."

"That's the spirit, Sugar. Winning is ninety-nine percent attitude. Are you ready?"

"Game on."

"Well, OK then. I want you to press your pussy up against my shaft and rub against it."

She tilts her head with a sly grin.

"All the way against it. I want you to slide up and down my shaft, so my tip tickles your clit, and move your hips until it touches your ass."

She exhales. "Shit."

"No, Sugar. Squirt. I'll make you come squirting and I won't even have to touch you."

CHAPTER TWENTY-ONE

CINDY

Focus, Cinderella.

I do not need that house, nor do I want it. But what if Pax wins and insists I call home when we're done to set up a time to meet my dad? He cannot meet my dad! He's *already* met my dad!

And I know damn well my uncle Vic will not play along with this. No fucking way. He'd take one look at Paxton, recognize him as Mr. Mysterious, and be on the phone to my father that same instant.

They'd probably kick his ass!

Well. They'd definitely try. But I have a lot of uncles. They'd all get in on it. Hell, Oliver would too. They would definitely kick his ass.

"Cindy," Pax says, breaking the roleplay. "You're just sitting there."

"Detective," I say, trying to give myself time to figure out how to get out of this game. "I really don't think—"

"You're gonna win?" He tsks his tongue. "I know you're not going to win, Sugar. But we're already playing. You want to be a tease? I can tease back. Now do what I say."

"Detective," I repeat, using my sweet acting voice. "It's just not fair that you get to tease me first."

"We're teasing each other," he says. "All you gotta do is make me come before you and you win. The more seductive you are, the more excited I get."

The whole problem with that is he knows how I am when his dick is playing with my clit. And he knows I can make myself squirt while I masturbate. So this is basically me masturbating with his dick.

"I'm so gonna win," I say.

But all I'm thinking is, *I'm so gonna lose.*

"Here," Pax says. "I'll help you get started."

"You're so considerate," I purr, slapping his hand away. "But you said—" Ah ha! I have a path to victory! "You said you'll make me come squirting and you won't even have to touch me."

"So that's the rule?"

I smile, smug. "That's the rule."

"Sugar, I've already won."

I let him think that as I move into position, cupping my breasts together the way I know he loves. He's got a lot of kinky ideas about my tits. I can tell by the way he fondles them while we fuck. He pushes them up towards my face, like he's hoping against hope my little tongue will just dart out and—

Shit, Cindy, stop turning yourself on. You're trying to win here.

But that's the problem, isn't it? Everything I can do to make him come also turns me on.

"Getting worried?" Pax asks, smirking up at me.

"Not at all." I take his hard dick in my hands and press it up to the wet lips of my pussy. He closes his eyes, just a flicker, really, and I know I'm the one with all the power here. He won't last. He won't.

I move my hips up and down, just a tiny bit. Sliding my juices all over his shaft.

"Fuck, yeah," he says.

Fuck, yeah, I think.

But I keep going. Pressing him against my folds, desperately trying to stimulate him without hitting my sweet spot.

"You're cheating," he says, pushing on his cock so that the head is right where I don't need it to be. "You have to hit the button, Sugar. That's the rules."

I move my hips, angling them so his tip just barely hits my clit, biting my lip so I don't get too turned on.

"Fuck," Pax says. "You have the prettiest pussy. So pink, and wet, and your lips fold around my dick like they want to eat it up."

Oh, God. I actually get wetter, if that's possible. He's gonna dirty-talk me right into losing this game.

Don't be stupid, Cindy. You have a mouth too. Use it!

"You know what I love?" I purr.

"Hmmm?" Pax asks, still concentrating on how my pussy looks hugging his cock.

"The way you look at my tits." I fist one, my other hand holding his cock tightly to my pussy so he gets the full effect of my movements. "And you know what I've figured out?"

"Hmmm?" he says again. "That you want me to touch you after all?"

I almost laugh. This might be easier than I thought. He's already wishing he could touch me.

"Because," he continues, "all I'm thinking about is how I'd like to grab your hips and drag your clit up and down my cock until you're whining about the agony of defeat."

He's good. I'll give him that. He's damn good.

171

"No," I say, bending forward and leaning down so my thighs straddle him and my tits press against his chest.

"If you stop moving, Sugar, I win by default."

"No," I say again, rubbing myself against him. That little lip of skin over the tip of his head bumps up against my clit and I exhale. Loudly. "I've figured out what you want me to do." And then I cup my breast, bring it up to my mouth, and trace my nipple with my tongue.

I feel his dick jump as his eyes go wide.

"Fuck," he says.

"Oh, yeah," I moan. "Do you like it?" I lick again. "You know how this feels when I do this to your cock?" I ask. "Well," I say, leaning all the way down into his neck so I can breathe the words into his ear. "That's how it feels for me right now too."

"Bitch," he says.

"Why play the game if you never want to win? I'm going to win this one, Mr. Mysterious."

"You stopped moving. Do that again and you forfeit."

Asshole. I move again, but damn, if the head of his dick isn't still *right there*. Ready to push my button.

I wince, then stop to calm down, but start back up again before he declares himself the winner.

"You're getting weaker," he says, maneuvering his legs so there's even more pressure and friction. Bending his knees and bracing his feet on the bed. "I might not be able to touch you, but—" He thrust his hips—hard—so his balls slap against my ass.

"Cheater!" I squeal. But holy fuck, that feels… so… *good*. I move faster, his shaft still sliding between the lips of my pussy.

Pax closes his eyes, so I keep going. "You like that?" I ask. "You like the way my pussy feels. All wet and warm and ready for your cock. Don't you just want to be inside me? Feel me squeeze you?"

"Keep going," he mumbles. "Keep talking."

God, it would be so easy to come right now. I bite my lip, trying not to let my own dirty talk be my downfall. How to win the game when losing means you get exactly what you want?

"I want to feel the slap of your balls again. I want your hard dick inside me. I want you in my mouth and I want your tongue in my pussy—"

"Do it," he says. "Turn around and do it."

Oh, man. I'm so gonna lose if I let his tongue touch me down there. But if I suck him off, there's a chance I can win. "I'm gonna take you deep in my throat, Detective. I'm gonna swallow your cock and make you choke me with your come."

His hips start grinding on me. My button is being pushed, over and over, and I know, in this moment, that if I don't do something quick, I will explode.

So I swing my leg over his body, turn around, and position myself over the top of him. His abs are hard, like a plank. And those irresistible hip muscles, forming a V, like they are pointing to his cock, are staring me in the face. I lick them without thinking, just as his tongue flicks against my clit.

My mouth covers his dick. I suck, but only because that's what he's doing to me, then gasp when I realize how close I am. My head dives down, taking in his whole shaft.

"Ahhh," he moans. "Ahhhh." Again. "Miss Cookie, you're a dirty whore if you can take my giant—ahhhhh—cock all the way into your throat."

Keep talking, I think in my head. If he's talking, he's not licking.

"I'm gonna come in there," he says, practically growling the words as he thrusts his hips.

But… "Oh, fuck," I mumble, thinking about his words.

"Sugar," he says, thrusting his hips again, forcing himself inside me so far, I fear I will gag and ruin all the hard work I just put in. "Mumble against my cock again and this game is over."

"Mmmmm," I say, feeling the vibrations as they bounce off his shaft.

And then his tongue is working. And I'm humming myself into a frenzy, and my hands are underneath his balls, my fingertips searching for that tender spot around his asshole that will end this game once and for all. But my hips are out of control as he licks, I realize. I'm rocking back and forth until I find his chin and… "Oohhhhhhh…"

That word goes on forever as I come, and in the same moment, his warm, salty semen is filling my mouth, spilling out from between my lips.

"Game over," he says, flipping me over as he fists his sticky cock so it stays hard. He hikes my hands up above my head, leans down to bite my nipple, and rams himself inside me with such force, my whole body moves. My head bumps up against the armrest of the couch.

I lift my knees up, giving him more access as he slams me with all his power. Balls against my asshole, and his lips on my mouth, kissing me and kissing me and kissing me...

We come again. I drag my fingernails down his back, making him roar.

We go still. He collapses on top of me, our hearts beating so hard, they are drums in my ears. The motion of the boat comes back to me, soothing us as the beat slows and the sea becomes music. Our hot, sweaty bodies the product of what we just composed.

"I win," he says. "I win."

"No," I say, and snuggle up to his chest when he angles his body towards mine and puts his arms around me. "We both won."

CHAPTER TWENTY-TWO

PAXTON

I didn't think she'd be so competitive, to be honest. I figured she'd call me ridiculous and we'd fuck around some more, then I'd just pound her against the wall.

Which is still not a bad idea, and I might be ready for another round real soon.

But... she did try real hard to win. And it's not the house.

Nope. I have a feeling Cinderella Vaughn is not the kind of girl who gives a fuck about owning a house. She was living in a trailer on the beach and seemed perfectly content.

She really doesn't want me to meet her family. And maybe later, when I'm not so happy and content, I might have to think about that some more. But right now I'm just gonna chalk it up to being some kind of Daddy's girl and let it go.

"I love your boat," Cindy says.

"Just wait," I mumble back, unable to open my eyes. "The other one is so much nicer. We could sail around the world on that one."

"That would be perfect. Alone with you for months and months," she says, her voice barely audible. She's tired. Hell, I'm tired. But we need to get going.

"I want nothing more than to lie here with you, but BRB."

I get out of bed, clean up in the head, then get a hot washcloth and go back to Cindy so I can wipe her sweaty face down. "Thank you," she says. But I'm not done. I open her legs up and wipe her inner thighs, then her glistening pussy. God, I'd like to fuck her again so bad. As soon as we get home, first thing on my agenda.

I lean down and kiss her on the lips. She wakes up just enough to kiss me back, and then I whisper, "I'm gonna change the heading and take us back to the marina. Stay here and sleep."

She sighs softly, then tucks her hands under her cheek and goes still.

I go up to the cockpit and change course, lingering a little, looking out at the vast emptiness of ocean, contemplative. After a few minutes we are heading back towards land, and it's weird how you can be looking at the end of the world one minute and civilization the next. We're not that far from shore. Only about an hour away. But it strikes me how easy it is to unplug. Disconnect. Become disconnected.

Isn't that what Cindy does? Isn't that why she lived in that trailer in what amounts to a parking lot? She likes her freedom. I hadn't really articulated it in my head when I offered up my house as her prize tonight. But this underlying difference between us isn't money. It's expectations. Or maybe just what you're willing to settle for.

Cindy is happy in her little trailer. She made that perfectly clear when we drove out there to get her clothes. It's a nice enough place, I guess. It's clean, and cozy. Decorated in a beachy cottage kind of way. Girly, if pressed to come up with a better description. Something she is and isn't at the same time.

I can't figure her out.

And what's more, I don't have much to go on. Her father makes sense in all kinds of ways. Tough guys raise tough girls, right? But naming her sisters after Disney princesses? That's not tough. Cinderella's name is the thing that doesn't fit. I don't really know the names of any other Disney princesses. Snow White, right? She's one of them? Poison apples? Or mirrors? I'm not sure. I'm ninety-nine point nine percent sure I've never even seen a Disney princess movie.

I know the Cinderella one. That's a book, and when I was little my mother read me stories every night before bed. So I've got Prince Charming's number. Dumbass who can't even recognize his girl unless he's got that damn shoe on her foot.

And what was with that comment about not having an office? She finds her clients through her brother's website? I didn't see a brother when I looked online.

I should really do a thorough background check on her. Figure out how she ticks. Where she came from. Why she's addicted to the nomadic lifestyle.

I could be a nomad. I like to travel.

But… there's this little nagging void in my head that says it's just not the same thing.

When Cindy travels she has a backpack of clothes and that's it. She leaves everything else behind, she said. Starting over is a hobby for her.

And if she decides to stop and stay a while, she just buys new stuff. Just enough stuff.

Besides, I still get the feeling she's hiding something. And whatever it is, I don't want to care about it. I really don't. Hell, I'm hiding a billion things about myself. Why would I go digging into her life if I don't want her digging into mine?

179

And yet I wish there was a way to prove we're the same, even though we're so different. I have houses all over the damn world. Those two islands. The boats. Two again. Paxton Vance has to have a backup plan.

I'm a collector, I realize. I might even be a hoarder. A house hoarder. Why do I have so many houses?

I have cars stashed away too. I should get one out of that storage facility in Long Beach and give it to Cindy. That VW Bug is cool for driving around Malibu, but you can't really *go anywhere* in a car like that.

That's the point. I hear her voice in my head. *Everything is disposable.*

How does she work like that? I mean, like... get clients and shit? If she's traveling all the time?

"Hey," Cindy says, coming up from behind and wrapping her arms around my neck. I smile up at her in the fading light. The reflection of the setting sun on the water makes her skin glow. "I thought you were coming back down?"

"Got caught up in the moment," I say, pulling her into my lap. "Realizing you just lost a twenty-one-million-dollar house in a bet is kind of sobering."

She slaps my arm. "You didn't lose anything. We both lost."

"No," I say, playing with her long strands of golden hair. It's got a little bounce in it today. "We both won. That means we both get the prize. I get to meet your mom, by way of your dad. And you get the title to my house."

"Pax. Please. I don't want your house."

"Why not?" I ask, reading way more into that statement than I should. "Because then you might have to settle down? Stick around? Get serious?"

"What?" she asks, pulling away from me. "Where's this coming from?"

"You don't even have an office. How do you work?"

"I told you. People get in contact and I go where I'm needed."

"You just pick up and leave?"

"Pax, you're being weird. I'm not going anywhere now."

"Why?"

"*Why?*"

"Yeah, why is now different? Because it's not old yet? Things are still shiny and new? What if you get a request for a job in like, Iowa?"

"I don't know." She shrugs. "If I do get a job in Iowa, I'll let you know and we can decide how to deal."

Hmmm. How to deal. I don't wanna have to deal. I want to nail this shit down like... right now.

"Well, the house is yours."

"That house is not mine. I won't take it."

"I'll just put your name on the deed and be done with it. You won't even know."

"I'm pretty sure I'd have to sign something."

"I'm positive I could fake your signature."

She shifts in my lap so she can look me in the eyes. "What is going on with you?"

I just look at her. How fucking beautiful she is. Not just her looks, which are incredible. But her whole... everything. Her everything.

I don't know what this feeling is. I don't have a word to describe it. It's bigger than anything I've ever felt before about a woman. It's everywhere and nowhere all at the same time.

"Hey," Cindy says, placing both of her palms on my stubbled face. "I'm not going anywhere."

For now, I say in my head. But when she gets tired of me, she's gonna sell that car, buy herself a plane ticket—hell, hitch that backpack over her shoulder and stick out her thumb on PCH. It could go that way. In fact, I can totally see her doing that.

"Detective," she says, kissing me on the lips. "I'm not leaving you. Ever."

"Miss Cookie," I say. "I'd just feel a whole lot better about that if you owned my house."

"You're crazy."

"They do say that."

"But I'm crazy too."

"That's the part that scares me."

"Why?" She giggles. "We're practically soulmates."

"Mr. and Mrs. Mysterious. That's who we are."

"Yeah," she says, leaning her head on my shoulder. "Yeah I like the sound of that. Mr. and Mrs. Mysterious."

We sit like that a little longer. Until I have to take the boat off autopilot and steer my way through the marina and back into the boat slip.

"I love this boat," Cindy says as I help her step back onto the dock. "I can't wait to see the other one."

I smile all the way back to the car. In fact, I smile all the way back up to Malibu over that little comment.

"You'll see all of it," I say just as we pull into Malibu Colony, even though she's been sleeping for the past fifteen minutes. "Every house, every island, every boat, every car."

Prince Charming is gonna deliver the fairy tale to his sweet-smelling Cinderella. Whether she wants it or not.

CHAPTER TWENTY-THREE

CINDY

"Hey," Pax whispers in my ear as he unbuckles my seat belt. "We're home."

Home. God, what was up with that whole conversation about giving me this house? I can't take this house. That's crazy.

I sigh, let him help me out of the car, then follow him into the house by way of the garage. This door leads straight out into the pool area, since the garage is street level and the guest house is technically on the second floor.

"You ready for some steaks?" he asks as we walk into the beach-side part of the house. He drops his keys on the kitchen island and walks to the refrigerator to pull it open and study what's inside.

"So hungry," I say. "I'll start the grill."

We went grocery shopping yesterday since he didn't have to go into the office to work and our take-out options in Malibu are limited.

Have I ever... grocery shopped with a man before?

Honestly, I don't think like that. I have had girlfriends who gush over a guy asking her to grocery shop with him—like it's something very meaningful. But even though I'm a romantic in many ways, I take love very literally.

Grocery shopping is... well, buying food to eat and nothing more. Now, letting me win a house from him in a silly bet—yeah, that gesture has some meaning behind it.

185

I just don't understand why he's so worried about me leaving. And it's not like I can even tell him how obsessive I've been trying to sneak my way into his life.

No. I can't tell him any of that. And he's right. I've got the past of a girl who takes off. A wanderer. A leaver, as my uncle Ford would say. I'm a leaver.

"I need to call that Liam asshole and let him know I'm out."

"You were in?" I ask from the patio. "You're not considering it for real, are you?"

"I told him I'd call him tonight and let him know. So I just have to wrap that shit up and get him off my back."

"You said text. I was there, remember?"

Pax backs away from the fridge as the door closes, with a package of T-bone steaks and a head of broccoli. "He's not really the kind of guy who takes no for an answer in a text. I'll have to call at least."

"Hmmm," I say.

"Hmm, what?" he says, tearing the plastic off the meat and walking towards me on the patio. "I can handle him."

"OK. I trust you completely." *I just wish you'd trust me back,* I want to say. But then he'll bring up all the things I really can't talk about. Like why I have no office and why I never stick around in one place. Why I bribed a teenager to let me deliver his food all summer. And why he can't meet my mom and dad, even if we did both win today.

Am I in too deep? Did I fuck this all up with my stalking?

"You wanna go surfing?" Pax asks. "After we eat? And watch the sunset from our boards?"

God. How does a man like this—tall, dangerous, mysterious—manage to say the most romantic things ever?

"Yes," I answer. "Yes, I'd love that."

He cooks the steaks to perfection while I wash the broccoli and squirt ranch dressing into little ceramic dipping bowls. And then we eat outside and watch a movie star toss a football with his two sons on the beach.

"You're gonna love it here," Pax says, once we're done. "It's your kind of place."

"I already love it here, Detective. And it's not because of the ocean, or the house, or the movie stars on the beach. It's because you're here. I'm not leaving, Paxton Vance." *Not after I worked so hard to get you in the first place.*

He looks at me for a long second. "How about you let me fuck your brains out on the kitchen counter and we'll save that sunset surfing for another day?"

I laugh, feeling more comfortable with this man than anyone I've ever known. "You're like a goddamned poet. Anybody ever tell you that?"

He stands up, pulls me to my feet, hoists me over his shoulder as he smacks my ass, and says, "Only the girl I fell in love with."

We fuck all over the house that evening. On the kitchen island, as promised. Then we take a swim in the pool and fuck in the outdoor shower, Pax pressing me up against the hard stucco wall until we laugh about the impressions it leaves on my back once he throws me down a lounge chair and starts rubbing lotion all over my body as he massages the tightness away in my wound-up muscles.

187

He fucks me during the massage, since the massage mostly consists of him playing with my pussy until I'm squirting and screaming his name. And some time after midnight he puts me into bed, drags the light cover over me, and kisses me on the cheek, saying, "Be right back. Just gonna make that call to Liam now."

I don't know what happens after that.

Because when I wake up he's gone and the only clue he left behind is a note.

I stuck it out for two weeks. Patted myself on the back and read that note over and over.

Cinderella,
I gotta do this job for Liam or he's just gonna get someone else to do it instead and the only way Corporate comes out of this alive is if I take over. Be back soon.

Mr. Charming
P.S. Don't leave.

I admit, the cute note was what made me stay so long, wondering what the fuck just happened. How I went from the best night of my life to… well, dumped. What else can I call it? I called him about a hundred times and it went to voicemail. I even hacked into his email just to make sure he wasn't dead. Because I thought he was dead for a good forty-eight hours before I got the new password to his email account.

He changed it. He knew I was hacking him and he changed it.

Which means we're over.

But nope. He's still alive. Because he's been checking emails. None of them with a reply, but every day some are marked read.

He's not even leaving me messages or texts in the middle of the night while I'm sleeping, so he doesn't have to talk to me. Not an email—I mean, he's online, right? He can't just bang out a few words? *Hey, it was fun, but moving on?* And there's always good old snail mail. I'm not expecting a Hallmark card, for fuck's sake. A few words scribbled on a Taco Bell napkin would suffice. And do I really need a slap in the face like that to take a hint? He's just not coming back.

So I left.

I packed up my backpack, sold my damn car, got on a plane, and left.

And I've been here in the Bay Area for almost ten days now, telling myself there are so many new things to do and see, I will never miss Paxton Vance. I will move on and chalk it all up to a bad case of delusional lust. And I have already answered ads for two jobs, and closed both cases with one hundred percent customer satisfaction. So, good omen, right?

But man, does my heart ache. My whole chest, really. Every guy I see who might be a reasonable alternative just gets compared. Like I have this checklist with Pax on one side and the whole world of men on the other.

189

And no one will ever come close to what I feel for him. All the billions of things I love about him, like the way he plays along with my crazy and calls me Miss Sugar Cookie while trying to give me his bazillion-dollar house on the beach. Or the way his head angles down while he walks, but his eyes are always aware of everything around him. Or that his mother bought him a baseball for Christmas last year with a card inside that said, *Remember that day I took you out of school early when you were eleven so we could go watch the Bats opening game? Well, my gift to you this Christmas is the memory of that day.*

Is his mother adorable or what? I mean, my mother is fucking adorable too. The best. But you gotta love a man who loves his mom. She gives him memories for Christmas, because really, what do you give a man who can buy himself anything he wants?

I'd like to think we were making memories that would last forever. That we'd be old one day and I'd write a note saying, *Remember that day we pretended you were a detective and I was Miss Sugar Cookie?* And make his whole life brighter just thinking about it.

I sigh as I look out at the ocean. I found another place to rent, this time a real house. Well, cottage. OK, vacation shack on the beach, if I'm being honest. But it's the same ocean as the one we had back in Malibu. And picturing him looking out at the Pacific is just about the only thing that makes my heart stop hurting.

Heartbreak is a real physical condition. Not a disease, exactly. But something worse. There is no cure for heartache except time. I am broken. I had never realized that the same love that pulls you together can break you in half. I literally feel broken.

I wish I kept my old phone number, but I was so angry when I left Southern California that I cancelled the account, burned the chip in the microwave, and tossed it in the ocean. The only way he can reach me now is... well, he can't. He said once if he left I'd never find him, and I guess he's right. But I'm just as elusive as he is. I can throw things away with the best of them. I didn't want to bring anything with me. Not even my clothes. So my backpack had nothing in it but the contents of my purse.

I won't call him again. I refuse. I just need to accept that it's over and move on.

I pick up a rock from the beach and skip it across the water. There are almost no waves this morning, so my rock jumps three times.

Maybe I should call Oliver and see if he can tell me what's going on?

But then I'd have to explain this whole fucked-up stalking thing to him. And I can't do that.

"Cynthia?"

I whirl around, startled. "What?" I say, not quite believing my eyes. "What are you doing here?"

Mariel Hawthorne is standing on the ridge that leads to my cottage, long coat pulled tight around her body and cinched at the waist with a belt. It's not a trench coat. She's too high-fashion for that. But it's got the same look and what I see is Pax the Detective when I look at her features. She's wearing sunglasses, even though the sun is just barely rising, and she slides them down her nose to see me better as I stare.

191

She starts walking down the embankment, her designer leather boots sinking into the sandy pebbles that line beaches up here. "I think we need to talk."

"Did Pax send you?"

"No." She laughs, and my heart hurts so bad, I have to clutch at my coat to try to numb myself from the pain. "No, I'm here for something else. Something I need to tell you. Probably should've told you that first day we met."

"Back in Del Mar?" I ask, happy that she's here. That some small bit of Pax is so close to me again. But confused. So utterly confused.

"No, dear. We both know you came to see me at Belmont a while back. I don't recall exactly when it was, but I never forget a face. Especially one as beautiful as yours."

"Oh," I say, letting go of my coat. "Well, thank you."

"Don't thank me yet. Not until you've heard the whole story."

"Story?" What is she talking about?

"Of why you're here. Why all this is happening. And what we might do about it."

"We?" I ask. "As in, you and *me*?"

"Yes, we, Cynthia."

"Cinderella."

"Oh, I know, dear. I just want to smile every time I say your real name, and what I have to tell you isn't anything to smile about. So Cynthia it is. Until all this is over, at least."

"Oh, God," I squeak. "It's Pax? He's dead? They killed him? That last job?"

"No, no, no," she says, coming within arm's reach, so she can pat my shoulder. "He's back from that. He's looking for

192

you, actually. But of course, he got drunk last night and told his friends who you really are and now I'm just not sure what to do. So I came here. To talk to you and see if we can't come up with some kind of understanding."

"Fuck," I say, forgetting who I'm talking to for a moment.

"Right. You're going to have to deal with that, of course. The next time you see him. But I'm here about something else entirely."

"What?" I ask, a chill riding up my spine. The kind of chill you get when you're about to hear bad news. "Why me? What could I possibly tell you?"

"Those silver envelopes. You said you'd never seen one before."

"I hadn't," I say. "Not until that day with you at the track."

"Think back, Cynthia. *Never*? Are you sure?"

I shrug. "I don't remember them. But then again, I was never on the lookout."

"Your sisters? They never got one?" She cocks her head at me, like she might think I'm lying. But I'm not lying.

"Not that I saw. Why?"

"I think we should take this conversation inside. Have a hot cup of tea. Some scones I brought with me from the bakery down the road. Something soothing."

Just picturing this makes me frown. "My mom used to do that when she had to break bad news to me and my brother and sisters. She'd bake all day, or make a big roast, something huge and delicious for dinner or dessert. And then she'd say, 'You're not getting money for that trip, Belle. Your father does not approve.' Or, 'There is no new car in your future,

Ariel. So put that illegal hacking site aside and get a real job.' So this must be your version of parental guidance night if you're trying to feed me tea and scones just to have a talk."

She smiles, like she's picturing my family dinner. "I think I will love your mother when we finally meet."

"I think you will too. If…" I say. "If you ever get to meet her."

Mariel pats my hand and then nods her head towards the cottage. "Come on, let's go inside. It's too cold and damp up here in the north. And I don't approve of your rustic accommodations, Cynthia. You're going to be in a five-star resort this afternoon. I'm not against roughing it, sweetie. But this is going too far. Your parents would never forgive me if I let you stay out here for one more second."

CHAPTER TWENTY-FOUR

PAXTON

Present Day - Mr. Perfect's House

"And that's the last time I saw her. Well," I amend, starting to sober up, "the last time I talked to her too. I went back home yesterday after our meeting at Corporate's house—"

"That was two weeks ago, Pax," Perfect says. "You've been drunk on mint juleps for two fucking weeks?"

But I wave him off. "Yesterday, two weeks ago… same thing. Once I figured out who she was I was gonna go home and confront her. But she wasn't at my house when I got there. So I drove to her trailer and it was empty. She ran, man. She picked up and ran." I sit down, my head in my hands. "Because I left her there. Just a fucking note, man. Saying I'd be back and to stay put. And now she's fucking gone. It took me weeks to take care of all that Corporate shit and she was like, 'Fuck you, dude. I'm outta here!'" I look up at Mac and Five, who are both staring at me like I've lost my mind. "Do you think you can call Oliver and ask him where she is?"

"Is he fucking serious right now?" Five practically growls at Mac. "You do realize I've know this girl since she was fucking *born*?" He's looking at me now. "And if you ever talk about fucking her again, Oliver and I will both kick your ass to—"

"I love her, OK? I *love* her. You guys are just gonna have to accept that she's mine now."

"Fuck that," Five says. "If you were fucking my baby sister, I'd kick your ass into next year. No," he says, pacing the room as he rubs his chin. "I'd blow your fucking head off with a shotgun."

Perfect rolls his eyes and mouths *drama* to me.

"Better yet," Five continues, "cut your goddamned balls off. Or your dick. I'd like to see you fuck anyone else's baby sister after that."

I let out a long exhale. "What's done is done," I say. "It can't be undone. I just need you to find her for me. Call Oliver's parents' house. Or…" I get excited with this idea. "Ariel! Yeah, Ariel will know where she is."

"Oh"—Five laughs—"you're gonna undo it all right." He stops pacing and points his finger at me. "You're gonna break up with her, that's what you're gonna do. Hopefully she's gone and won't ever bother with you again. But if she does show up, you're gonna cut all ties, send her ass back home to Colorado, and wash your hands. Do you hear me?"

I stop to think for a minute. "The Little Mermaid. Ariel is named after the Little Mermaid. Which princess is Belle?" I suddenly have a need to know all the Disney princesses. So I take out my phone and start to look it up.

"You know, Pax," Perfect says, ignoring my question.

"Beauty and the Beast!" I say, so proud of my skills.

"You're the next one they're gonna fuck with, right?" Perfect continues. "If Cindy's around when that happens, she might—"

"I'll kill you," Five says. "Dead. If anything happens to Cindy Shrike, I will kill you. You're gonna forget you ever heard of a girl named Cinderella."

I want to object, but Perfect's words are ringing in my head. Could they use her against me?

Could? *Could?* More like, they absolutely *will.*

I get up, walk to Perfect's bar, make myself a bourbon, and drink it down in one gulp.

"Yeah," Five says, practically spitting the word out. "And if I see you drink another mint julep, I will kick your ass just for being so goddamned wussy. You understand me, Mysterious? Am I making myself clear?"

I pour another drink, down that one too, and then let the burning sensation in my gut numb me from the waist up.

"Oliver can't ever know about this," Five says. "Thanksgiving is coming up next month, so she'll come home for that and I'll take her aside and explain things. OK? You don't tell her shit if you find her. Not one word. If you have to say something, then you just say, 'Sorry, I'm an asshole. I cheated on you in—'"

"I'm not telling her that, you dick. Fuck, no."

"Oh, I don't give one fancy fuck what you think you're gonna tell her. I'm the one with access. So I'm gonna find her and I'll be the one to tell her you're a cheating motherfucker and she will never look at you twice again."

"Five," Perfect interrupts. "You're not doing any of that, OK? Just calm down." He turns to me. "Pax, you have to see you need to let her go, right? You can't take the chance that our enemies might drag her into this shit we're in." His eyes plead with me. "Right?"

197

I just stare at him.

"Right? You don't want to get her hurt? I know you don't. So you're gonna do the right thing. No one," he says, looking over at Five, "is gonna babysit you. We're not gonna call her or do any of those things Five just said. Because you're a grown-ass man, for fuck's sake. And you know you have to do the right thing. So leave her alone. Pretend this never happened, and if you do bump into her, you say, 'Sorry, Cindy. I'm just not into you.'"

I'm not saying shit while Perfect talks up his plan. I can't promise that. If I see her, I'm handcuffing her ass to me and throwing the goddamned key away. That's what I'm gonna do. Fuck everyone if that happens. We'll get on that boat in Del Rey and just say, "Show's over, folks. Nothin' to see here." And sail our merry asses around the world—or at least to another port so I can pick up a suitable yacht—and just say fuck everyone.

I look up at Five and he's got a pained expression on his face. I'm just about to lie and say, "Yup, that's a great plan, Perfect," when Five opens his mouth and says… "What if they already have her?"

"Who?" I ask. "Liam? Fucking Lucio Gori Senior? Why would they even know about her?"

"Don't jump to conclusions," Perfect says. And then he looks at Five like he's sending him a secret message.

"What the fuck was that look for?"

"What look?" Perfect says.

"Don't play stupid with me," I say. "You just shot Five a *look.*"

"I'm just saying, there's a lot of shit going down right now," Five says. "And a missing Shrike girl isn't something I can just pretend not to know. You have to understand that, right?"

"Five—" Perfect says.

"What the fuck are you saying?"

"Pax, man," Five says. "If she's missing, then I gotta call home."

"Home?" Perfect is scrunching up his face like this is a very bad idea.

I agree. "You're calling Oliver?" I laugh. "You fucking piece of shit."

"No," Five says. "I'm calling his fucking father."

"Cindy's father?" I scrub my hand down my face. "You can't do that."

"The hell I can't. I will get my ass beat if I don't report in on this one, Pax. Sorry, there is no way I'm not—"

"Five," Perfect says again, only this time he raises his voice. Scout starts barking and jumping around, the agitation in the room clearly palpable. "You're Mr. Shut-the-fuck-up. And now, all of a sudden, you're eager to share? No. I don't fucking think so."

I'm opening my mouth to agree when my phone vibrates in my pants.

I look up at Perfect, then Five, and then his phone vibrates in his hand. I pull mine out as Five studies his screen.

"Who is it?" Perfect asks.

"My mother."

"Oliver," Five says.

We just stand there looking at each other for a few seconds, both phones going off simultaneously.

"Well, don't just stand there looking stupid, answer them!" Perfect says. Scout barks her agreement.

"Hello?" Five and I say together.

"Paxton," my mother says. "I need you to come to the Hundred Palms Resort."

"What? Mom, I'm a little busy right now. Can I call you back…" I look outside and realize it's morning. I was talking all night long. "After lunch or something?"

"No, Paxton, you may not." Her voice has a hard edge to it, like she's pulling the mom card on me. "I'm here," she says, "with Cynthia, Nolan, and that sweet girl, Ivy. And we require the presence of all the Misters, with their respective Mrs., for an emergency meeting."

"You have Cindy? Hey," I say, looking at Perfect. "I found her. Cindy's with my mom and Romantic at his desert armpit of a resort."

"Well," Five says, pocketing his phone. "That was Oliver looking for Ariel."

"She's in the mountains with Ellie," Perfect says. "Be back this afternoon."

"Told him that. But he's on his way here because I called a private meeting."

"Mom," I say. "We'll be there later today. But… is she OK?"

"She's fine, Paxton."

"Can I talk to her?"

"No."

"No? Well, why the fuck not?"

"Because your personal issues need to be put aside until we discuss the job you just finished." How the fuck did she know about that? "Call your Corporate friend and tell him to drive down to the resort as well. And we need his Mrs. She's definitely a player."

"Victoria?"

"What?" Five asks. "What's going on?" He grabs the phone from my hand and says, "Hello? This is Five." But he just looks down at my phone and tosses it back. "She hung up."

"She's called a Mister meeting at Nolan's resort."

"She can't call a Mister meeting," Five says. "She's not a Mister."

"Neither are you, dumbass. But if you'd like to call my mother back and explain that to her, be my guest. I'm going. Cindy's there and I need to talk to her."

"We'll, we're not going anywhere until Oliver gets here."

"And the girls need to get back from the mountains," Perfect says. "Maybe I should take the helicopter and pick them up?"

"Good idea," I say. "I'll take the Mister jet out to California, while you guys take care of your end." I'm anxious to get the fuck out of Colorado.

"I don't think so—"

"Fuck you," I tell Five. "Who the fuck made you the boss of this operation? This is my issue, remember? 'You're next, Mysterious,'" I say in a fake Five voice. "OK, I'm next. Clearly. So if everything that's happening is due to it being my turn, then I'm in charge. And I say Perfect gets Ellie and

Ariel, you get Oliver, and we meet in the desert. I'll call Corporate and let him know his presence is required."

I stop and wait for Perfect to object, but he just throws up his hands at Five and says, "We'll do it his way. Can't hurt."

But Five narrows his eyes at me. He's not used to being challenged in these matters. Even Corporate deferred to him during that last episode of bullshit. He points a finger at me. "I'm telling Oliver the minute I see him."

"You do that."

"And then the two of you can sort it out."

"We most definitely will."

Five turns to leave, opens the front door, then stops and turns to look over his shoulder. "And by the way, you're welcome for carting your drunk ass all over Colorado in a helicopter last night. Which I'm taking with me."

He walks out, slamming the door behind him. Scout barks at that. I look at Perfect.

"I'm gonna have to bring the dog," he says. "And Five isn't gonna like that one bit."

We laugh, picturing Perfect's giant Old English sheepdog on Five's fancy jet, and say, "Fucking Five," at the same time.

"I'll see you there," I say, then help myself to some car keys from the table near the garage door. "I'm gonna borrow your car."

CHAPTER TWENTY-FIVE

CINDY

I am looking out the window of Nolan's second-floor office, staring at the long, palm tree-lined driveway leading up to the resort, desperately willing Paxton to appear. I know he landed—the pilot called, per Nolan's instructions, as soon as he left the tarmac in the limo—but that feels like an eternity ago.

My heart still hurts, although Mariel has eased it a bit since this morning. It has been quite the messed-up day on my end. All the things she told me. I just don't know what to make of it. But it doesn't matter. We have other issues to deal with first. Namely, the people responsible for the whole Mr. Corporate fuck-up, as it's now being called by Nolan, who was very pissed off he was not informed of what was happening, since there was a Mr. Romantic fuck-up last summer and a less dangerous, but equally suspicious, Mr. Perfect fuck-up about a year ago.

Ivy explained them both to me. And Jesus. I don't think I can look at Nolan Delaney the same way after the things she disclosed under the Mrs. to the Misters pact I had to swear.

Am I a Mrs. to a Mister?

"Knock, knock," Mariel says behind me.

I turn and find her standing in the doorway with a tall, strikingly beautiful woman with dark hair and the most mesmerizing violet eyes I've ever seen. "Hey," I say, uncertain what to make of her. I know who she is just from the description Mariel gave me earlier. Victoria Arias, aka Mrs. Corporate.

"Cynthia," Mariel says. "This is Victoria, Weston Conrad's better half."

The things Mariel disclosed about her… It all renders me speechless. I was hoping to see Pax before having to meet her, just to give me a bit of courage. I mean… how to process it? I just don't know. But I suck it up and walk over to her, extending my hand. "Nice to meet you, Victoria. I'm Cynthia. I mean"—I laugh—"Cinderella. Oliver's sister. And…" I shrug. "Pax's girlfriend. Maybe."

"You can call me Tori," she purrs in a sultry, sexy voice.

"Oh, OK. Well, you can call me Cindy. Everyone does. Except…" I nod my head to Mariel.

"I'll just leave you girls," Mariel says. "So you can get to know each other better in *private*."

Mariel leaves, closing the door behind her.

And then… shit. What to say?

Victoria walks forward and takes a seat in a chair, straightening out her lavender top as she does it, then crosses her racehorse legs that spill out of her micro-mini skirt and folds her hands in her lap. "She said you wanted to talk to me?" Tori looks up at me expectantly, full of fire and defiance.

"I do," I say, taking a seat next to her in the other chair. Jesus. Does she have to be so beautiful? And sophisticated in her fluttery blouse and giant diamond ring?

I resist the urge to look down at my gaudy silver bracelets clinking on my wrist. Or my old, worn Frye boots that most definitely make me look like a cowgirl hick, since I'm wearing them with a red flirty skirt and black and white tank top that says, *Cute but Psycho* across my giant tits.

I'm not even gonna bother trying to justify the two pigtail braids I have my hair in today. I thought it was cute this morning. Now, standing in front of Mrs. Corporate, I just feel childish.

"Well, I'm all ears, Cindy. Give it your best shot."

She's intimidating. Definitely intimidating. I'm suddenly wishing my mother was here to say what I need to say. She'd know how to handle this woman. She'd talk circles around her and threaten to kick her ass if she stepped out of line.

But I'm not that talented in the tough-chick department. I'm more of a kill-'em-with-quirkiness kind of girl. I'm not sure that's gonna work with Mrs. Corporate.

"I'm…" Shit. *Get it together, Cindy. You're capable, and smart, and very good at what you do.* "I'm just a little worried about what happened out there on Pax's islands in the Exumas."

"Define worried," Tori says, her voice smooth. Calm. Confident.

"Well." I laugh nervously. "You almost got him killed."

"He almost got *us* killed." She takes a deep breath—and a moment—to compose herself. "So I'm not sure we have anything to discuss about that incident."

"But the reason, Tori. Surely you can see the problem I'm having."

"Not quite, Cindy," she says, unrattled. "Why don't you explain?"

"He was doing it to protect Weston, Tori. You know that, right?"

"Do I know that?" she says, a little bit of bitchiness leaking through in her tone. "All I know is that Mr. Mysterious set us up to be ambushed out in the middle of the ocean. They had machine guns, Cindy. Does that sound like protecting us?"

"Nobody calls them machine guns, Tori. Please. And from what I understand Pax had no choice. That Liam guy came to our house. Our office. He was relentless. I heard the entire conversation. It's not like Pax did it for money. He did it because Liam threatened to hire someone else if he refused. And the reason Liam was so pissed off was because West had something he wanted."

"Well, Liam Henry beat the shit out of West when he was a child, killed his father, and then sold him to another family. Does that sound like something a seven-year-old can control?"

"Of course not," I say, backing down. "No. I didn't mean…" Shit. "I didn't know that part."

Tori remains silent for a second.

"But you," I say. "You don't know the whole story either."

"So tell me," she says, gritting her teeth. "If you know what's happening, then tell me. *Please*. Because West refuses to talk about it anymore. He says it's behind us."

"Clearly it's not behind us," I say.

"Clearly."

And this is why I'm here. To fill her in. I'm the only one, aside from Mariel, who knows what's really going on here. I've been mulling everything over all day. Willing it not to be true. Wishing I could just write off Mariel Hawthorne as some delusional rich snob who's seen too many detective movies or read too many crazy books.

But everything she told me makes sense. Everything makes so much sense right down to the part that involves my family.

"And if you'd like a more accurate rundown on what happened," Victoria snaps, "I'll say this. I was running for my life. I thought West was dead at one point. I thought Paxton Vance was going to kill me. And that's *before* all the shit went down. Imagine people you love being tortured in front of you. Imagine the one person you fear most being responsible for it. Imagine," Tori says, the anger practically pouring out of her, "the worst possible outcome after all that happened."

I swallow hard and take a deep breath. "I'm sorry."

"I don't care about apologies, Cindy. I have a plan." She looks me dead on. "And West won't even listen to me because he wants to think this is behind us. Well, I've got a child to think about. My son isn't going to grow up with this shit hanging over his head. And so the reason we're all here together right now had better include the words *end* and *game*. Because that's where I'm at right now, Cinderella Shrike. End. Game."

It takes me a few seconds to let all that sink in. Why *are* we here? Mariel gave me strict orders not to open my mouth to any of the Misters until she has a chance to talk to Pax about it, but she did want me to discuss it with Tori, since she is the only one of us girls who was there when that whole rape charge actually went down.

Plus, after hearing everything Mariel had to say about Tori, I've come to the conclusion that she's badass. Victoria Arias is a Nikita. She reminds me of Five's oldest sister, Sasha, for some reason. Capable, smart, and... dangerous.

"What kind of plan?" I ask.

Tori looks away. Stares out the window like she's trying to figure out if she can trust me. But I'm Cindy Shrike. I'm in this group whether she likes it or not, whether Paxton and I are a thing or not. My brother is involved, and by extension, my sister Ariel. Because they are in business—have been in business—since this whole thing started. And even though no one ever told me, no one needed to tell me. I know it's the business that got Oliver involved in all this. Whatever happened to him at Brown is the reason he is the way he is today. He was never so standoffish before that rape charge. He was sweet, and funny, and charming just like my dad. And now Oliver is dark, withdrawn, and secretive.

I need to fix that. And I *can* fix that. I know enough now, thanks to Mariel, to get to the bottom of this and set things right.

Tori looks back at me. "I know how to kill them both."

My gut clenches. I don't want to hear this. I really don't want to hear any of this. But I have to. Running away won't fix this problem. I can't fall back on my old habits. Sure, it's great to walk out when things start to feel overwhelming. Sell your car, donate your clothes to a thrift store, and hit the road with a backpack and a bank account knowing you can replace everything you just walked away from with very little effort.

But if I want to fix Oliver I need to stay here and participate in the solution. And I can't replace Paxton Vance. No matter how hard I try to talk myself into that plan, it's not happening. Somewhere along the way these past two months, things changed. I can't pinpoint the exact moment. It might've been that night we were jumping rooftops in Malibu. It might've been the first legit case we solved together. It might've been the day at the races. I'm not sure, but it doesn't matter when. The only thing that matters is that it did.

So I suck it up and ask, "Both who?"

"Liam, the guy bothering you and Pax. And Lucio Gori Senior. The guy after me."

"That's who's responsible for all this bullshit?" I make a face. That's not what Mariel told me.

Tori nods. "They need to be taken out."

"You're going to… have them *killed?*"

She smiles. "That's the best part, Cindy. I won't have to do anything illegal myself. None of us will need to do anything illegal. Don't you see? We can fix it. All of it. But I need help to pull this off."

"Whose help? The Misters? I don't want Pax doing this kind of thing anymore. I want him out of this crazy fixer business. I've got big plans for us and none of it includes putting his life on the line just to wipe away other people's mistakes."

"Oh, Paxton Vance has no role in this job,"

"Then who?" I'm getting frustrated now. I need answers and she's being cryptic.

Victoria Arias smiles and wow, she really is the most striking woman I've ever seen. I'm no wallflower. I was born to a mother who puts the bomb in bombshell and I look just like her when she was my age. But Tori has another kind of beauty. Something timeless and elegant. She is Grace Kelly to my Brigitte Bardot. "Us."

"Us? I'm not sure I like where this is going. You need to know more. I don't—"

"Look," Tori says, cutting me off. "I know how to fix this but I'm the only one who can do it. Trust me on that."

"But you just said us. As in *me*—"

"Listen, Cindy." But there are voices downstairs and she stops talking to look warily at the door for a second before turning her attention back to me. "Whatever is going on with you and Mariel, that needs to wait. This is an immediate threat and I'm just lucky that Liam Henry and Lucio Gori haven't struck yet. They will kill me. Do you understand? They will kill West and my newly adopted son Ethan and then they will come looking for all the loose ends like you, and Pax, and Ivy, for fuck's sake. Do you want that sweet girl to be collateral damage? These people are dangerous. They do not give one shit about who they hurt as long as they get what they want."

"Well, what the fuck *do* they want?"

"Something we can't give them, Cindy. That's the only thing that matters. What they want, they can't have. And it's not because we're partial to it and won't give it up. We don't have it and we can't get it. But people like this don't care, do you understand?" She stops to take a breath because she was getting a little intense there for a second. "They don't care.

They will hurt us anyway, just because they can. Just to prove a point. Just to make sure everyone knows there's no way out once you're in."

I exhale. "Well, what do you need *me* for?"

"Backup," she says immediately. "I need you for backup, Cindy. You're a Shrike and I know what the Shrike family is capable of."

All the hairs on the back of my neck prickle and take offense. "What's that supposed to mean?"

"That you're one tough bitch, Cinderella. That's what it means. And I need you. Ellie is not like us. She's not street-smart the way we are. And Ivy is pregnant, so even if she had it in her, she can't help. I need you."

A knock at the door makes us both look at it.

"Hey," Pax calls. "You guys in there?"

"Come in," we say together.

I nod to Tori and she mouths, *Talk later*, as Pax opens the door.

CHAPTER TWENTY-SIX

PAXTON

I need you? What could Victoria possibly need with Cindy? I knock on the door to Nolan's office. "Hey. You guys in there?"

"Come in," they both chime at the same time. Like they're nervous. Hiding something.

I look at Tori and squint my eyes. "Victoria," I say, greeting her with cold suspicion.

She squints her eyes right back. "Paxton," she says. "Who are you supposed to be? Dick Tracy?" She huffs some air. "Well, you and Sparkle Plenty here have a good time. I have to get back to my family."

Victoria pushes past me and leaves before I can say anything else.

I look at Cindy and sigh. "I'm sorry."

She looks me up and down and tries to suppress a smile. "Are you Dick Tracy?"

I look down at my trench coat and then take off my fedora. "I didn't mean to be gone so long. We just… ran into a few problems." Cindy says nothing and I get a bad feeling about what she and Victoria might've been talking about. "Did… did Victoria fill you in?"

"No," Cindy says sweetly. "No. I was up here looking out the window waiting for your car to arrive and she came up with your mother to introduce herself."

"Hmm," I mumble. "She's wild and dramatic. So it's best to take anything she says with a grain of salt. Why didn't you answer my calls?"

Cindy twists one of her long blonde braids. "I got rid of my phone. I was mad."

"Are you still?"

"How can I be mad when you show up here just in the nick of time, Detective?"

"Cute but Psycho, Miss Cookie?" I ask through the smile as I nod at her outfit. Goddamn. Her tits look spectacular in that tight t-shirt. "On anyone else I'd chalk that declaration up to a quirky sense of style, but on you it makes me nervous."

Cindy takes a step towards me, her boots thudding on the hardwood floor. Which makes me notice the rest of her. The long, tanned legs peeking out from that short flirty skirt. The jingle of her bracelets that remind me of all the times she showed up at my house in that zipper-clad leather jacket.

It makes so much sense now, how didn't I see it before?

"Cinderella Shrike," I say. And then a chuckle comes out. "It's every bit as sexy as Miss Sugar Cookie."

"I'm sorry," she says, like it's her turn to explain. "I shouldn't have lied about who I was. But I knew you'd never look twice if you found out."

"Everyone looks twice, Cindy. *Everyone.*"

We stare at each other for several long seconds and I can't help but wonder if things have changed now that I know.

They haven't for me, that's for sure.

"I love you," I say, taking off my ridiculous fedora and holding it to my chest. "But it makes me nervous."

214

"What does?" Cindy says, crossing the distance between us and placing her hand on my arm. She is heat. Even though my trench coat costume, I can feel her touch like we are skin on skin. "Me? Because I'm Oliver's sister? Or because you're involved in something bigger than you thought?"

I scowl. "What did Victoria tell you?"

"Is that what you want this conversation to turn into? The jobs? The work, Pax? What you do? What I do?"

"I just want to know how much I need to say right now."

"About where you were? What you were doing? Or how it turned out?"

"Cindy—"

"No," she says softly. "Don't. You don't need to protect me, OK? I'm Cinderella Shrike. I grew up with this shit, Pax. Do you really think I don't know what my family was into before I was born? I do."

"What are you talking about?"

Cindy shuts up as her eyes widen.

"Cindy?" I say. "What does that mean?"

"You're my brother's best friend, right? He never… talked about us? My mom and dad?"

"I've met them, of course. Nice people. Your dad is cool as fuck and your mom is… well. It's probably not appropriate to say anything else about your mom."

She stares at me and for a second I think she's going to get mad at how I might perceive her mother. But then she laughs loudly and looks down at those adorable boots on her feet. "They call me the Baby Bomb. I mean, you've seen my sisters, obviously, so we are all little baby bombs. But I am

215

so much like her in so many ways. Rory was such a princess—"

"Princess Rory," I say, smiling. "Aurora. Why the fuck didn't I figure this out?"

"But we're so opposite. My sisters are classy and I am…" She looks down at her outfit. "Well… not. I'm nothing but an explosion waiting to happen."

"I want to fuck you."

Cindy laughs. "Why, Detective," she says. "That's not what this conversation is about."

"I don't care, Cindy. I don't give a fuck whose sister you are. I don't give a fuck what Oliver thinks. And even if I'd known that first time you came to my door with my food, there's no way in hell I'd ever look at another woman again."

"He's coming here, you know."

"I know. And I don't care what he thinks. I'm good for you. I am. I wouldn't do anything to hurt you, Cindy. Or put you in danger. You're not part of this, OK? You're not going to get mixed up in this whole Mister world. You won't. I can keep you safe. No one," I say, pulling her into my chest and wrapping my arms tightly around her, "will ever hurt you as long as I live."

She rests her head on my shoulder and hugs me back. I can smell her hair, and her skin, and her clothes. And everything about her is sweet and good and delicious. "It's cute that you think I need protecting. We'll be fine. We'll figure this out and take care of it. We'll—"

"No," I say, pushing her back a few inches so I can look down at her face. "No. You're not understanding me. There is no *we* in this Mister problem. Yes, the other guys and I will figure it out, but you're staying here with Ellie, and Ivy, and Tori. Oliver really would kick my ass if I dragged you into this."

"Paxton," she says, grabbing hold of my biceps with both hands. "He's my brother. What happened to him happened to me too. And yeah, I was too young to understand what it all meant at the time. But I get it *now*. I understand. I'm as much a part of this as anyone. I'm not going to just sit back and let these people put him in danger. Or you, for fuck's sake."

I want to shake her right now. Ask her what the fuck Victoria Arias said. What little plan she might be hatching and how she might've tried to involve Cindy. Because that's the kind of woman Tori is. But I don't want to fight about this bullshit now. "I haven't seen you in weeks, Miss Cookie." My hands slide down to her ass and lift up that flirty little skirt until they are cupped against her cheeks with only her silky panties holding me back.

"The first time I walked in his office I wanted nothing more than to have him bend me over his desk and fuck me from behind."

"Jesus," I say. "Yes."

"I wanted the window shades wide open so anyone passing could see us."

"Fuck," I say, my dick getting hard. I have a feeling she's just trying to change the subject away from our real-world problems but I don't really care.

"I wanted him to slip his fingers under the elastic of my panties and pull them down to my knees—"

217

I drop my hat on the floor, turn her around, and push her face first onto the desk, lifting her skirt up, as I grab her panties. "Like this, Miss Cookie?" I tug on them. Hard, making her gasp as I drag them down and kick her legs open with my foot. "Spread 'em, ma'am."

She giggles, but complies, so her panties are stretched taut at her knees. "I hope you have a warrant for this illegal search, Detective."

"I don't need a warrant, Miss Cookie. You're mine now. And I'll search you whenever I want." My fingertips lightly trace her inner thigh as I bend down. She shivers and arches her back, sucking in a breath at my soft touch. "I think you might be hiding something."

She giggles again as I kiss that little dent behind her knee and make my way up the back of her leg. "Where could I possibly—Oh," she sighs, when I nip her ass cheek.

"Yeah, 'oh' is right," I mumble, inhaling her sweet scent as I place both hands on her ass and begin to lick between her legs. She trembles when my finger finds her clit and begins to stroke.

"My God," she says, her breath coming quicker. "I'm ready to confess."

"You're not getting off that easy, you little trollop." Her laugh is loud. And happy. And holy fuck, she makes me so damn happy back. "I know you won't tell me the truth unless I ease it out of you. So maybe I need to ease something into you"—I insert a finger into her pussy, searching for the trigger to make her crazy with lust—"to get your full attention."

"Pax," she moans.

"That's Detective Pax to you."

"Detective—" But she can't finish because my tongue is swirling around the rim of her perfect little puckered asshole. Her arms go above her head on the desk and she stretches forward, giving me more access. "I want to come right now. All over your face."

I stand up and smack her ass, leaving a perfect red handprint on her right cheek. "Not yet, my pretty little cookie. I'm just getting started. Dessert can come later. Much later."

I pull her up and quickly spin her around, her big blue eyes wide with surprise, and want, and everything that makes a man happy when he's with a woman. I lift her shirt up, find a sweet, pale-pink bra under that graphic tee, and lick my lips as I study the way her breasts practically spill out around the white eyelet lace.

"I'm gonna have my cake and eat it too, Sugar. They say it can't be done, but it's happening. Right now." I push her so she is forced to lie back on the cold, hard surface of the desk. Her chest is rising and falling with the anticipation of what's coming. God, she is so damn hot. "I missed you," I say impulsively. "Did you miss me? Or was it easy to move on and forget?"

"Detective," she whispers. "If I didn't know better, I'd think you were smitten with me."

"You have been the only thing on my mind for weeks. Call it whatever you want," I say, looking down and noticing that her panties have dropped to her ankles. I reach down, tug them around her boot, and then put them in my trench coat pocket for later. She gives me a knowing smirk, but I

219

don't care. I kick her legs open again, then reach down, grab under her knees, and hike them up to her chest.

Her eyes track mine as I lower myself in front of her open pussy. She's glistening with readiness, but I'm just getting started.

One sweep of my tongue is all it takes to make her moan. "If you make me squirt on this desk—"

I laugh loudly just picturing it. "Miss Cookie, if I make you squirt all over Nolan Delaney's desk, my life will be complete. I will hold that over his head for decades to come. Pun intended."

She laughs, reaching for the collar of my coat, pulling my face to hers before I can object.

The kiss is sweet. Her full lips taste like strawberries. Our tongues dance together like we've been practicing these moves for a lifetime. Her hands are in my hair, on my face, then her fingernails dig into my arms. "You have too many clothes on. I want to feel your skin. Take off that ridiculous coat."

"Are you ordering me around?" I laugh into her mouth as I kiss her again.

"Please," she begs. "Take it off."

I stand up, shrug the coat off, and then slip my t-shirt over my head. She stares at my chest before lowering her gaze, eyes lingering on the precise muscles of my stomach. She flattens both palms onto my skin as heat creeps into my body.

"You're beautiful," she says. "You know that?"

I shake my head. Very slowly. "You're lookin' in the mirror, Sugar. It's not me you're seein'."

She bites her lip, eyes bright with mischief. "And sweet too."

"I'm not the one covered in sprinkles, Miss Cookie."

"I'm going to marry you, ya know."

I lean down and take her face in my hands, fingertips brushing small circles against her cheeks as I stare into her blue eyes. "And have my babies?" I ask. "Little baby sugar cookies?"

"Maybe little baby brownies," she whispers. And then she frowns. Deeply. And whispers, "Don't leave me like that again. I was so sad."

Oh, God. I am sad too, just thinking about it. "I'm really sorry I did that. I was just busy, Cindy. And it was confusing and being hired to kill a friend is kinda fucked up."

"I would've helped you."

"No," I say. "I mean, I know you're capable. But no. I don't want you involved in any of this."

"I'm already—"

"Shhh," I whisper, kissing her mouth to stop this conversation. "Later. We have forever to talk about this. But right now all I want to do is enjoy everything about you." *Before your brother gets here and we have to duke it out*, I don't add.

She sees—or maybe senses—what I'm thinking and frowns again. It makes creases in her forehead as her little nose scrunches up. But she doesn't push it. Instead, she reaches down and begin unbuckling my belt. She says, "I want to take off your pants."

CHAPTER TWENTY-SEVEN
CINDY

My fingers fumble with nervousness. I suddenly am shaking, unable to control my body's reactions to everything that has happened over the past several weeks.

"Cindy," Pax says, his hands taking over for the task I am seemingly unable to complete. His belt opens, the buckle jingling as he guides my fingertips to the button on his jeans. I manage that, the rapid beating of my heart still making me uneasy, and then drag the zipper down.

Pax is eager and ready for me, pulling his hard dick from his boxer briefs and pumping himself a few times before once again guiding my hand to where it should automatically be.

I gaze up at him, expecting him to ask questions. But his eyes are half-mast and filled with desire. "You really are beautiful," I say. The part of me in the moment is unable to deny what I feel when I look at his face or his body. "I really do love you."

"I really do love you back. I don't care what Oliver says about this. It's real. And it's ours, not his. He has no say in anything." His smile resets the uneven beating of my heart, and just as suddenly as it came, my anxiety passes. The *thumpety-thump* is normalized to just plain old *thump-thump*. "I wanna be with you. Not just today, but forever. I wanna wake up every morning thinking about the moment we will fall asleep together that night. I want to drink mint juleps with you, and margaritas, and start a new life that has nothing to do with the past. I want all of that. But right now I just wanna watch you, Cindy. Suck my cock, take it down your throat, swallow me. And then I'm gonna fuck you until you scream."

I am nothing but heat. My whole body floods with warmth. My pussy is wet and throbbing for him. Ready to forget, if just for a moment, what's really happening here.

I deserve this moment. I really do.

So I grab his biceps and sit up. I place both palms flat on his chest and push, just slightly. Just enough to make him take one step back and give me room to sink to my knees between him and the desk.

When I look up I'm the one who's smiling now. "Are you ready to pick up where we left off?"

"So fucking ready."

I open my mouth. He lets out a long breath of anticipation and slowly pumps his thick cock up and down as my tongue reaches for his tip. I lick. Once. Twice. My eyes trained on his as they close. His hands are on my head, fingertips tracing down my long braids as I take the head of his cock in my mouth and suck. He fists my braids, opens his lust-filled eyes for a moment, then slowly urges me to take him deeper.

I open as wide as I can, taking him the way he wants. Letting him fill me up until I can't take any more and begin to gag.

"Breathe," Pax says, encouraging me.

I do. I breathe through it, placing my hands flat on his thighs so I can push him away if it gets to be too much. But just as I do that, he lets got of my head and places his hands on top of mine, slowly moving his hips back and forth as he guides my fingers to his balls.

If I didn't have his cock in my mouth, I'd smile. Instead, I chuckle, the vibrations of my vocal cords hitting him in just the right way, because he moans and his hands resume their position on my head. Urging. More and more urging to take him in as far as I can.

Drool starts slipping past my lips, dripping down onto my right knee, and it only makes me want to try harder.

"Mmmm," I murmur around his hot flesh.

Pax reaches down and twists my nipple, making me groan with surprise at the acute twinge of pain. I draw back out of instinct, but his hips follow me, keeping us connected. "Stop me," he says. "Stop me if you don't like it. But I like it."

I look up at him and find a genuine look of concern on his face. My head moves forward, taking him deeper. One hand still fondling his balls as the other slides his pants down farther so I can play with his asshole.

"Fuck," he says, throwing his head back. "Fuck. Cindy—"
"

I know he likes it. I know he wants more. I know he wants it to be dirty, and sweaty, and sticky.

I want that too. So I pull back, then thrust forward. I let the tip of his dick bump up against the back of my throat. I welcome the gag reflex. I welcome the drool spilling out of my mouth. I do it again, and again, and again until he is gripping my head too tight, so my scalp begins to tingle.

The last thrust forward ends with me pulling all the way back until his long, hard cock falls out of my mouth.

225

Pax opens his eyes, but I hold up one finger and say, "Just be patient."

And then I get underneath him. His huge balls dangle in front of my face and my tongue flicks out, reaching for them. Flicking against them until my hand grabs hold and I open my mouth wider and suck them.

"I'm gonna come," he says. "I'm gonna come down your throat."

And I'm gonna help him do that.

My mouth goes searching for his cock again. I take him in all at once this time. My head bobbing back and forth, the drool coating my chin, falling onto my breasts as my finger is still tracing the outline of his asshole.

He grips my hair tighter—if that's possible—and the salty taste of semen fills my mouth, then my throat.

I swallow all of it as he thrusts his hips at my face. And when the wave of contractions slows to almost nothing, I pull back and look up to meet his gaze when I lick my lips.

"Your turn now," he says.

A moment later he's pulled me to standing and he's walking me around the side of the desk where the large executive chair is waiting. He sits, holding my hand, and then points to his lap.

"I want to smack that ass, Cindy Shrike. Not because you're bad. Just because I like it."

"Ummm…"

"Lie across my knee, Cindy." His eyes are still heavy from the orgasm but his voice is clear and commanding.

"You want to spank me?" I ask through a smile.

"Turn that fucking ass red." He pauses. "You'll enjoy it, I promise." Then he pats his knee with one hand and encircles my waist with the other. "Right here, Sugar."

I stumble forward, kinda turned on. Kinda turned off. Not sure what this means or why he likes it. But I bend over so my hips are centered on his lap, and let my head and legs dangle over the side of the chair.

"You're doubting me, aren't you?"

"I just don't get it. But proceed, Detective. Perhaps you know something I don't."

He leans forward so his mouth is close enough to my ear to hear him whisper, "I know all the ways, all the things, all the secrets, Cinderella." His hand slides my skirt up and the cool air from the AC hits my bare ass. "So don't rush to judgment." The light pressure of his fingertips tracing a line down the crease of my ass and into the heat between my legs makes me suck in a breath.

"Keep going?" he asks. I can practically hear him smile.

I swallow. "Yes. Keep going."

He withdraws his hand from between my legs and I'm immediately wishing for him to do it again. But instead of going right for my most sensitive parts, his palm glides across the round curve of my cheeks, barely skimming the small opening between my thighs.

"You're going to tease me?" I ask.

No answer from Mr. Mysterious. Just another light pass of his hand across the place where my legs meet my ass. Then another, and another. Until I'm relaxed, my eyes closed, enjoying the sensation. And I can feel his cock underneath

227

me growing bigger, and getting thicker with each passing moment.

I hear the crack of his hand before I even realize the pain. My back bucks a little, making me wobble on his lap. "Damn, Paxton."

"Shhh," he says, continuing with his light touches. My ass is heating up and the kink has barely started. This time his fingertips dip just a little deeper into that space between my legs and once he even bumps up against my clit.

I bite my lip and wish for more when he doesn't do it again.

"Do you like it?"

"You're teasing me."

"It's a good tease though, right?" And just as the last word is out of his mouth, that flick of his finger on my pussy as his hand passes over my cheeks.

"Yes," I say. Another crack echoes off the tall ceilings of the office. And then another. "Ow!"

But again, his fingertips are there on my clit. A small, barely detectible tickle that has me squirming.

"Hold still," he says, another smack landing hard. And I'm just about to sit up and smack him back when his palm flattens out over the stinging heat radiating across my bottom. "I'm not letting you get away, Cinderella. Someone has to learn who's in charge here."

"Who's in—Ow! Jesus fucking Christ, Mysterious! What the hell?"

"I told you stay put, didn't I?"

"Paxton, you said you wanted to do this because it was—Ow!"

"Fun?" he asks. "It is fun. But when I tell you to stay put, Miss Cookie, I need to know you'll stay *put*. Otherwise how do I know you're safe?"

I turn my body just enough to look up at him. "You are punishing me?"

His fingers are tracing that pattern along my legs again. Teasing. Again. Because nothing even remotely comes close to touching my pussy this time. "I'm not punishing you. This feels too good to be punishment. I'm just showing you that you can trust me. So the next time I want you to do something that will keep you safe, you'll do it without question."

"That's not fair," I say. "You're the one who left and didn't send a message."

"Which is why we're having fun right now. And why you only have one ass cheek red instead of two."

"You can't threaten me, Paxton."

"Do you want me to stop?" he asks, raising an eyebrow. "Really? Because we haven't even gotten to the good part yet."

I squint my eyes at him. "What good part?"

"The part where you come, of course. I came, now it's your turn."

"But you want to smack the come out of me?"

Another crack on my ass and I'm about to jump up when he leans over and traps me there beneath his chest. "Stop resisting, Cinderella. Just give in and trust me." He leans closer to my ear and whispers, "Do you trust me?"

I relax and drop my head. "Yes." Because I do. I know he's got a plan here. And I know it ends with satisfaction. So why bother fighting it?

He rubs my ass again, his touch rougher, his circles over my skin larger. And then another smack. This time I suck in air and bite my lip, but don't buck my back in protest because he's got his fingertips between my legs and this time the light pass over my clit lingers and he plays with it.

"Whatever Victoria told you when you were alone in here with her needs to be forgotten. Do you understand?"

I want to say, *What do you mean*? Or, *She didn't tell me anything*. But I know what he means and she did tell me something. He's got every right to be suspicious. She's asking me to help her do something none of the Misters will sign off on. It will put her in danger, it will put me in danger, and it might put everyone else in danger too.

"Deal?" Pax asks after letting me think for a few moments.

"Deal," I say.

"Good," Pax says, urging me to get up off his lap. He helps me, and then we both get up.

"I thought you were going to—" But he's got me bent over the desk again before I can finish.

"Oh, I have no intention of denying you anything, Miss Cookie." He lifts my skirt once more and grabs my hips and positions me by kicking my legs open. "I'm happy to fuck you now."

His cock finds my pussy wet and ready. He eases into me way too slowly for how turned on I am right now. I can still feel the sting of his spankings. I can still imagine the tickle sensation of him playing with my clit. And it's throbbing right now. My lower body is staggeringly weak as I wait for him to fully enter me.

His cock is rock hard, his girth stretching me, making me open my legs wider to accommodate him. He leans forward, takes my hands, and slides them along the surface of the desk until they are above my head. He tightly grabs both wrists with one hand and then both my long braids with the other.

"Hard?" he asks. "Or soft?"

I don't even need to think about it. "Hard," I say.

He pulls out, almost all the way out, and then rams himself back inside me with so much force, I slide forward on the desk. I grunt, but he's doing it again, so the grunt turns into a moan, turns into a long, whimpering song of, "Yes, yes, yes…"

Our skin-on-skin contact makes a slapping sound. His large, hard balls are slamming against my clit. One hand is fisting the skin of my hip, while the other has my braids and he's pulling my head back, and back, and back… until he says, "Open your eyes, Cindy. And watch what you do to me."

I do. I open them. And his face is everything I ever dreamed of when I pictured myself with Mr. Mysterious as a teenager. Pure, testosterone-filled maleness. He leans down to kiss me, biting my lip, then my tongue, and then he says, "Come."

I wail. His hand clamps over my mouth as everything I've ever wanted comes to fruition. Wave after wave of spasming orgasm. His fingers are there on my clit to bring it all home and the ensuing flood of wetness can only mean one thing.

I did, in fact, squirt all over Mr. Romantic's desk.

Pax is laughing, I'm collapsed on the desk, my legs so weak, they tremble.

But then there is a loud ruckus outside the door.

"Shit," Pax says.

"What? What is that?"

But Pax has let go of me and he's pulling up his pants. "Get dressed," he says. "Quick! It's your brother."

Oh, fuck.

I scramble around looking for my t-shirt, then hike it over my head just as someone pounds loudly on the door.

"Pax?" Oliver yells from the other side. "What the fuck are you doing?" The doorknob jiggles as he tries to open it, but thankfully it's locked.

I glance around as I smooth down my shirt and make sure my girls are both tucked neatly into my bra. But then I catch sight of my reflection in the glare of the window and realize there's no way out of this.

My hair is a mess. I look as well-fucked as any cheating wife I've ever followed after pulling a nooner with an illicit lover.

I whirl around to find Pax just as Oliver begins crashing his body into the door, trying to break the lock. I'm reaching for Pax, desperate to smooth down his hair as he straightens his shirt, when Oliver comes crashing through.

He glares at Paxton for a moment, breathing hard, nostrils flaring, eyes as angry as I've ever seen them. And then he looks at me.

And every bit of that evaporates. "Cindy," he says, calm, pulling on the end of his shirt a little, like he's trying to compose himself.

"Oli," I say, smiling. Hoping like hell he's not going to start shit. "What are you doing here?"

Oliver glances at Paxton, grinds his teeth and clenches his jaw for a second. "Just looking for my best friend." He looks back at me. "Hey, Cin, we've got a few things to talk about here. Why don't you go join the other Misses in the kitchen? I hear they're making dinner… or something."

My mouth opens in shock. "Did you just tell me to go to the kitchen?"

"Cindy," Pax says. I look over at him and he shakes his head. "Go. I'll catch up with you later."

"Yeah," Oliver says, cracking his knuckles. "He'll catch up later."

I sigh, resign myself to the fact that I was just dismissed, and walk out into the hallway where all the Misters are waiting, wide eyes, mouths hanging open—I get an angry look from Mr. Romantic as he figures out we just fucked in his office—and then I spy Victoria beckoning me at the bottom of the stairs.

I don't look back when the office door slams and I pretend not to hear the yelling that comes after. I just follow Victoria through the bustling hotel, past the restaurant, and down a long hallway where we stop in front of one of those double swinging doors you find in commercial kitchens.

"Well," she says. "I guess that's the end of that friendship."

233

"That's not true," I say, immediately irritated with her. "They're best friends. They're gonna work it out."

"Hmm," Victoria says. "A best friend doesn't usually fuck the baby sister in his other friend's office. But whatever. They can have their little fight. All the important stuff is going on in here anyway." And then she swings the door open and I see all the other Misses, plus my big sister Ariel, huddled around a long stainless steel table.

"Well," Ariel says, once they all notice us. "Look who it is. The wandering princess has finally been corralled."

"Don't be dramatic, Ari," I say, waving a hand at her. "But what are you doing here anyway? What's all this stuff got to do with you?"

She grabs something off the table and holds it up in the air. It takes every ounce of self-control not to double over and get sick at the sight of what she's holding. "What the— where did you get that?" I whisper, my hand over my heart as I stare at the shiny silver envelope.

"It came to the office in the mail, Cinderella. And it's addressed to you."

CHAPTER TWENTY-EIGHT

PAXTON

Both Oliver and I watch Cindy retreat through the door. I catch a glimpse of Nolan, Mac, Five, and West lingering just outside the door before she closes it behind her. And then we turn and face each other.

"Fuck you," Oliver says. "Just fuck you. Fuck you. Fuck you. Fuck *you*." He pokes me in the chest with his finger each time he says it, but the last time he pushes with his whole palm and I have to take a step back.

"Look—"

"No, *you* fucking look." Oliver snarls the words out. "You fucking look, asshole. My sister?" He pauses like he's still unable to come to terms with it. "My baby fucking sister, Pax? Just what the fuck? Why don't you just rat me out to the police while you're at it? Huh? Or chop me up and feed me to the poor? Hey, I got an idea, why don't I just fucking punch your lights out?"

The blow comes hard, smacking against my jaw. I'm not expecting it, so my head snaps to the side and my ear starts to ring.

The second blow clips my lip and blood sprays out onto Oliver's white thermal shirt.

I see red. I duck my head and bull-charge him, straight into the desk. He goes flying over it backwards in some kind of circus somersault and actually lands on his feet on the opposite side.

235

I lean over.

He meets me in the middle.

Eye to eye.

"What the hell is wrong with you?" he asks.

"What the fuck do you want me to say, Oliver? I like her, OK? She came to me. I didn't… like… seek her out or anything. She came on to me, man. At my fucking house in Malibu. I didn't know!"

"That's funny," Oliver says, his rage about to spill over. "Because I distinctly remember you spitting out your drink at Corporate's house two weeks ago when I mentioned I had a sister named Cinderella." Oliver starts walking around the desk as he talks. "You didn't think it was relevant then? Instead you decide to keep it a secret, tell fucking Perfect before me, and then proceed to bang her in Nolan 'sick fuck' Delaney's office while everyone else is downstairs!"

He's standing in front of me again. Fists clenching.

"If you swing," I warn him. "I'll swing back."

He's in motion before I finish and he connects with my cheek before I can block.

But OK. I get it now.

It's a fight.

I swing back, clip him in the jaw just before he ducks, and then he rams me, head first, pushing me into the wall. Pictures fall off, and the door flies open. Nolan is standing there pointing at us as he roars, "Knock it the fuck off!"

But I barely hear it because Oliver's next swing also connects, this time with the side of my head. My ear absorbs the second shot in less than two minutes and rings even louder.

Then Mac and West have me by the arms and Five and Nolan are pushing Oliver back to the other side of the room.

"That's enough," Five says, when Oliver continues to shout at me. "That's enough."

Oliver turns on Five then. "How long have you known about this?"

"Me?" Five laughs. "I found out last night. I came to you today. And now you know too. So don't go mixing me up with the rest of this bullshit, Oliver Shrike. Remember who the fuck you are."

"I know who I am," Oliver says, swiping the back of his hand across his bleeding lip. "But"—he points to the rest of us—"I don't know who the fuck these guys are anymore. I'll tell you that right now. I have no fucking clue who you guys are. I think I'm done here. I think I'm out. Fuck you," he says, pointing to me. Then Nolan. "And you and your sick shit. And you too, asshole"—to Perfect—"you and your do-gooder bullshit can just all go to hell."

"What about me?" West says.

"You're the worst of all of them, Corporate." Oliver sneers his name. "You lie like a motherfucker. I hate liars."

"Just calm the fuck down," I say, shrugging West and Mac off me. "It's not the end of the world. And you're one to talk, dickhead. None of us are innocent, OK? Not even you."

"Not even me?" Oliver says, spitting blood onto the floor of Nolan's office.

"Nice," Nolan says, taking a swipe at Oliver's shoulder. "Nice fucking manners, Shrike."

But Oliver doesn't even notice. He's glaring at me. His blue eyes are tiny slits of anger and he peers at me from under his messed-up blond hair. He's a big guy. Not as tall as me, but a damn big guy. He looked like a linebacker even as a freshman in college. He looked rough. But now—with his biceps bulging against the tight fabric of his long-sleeved Shrike Bikes thermal, tattoos peeking out from underneath the collar, sweat pouring down the side of his jaw as he tries to contain his anger—he just looks… dangerous.

"It's not the end of the world," Oliver says, repeating my words. "To you. But I had one sister, Paxton Vance. One sister who was smaller than me all growing up. One *baby* sister who looked up to me as her protector instead of down on me like an annoyance. And you just stole her away."

"Oliver," Mac says. "Come on, man. It's not like that and you know it."

But Oliver shrugs him off when he tries to clap him on the shoulder. "How the fuck would you know?" And then he looks at all of us. "How the fuck would any of you know?" He points at Mac. "Do you have a little sister? Or you, Nolan? Who the fuck knows with West, he's such a goddamned liar."

"Hey," West protests.

"I do," Five says.

"I know you do, asshole." Oliver doesn't take his eyes off me.

"So I get it. Which is why I told you right away. But look, you're best friends with Pax for a reason, right?"

Oliver just shakes his head.

"You know he'll take good care of her."

Oliver breaks his death stare at me to look at Five. "Take good care of her? Are you fucking kidding me?"

"Oliver—" I say.

"No." He cuts me off. "No. You *can't* take good care of her. You just fucked her, Vance. You just fucked her."

"Look," I say. "I get it. The office wasn't appropriate—"

"No, shit, asshole," Nolan says. "We *are* a fucking hotel, you know."

"I can't believe you guys," Oliver says. "You think this is funny?" He stares at us. All of us, one at a time. And then his gaze lands back on me. "I'm not talking about fucking her, Pax. I'm talking about fucking her *over*."

For a second I think he's talking about me cheating or something. I'm about to protest when it finally hits me.

"You ask everyone if I'm normal," Oliver says, pointing at West. "'Why doesn't he date anyone? Why doesn't he have a girlfriend? How can a guy run a dating site and not have a girlfriend?' Well, I'll tell you assholes *why*," he says, snarling the last word like a wild animal. "Because you don't pack other people into your fucked-up baggage and take them on the trip. If there's one thing my dad made me understand when all that shit went down ten years ago, that was it. You travel to your destination alone. You don't bring anyone along for the ride."

He looks back at me and everything becomes clear.

"You just got her involved, Pax," he says, poking me in the chest so hard I have to take half a step back. "You just packed her bags and put her on a runaway train to nowhere. Whoever is doing all this, they're gonna come after her too. So congratulations, Mr. Mysterious. You're probably gonna get my little sister killed."

CHAPTER TWENTY-NINE

CINDY

Victoria snatches the envelope from Ari's hand and flings it onto the table. It goes sliding across the stainless steel and drops off the edge onto the floor, out of sight. "She can worry about her junk mail later, OK? We have a serious fucking problem."

"Wait," I say, looking at my sister. "Do I get mail at the office often?"

"Nope," Ariel says. "This is the first time that I know of." And then she narrows her eyes at me like she's got a follow-up question.

"OK," a cute blonde woman says, refocusing our attention. "Look, we're all on edge right now. None of us know what's going on—"

"I know what's going on, Ellie," Victoria snaps. "I know exactly what's going on."

And then she's rattling on a mile a minute about Liam Henry and that guy named Gori and the fact that her father was tortured to death.

Which totally sucks. Completely sucks. But I'm slowly edging my way around the table until the silver envelope lies like a bad omen on the floor next to my feet. I want to bend down and pick it up, but I can't. Not without being noticed. So I kick it under the table and try to follow the conversation. Try not to think about what's inside that envelope. Try not

241

to imagine all the many, many ways this situation just got infinitely worse.

"What can we do?" Ivy asks.

"You're not doing anything," Victoria says. "You're pregnant so you're not doing anything. And you"—Victoria nods to the one called Ellie—"you're just not cut out for stuff like this, OK? I need Cindy and Ariel."

"Wait," I say, finally catching up. "What's Ariel got to do with this?"

"Jesus, Cindy," Ariel says. "If you'd stop by home once in a while, maybe you'd know."

"Know what?" Please tell me she didn't get a silver envelope too.

"I've been working with Pax and Oliver on this shit since it happened. I know everything." Ari nods to Ivy. "I know about what happened to you on Martha's Vineyard—"

"Wait. What?" I ask.

But Ari ignores me and nods to Ellie. "I know that Allen jerk reappeared in your life and Ellen Abraham was causing trouble at your work."

"Who is Ellen? Allen? What the hell is—"

"I know about the island, Tori. Everything. Including what happened to your father. But most of all, I am the only one who knows what happened to Oliver that night."

That night.

Just hearing those two words makes me sick.

"What happened?" Ivy asks. "What part did he play?"

But Ari just shakes her head. "Sorry, it's not my story to tell."

242

"Well, good for you Ariel," Victoria says. "But I know who's responsible. Liam Henry set up West and I because Lucio Gori Junior wanted me dead. Now he's dead, but his father is still alive. And I'm sure West wants to think his parents"—she does air quotes as she says that word—"are good enough people. But they're not. No one *buys* a child. So can we please put all this bickering bullshit aside and get on the same page for once?"

"What do you want us to do?" I ask, completely frustrated with all the details I've been in the dark about. "What can we do?"

"I have a plan," Victoria says. "And it's a really great one that will get rid of Liam Henry and Lucio Gori Senior for good."

"You want us to… kill them?" Ivy asks. She's stunned.

"Not us, Ivy." And then Victoria smiles a smile that reminds me of Paxton when he's got someone in his sights. "That's the best part, I told you. We don't have to kill anyone. We just need them to kill each other."

"We—" Ellie starts. But Nolan comes bursting through the double kitchen doors and she stops short.

We all go silent.

"What?" he asks. "What's going on in here? I thought you busy were making dinner?"

"Don't be silly, Nolan," Ivy says, recovering first. "We have Elizabeth for that. And she prefers the regular kitchen when she cooks, remember? I mean, why employ a first-rate chef if you can't show her off to your best friends?"

"Oh, yeah," Nolan says, looking us all over as he tries to appear calm. "Right. Sorry, I just figured you were busy

243

making dinner when you all disappeared to the catering kitchen."

"What are you doing in here?" Ivy asks. "Aren't you supposed to be mediating the Mister meeting?"

"Ahhh, ice." Nolan smiles sheepishly at Ivy. "I need ice. Two bags, please."

"Why?" Ellie asks.

"You know." Nolan sighs, then shrugs. "Just... guy stuff."

"They beat the shit out of each other," I say. "Didn't they?"

"Nope," Nolan says, putting a hand up. "Nope. Just a few swings and some shouting, that's all. It's cool now." But his gaze lingers on me for a moment and he frowns.

I squint my eyes at him, and he redirects his attention to Ivy, who is busy scooping crushed ice from the ice maker into baggies. She hands them over and Nolan is just about to leave when a chef appears through another set of doors and says, "Dinner's almost ready. I need everyone out so my servers can prep. So please go grab a seat in the Sapphire dining room and the servers will be in shortly."

She disappears, but the doors Nolan came through swing open once again. Pax appears, that ridiculous detective coat swinging out behind him as he strides into the kitchen.

"Pax," I say, walking towards him. "What happened?"

"Nothing," he says, putting his arm around my waist and pulling me close. "Nothing. We're all good now."

Ivy hands him an ice pack for his swollen face and then she and Nolan disappear, presumably to deliver the other ice pack to Oliver.

"Do you ladies mind," Pax says, looking at Ellie, Victoria, and Ariel, "just… giving us a minute?"

"Sure, sure," the three of them say, exiting the way Ivy and Nolan left.

When they're gone I take the ice pack from Pax and place it on his jaw. "You fought."

"Just a little bit, Sugar. It's fine, I swear. We're OK now. He just…" Pax sucks in a breath. "He just needed to say what he came to say and I said what I had to say. And… we're good now. We're just gonna stay here at the resort for a few days to try to figure all this shit out, and then we'll go back to Malibu and live happily ever after."

I stare up into his eyes. "You're lying."

"I'm not," he insists. "I swear. It's gonna be fine. Oliver's not mad, he's just worried about you."

"About me? Why?" But I don't even hear Pax's answer because my mind is back to the silver envelope hiding underneath the kitchen table.

"I think you better put these back on." Pax pulls my panties out of his trench coat pocket and hands them to me. "I mean, I sorta dig the thought of you sitting next to me at dinner with no panties on, but I'm pretty sure Oliver would kick my ass for real if he ever found out." He kisses me on the lips, his tongue seeking mine out. We linger like that for a moment. But then he pulls back and says, "So better to head that little complication off at the pass."

We meet everyone else up in the dining room. There is a large blackboard decorated with colored chalk on the far end of the room with a seven course meal elaborately written in perfect calligraphy. I'm starving, and everyone else is already sitting, so Pax and I take the two empty chairs at the table.

I stare at Oliver across from me, who is sitting next to Ariel, unable to look up and meet my eyes. Ivy and Nolan are to my left and Pax is on my right. Victoria is on the other side of Oliver and West is to her right. Ellie is next to Ariel, Mac is across from her and Five is at the head of the table like a boss. Victoria looks at me as I place my napkin in my lap, and gives me a slight nod of her head. Like we are co-conspirators or something.

I don't know what her plan is, but it's all wrong. It's all wrong. Maybe Liam Henry and this Gori guy are both involved somehow. And I'm not sure what to make of that comment about Weston's parents. So who knows about them. But nothing she's said—nothing any of the other Misses have said—leads back to Mariel Hawthorne and her shiny silver envelopes.

"Hey," I say to Pax. "Where's your mother?"

"My mother was here?" he asks back. "When? I didn't see her."

"I didn't see her," Oliver growls. "You need your mommy, Paxton?"

"Fuck you, asshole."

Oliver narrows his eyes at Pax, his lip still bleeding a little from their fight.

"She left," Ivy says. "She said she'll be back tomorrow, I think? Or tonight? Nolan? Which did she say? You were there."

"I don't know," Nolan says. "Like I pay attention to Paxton's mother."

"Well, this is a lovely reunion," Ellie says, her chirpy voice and easy smile trying to diffuse the situation. "I'm so happy to meet you, Cindy. And Ariel is already one of my most favorite people ever," she says, nodding to my sister. "The three of us really need to stay close after this, since we're all in Colorado, you know."

I manage a smile in return, but I can barely pay attention to the conversation while we wait for the first course to be served. I mostly zone out, wondering how I can get back into that kitchen to recover the envelope.

It has to be related. It has to be.

"Hey," Oliver says, kicking my feet under the table. "It's really good to see you again, Cin."

"Yeah." I smile at my big brother. "Yeah, it's good to see you too. I should've come home more often."

Oliver shrugs, then looks over at Ariel, then Pax, before coming back to me. "Do your thing, sis. We know you love us. But you really should come home for the holidays this year. And I guess…" He looks at Pax again. "I guess you can bring this asshole too, if you want."

"Invitation accepted," Pax mumbles. "But if you swing at me again I won't go easy on you next time."

"Shit," Oliver says, and not in a joking way. "You wish you could take me. And my dad is still gonna kick your fucking ass."

"OK," Five says. "I think this would be a good time to bring it all out in the open. Say what we've got to say.

247

Implicate who we think is involved. And try to come up with answers."

It's weird being around Five like this. I've known him my whole life. He's like a brother, but a much older one. He was already fifteen when I was born, so we never hung out socially at all. All my sisters but Ariel were so much older, I barely know them. Only Oliver and Ariel were close enough in age to be a major part of my childhood.

"Who are the players?" Five asks. "We'll start with West and go around the table."

"Liam, of course," West says.

"And Lucio Senior," Victoria adds.

"Yeah," Pax says next to me. "Liam is definitely involved. I don't know about Gori though. He's so…" Pax stops like he's searching for a word. "Lower class, you know? I mean, he's the only outright criminal on the list, right?"

"Why," Tori blurts out, "do you guys have such a hard time believing me?"

"We get it, Tori," Nolan says. "He's a bad guy. But is he *our* problem?"

"My mother pledged me to his son, Nolan. He raped me repeatedly as a kid until my father got me out and gave me a new life. And the night before The Night, he suddenly reappears? No. This is not a coincidence."

"Well," Mac says, "maybe if West actually came clean about his past, we'd be getting somewhere."

"I did come clean, asshole," West says.

"You're hiding things," Five says. "We all know it. But hey, if you want to get all of us killed because you can't come to terms with your secrets, then you go ahead and do that."

"I agree with Five," Victoria says. "Weston's parents are definitely involved."

"They are not—"

"They are," Tori insists. "You don't *buy* children, Weston!"

"It wasn't like that."

"Then what was it like?" Oliver asks. "Now is a very good time to tell us the rest of the story."

"No one knows *your* story," West retorts. And then he nods towards us. "No one knows Paxton's story either. Why don't we start with you two? Because we already know how Mac and Nolan fit it."

I wait for Pax to tell them about his silver envelope, but he doesn't. He and Oliver look across the table at each other stoically. Poker faces, both of them.

"What about that bitch Claudette?" Ivy pipes in, breaking the silence.

"Yeah," Nolan says. "It bothers me that she's still at large."

"And she got Boring Richard involved. I bet it was her." Ivy looks around with a convincing look on her face.

"Well." Ellie sighs. "I had all that fun with my co-worker, Ellen, don't forget."

"And Allen," Mac adds. "It just makes no sense. Who is running this operation? And why? Why were we falsely accused of raping that girl? Why us?"

We all look at each other, unable to answer, when the chef and her servers appear with plates of crab salad canapés. We are all suddenly quiet as they serve us, and then they disappear into the kitchen.

"I still think it's Weston's problem," Oliver says, looking down at his place setting, scowling at the tiny finger-food sandwich, and then shoves it in his mouth in one bite and chews as he talks. "He's still keeping secrets."

"You wanna know my secrets?" West says. "You think I'm the problem? Well, here you go. I might've killed Stewart Manchester."

"We already knew that part—" Oliver interrupts.

"But they don't," Weston counters.

"Who the hell is Stewart Manchester?" Ellie asks. I'm glad, because I feel like I've been dropped into an episode of *The Twilight Zone*.

"A guy who figured out who I was back in prep school. He knew the Conrads weren't my real parents and he blackmailed me for something I found a long time ago. But when we met in our separate yachts out in international waters to hash it all out, he fell over the side and never came back up. I assumed he was dead. I left and never saw him again. That was just before we were accused too. So it's like, my life was all fucked up, then it wasn't because my problem died, and then it was again, because of the rape charge."

"And Victoria," Pax adds. "She definitely contributed something to that night too."

"This is what I've been telling you assholes all along!" Tori says. "We are all connected! We need to take out Liam and Lucio Gori Senior. They're the ones behind all this." She glances at West, sitting next to her. "And your parents."

"Goddamn it, Tori—"

"West," Pax says. "You need to come clean about whatever it is you left out the last time we spoke."

"It's not even relevant," West says. "I blackmailed Liam a few years later, OK?"

"Blackmailed him, *how?*" Mac asks.

"He was pressuring my father about money, OK? The money I never gave up to him, right? So I took him aside one night at a party, back when my business was still struggling, and told him I could use some help. He laughed, of course. But I had an ace in the hole. One more gold coin from my little childhood treasure hunting days. And I told him I planted more treasure on property he owns somewhere and he'd never find it. And if he didn't leave my parents alone— and help me by giving me all his headhunting contracts—I'd call the FBI and tell them where all that treasure was. He'd be arrested for violating the Archeological Resources Protection Act of 1979. Which states pretty much everything you find treasure hunting belongs to the government. So…" West looks at all of us around the table. "Yeah. I blackmailed him. And he made good on that promise by giving me all those contracts until—"

"Until I showed up as your competition," Victoria says. "And then you knew something was wrong."

"Exactly," West says, reaching under the table to take Victoria's hand. "I knew he was on to me, or had me in some way."

"Or was just trying to kill you off," Pax finishes.

"Right." West sighs. "I was in denial at first. It was some misunderstanding, or maybe he was just obsessed with Tori's looks and was trying to piss me off? Or whatever. I didn't want to believe all that shit from the past was finally catching

251

up with me. So you see, I don't really think he's our guy, Tori. I fucked with him, he fucked with me back. It's that simple."

"But he came to our house too," Pax says. And now he's the one reaching for my hand under the table. He squeezes it and I squeeze back. He said "our house," which, given the circumstances, shouldn't make me all fluttery inside, but it does. "So why did he involve me?"

"And Cindy," Oliver adds.

"Cindy might not be involved. There's no evidence that she's involved," Five says.

Except that silver envelope that came addressed to me at the dating site office today. I look over at Ariel and find her already staring at me. She cocks her head, like she might be putting all these pieces together, but she says nothing as I quickly look away.

If Pax happens to mention his "evidence" from when they were all accused of rape, she'll figure it out.

But it's not Pax who directs the conversation to the exact place I don't want it to go. It's Ivy. "What about that silver envelope?"

"What silver envelope?" Oliver asks.

Shit. Shit. Shit.

"The one at the house on Martha's Vineyard? You know?" She looks at Nolan. "Remember? Pax picked it up when he got all the other evidence of our..." She blushes. "Our fantasy night out of the way before the cops saw it. What was in that envelope?"

I chance a glance at Ariel and she's got her mouth open, ready to say something.

But Ellie beats her to it. "Silver envelopes?" Every head turns to look at her. She looks across the table at Mac. "Didn't you use silver envelopes for our scavenger hunt on our first date?"

"Yeah," Mac says. "Pax already asked me about it, but you know what? I don't really know why I used silver envelopes. Maybe because it reminded me of The Night?"

"Well," Nolan says, "I guess the next question is… why the hell is Paxton asking about silver envelopes? He asked me too. When Ivy was invited to apply for the job here at the resort, she said it came in a silver envelope."

"Yes," Ivy says. "It did!"

I look at my sister again and now she's scowling. I shake my head.

She shakes hers back.

Later, I mouth silently. Mariel gave me specific instructions when we had our discussion. And it did not involve telling everyone about what she knows.

"Well," Pax says. And I just know he's going to tell them about our day at the races with his mother. But he doesn't. He might, in fact, sort of tell a lie. "It's just odd, don't you think?"

He squeezes my hand, like he's trying to keep this a secret as well.

I squeeze back, relieved to get to the end of the silver envelope discussion.

"Cindy," Ariel says, standing up so fast her chair scrapes on the floor. She places her napkin next to her untouched canapé and says, "I have to go to the little girl's room. Can you come with me?"

"Um, the food is coming soon," I say weakly.

"Fuck the food, Cinderella. Get your ass up and join me."

Oliver laughs. "Fucking sisters. They are incapable of peeing alone."

"Mac," Five says as Ariel grabs hold of my arm and practically drags me across the dining room. "You never did explain why you were using silver envelopes for that scavenger hunt."

"Well," Mac says… But then I can't hear anything else because Ariel has me out in the hallway.

"What the fuck, Cindy!" she whisper-shouts. "I knew you had a funny look on your face when I was holding up that silver envelope."

"Ariel, look—"

"No, you look! You have a crucial piece of evidence and you're withholding it."

"It was junk mail," I say.

"No, it wasn't."

"I opened it when you were arguing with Victoria, OK? It was a credit card offer in a pretty envelope, that's all. I threw it away."

"Then we're gonna go get it out of the trash. Because I don't believe a word you're saying."

"Fine with me."

I let Ariel drag me through the hallways back to the catering kitchen, which is now bustling with cooks and servers who are getting our dinner ready.

"Can I help you?" Elizabeth, the chef, asks, when she spots us at the doorway.

"Yes, Elizabeth. Sorry to interrupt you guys in here. But my sister left something in the trash that we need to recover. Do you mind if we look?"

"Oh, sorry. We emptied the trash."

"Where did you take it?" Ariel asks, her voice stiff and cold. "We really need it back."

"It's been compacted." Elizabeth shrugs. "Sorry. We have very strict trash regulations on the resort. Everything is compacted to save landfill space."

"See," I say, pulling my arm so Ariel has to let go of me. "It's nothing. I'm not lying."

"Is something wrong?" the chef asks.

"No," I say. "We're just a little edgy tonight, Elizabeth. That's all. Isn't that right, *Ariel*?"

Ari huffs air but turns on her heel and walks back out the door.

"Sorry to bother you," I call back over my shoulder as I follow her. She is waiting at the end of a hallway, seething with anger.

"You're lying."

"I'm not! I swear! Why would I lie about a stupid piece of mail?"

She looks me up and down, then turns once again and starts walking back to the dining room.

"What if we're looking at it all wrong?" Five is saying when Ari and I return.

"What do you mean?" Nolan asks.

"Look," Oliver says, getting up, dipping his napkin in his water glass to get it wet, and then walking over to the menu chalkboard. He wipes it clean, picks up a pink piece of chalk

255

from the tray, and begins to write down names. "Claudette, Allen, Stewart, Ellen, the Conrads, Lucio Gori Junior, Lucio Gori Senior, Liam Henry, and Boring Richard."

"Wait," Ivy says, a sad look on her face. "Do you think my father was involved?" She turns to look at Nolan. "Remember those girls you told me about? The blogger who tried to set you up? And the one who lied about being pregnant?"

"Yeah," Nolan says, scratching his chin. "How the fuck do all these people connect?"

"And, more importantly, who's in charge?" Victoria asks. "Because it looks pretty clear to me that it's all about Liam and Gori. They are the bosses, everyone else is just a player."

"Maybe," Five says, getting up to join Oliver. "If you look at it like a flow chart—" He draws squares and circles around each name, then starts connecting them with lines. "Then it barely makes sense."

"Jesus fuck," Mac says. "That is complicated."

"Right," Five says. "But—" He erases all the names and lines and then draws a big circle in the middle, attaching each name to it on the outside with one short line so it looks like an elongated sun a child might draw in pre-school. "If you look at it this way, it's really rather simple."

"It's not a *who* inside that circle," I say before thinking.

"But a what," Ariel finishes for me. "Some kind of organization, or company, or…" She trails off. I don't look at her. But it's true. Everyone knows it. There is a cacophony of *oh*, and *yes*, and *of course* coming from everyone at the table.

"We only have one more question," Oliver says. "What's the name of the entity inside the circle? When we figure that out we'll know," he says. "We'll know everything. Why they set us up, who was responsible, and what we need to do about it."

Pax reaches for my hand again. We squeeze together this time.

Because we already know what goes inside that circle.

The Silver Society.

And this can only mean one thing. There is one more missing name on that list of people.

And it's his mother.

CHAPTER THIRTY

PAXTON

The conversation lags through dinner after that. Presumably the group is busy mulling over who this mysterious entity in the center circle might be.

But the name is repeating itself over, and over, and over in my head.

The Silver Society.

I have so many questions for Cindy. They are spilling out of my mind and filling up my head until I feel like just grabbing her arm and pulling her out of the dining room.

But I can't do that.

No. I can't do that.

Because everyone will know I know something and then they will start asking questions. And Cindy might let something slip about the silver envelope my mother showed us at the races. And one of the guys—Corporate, probably, because we've never exactly been friends and he's probably still pissed off at me about that whole island mercenary contract I had on his life a few weeks ago—will put two and two together and come up with Mariel Hawthorne. And then I might really have to kill him.

And, and, and. It goes on, and on, and on like that from there.

"How's the food?" the chef, some fresh-faced thirty-something woman, says, beaming a smile at all of us as she claps her hands together in anticipation.

"Oh, it's lovely," Ivy says. I can't see her, she's on the other side of Cindy, and I don't try, anyway. I just look back down at my plate as Nolan tries to convince the woman everything is perfect even though there is nothing about us that says anything is perfect.

I cut a piece of steak and shove it in my mouth.

Cindy turns her head to look at me, just as Ellie, Mac, and Five begin talking on my end of the table. She leans in and kisses me on the cheek, but instead of turning away, she lingers close to my ear and whispers, "I have to tell you something."

I pull away and look her in the eyes.

Alone, she mouths to me.

After dinner, I mouth back.

Cindy takes a deep breath and nods her head, then goes back to picking at her steak. We have one course left. One more course and then I can get out of this fucking room, get away from all these fucking people, and just clear my head and think.

Think.

I really need to think.

Cindy and I are conspicuously silent after that, and Oliver does not miss this. He's mostly scowling through the rest of the main course and when our plates are finally taken away, he says, "So…" looking straight at me. Only a few people notice. Cindy, of course. And when I look to my right at Five, he scowls and steeples his fingers under his chin like some kind of epic villain in a superhero movie.

"So," I say back. Mac and Ellie are engaged in a conversation about their dog, who was herded away with

Corporate's new insta-kid the moment they got here. But Ariel is directly across from me, and she's paying very close attention.

"Do you love her?" Oliver asks. "Because if you don't, you need to back. The fuck. Away."

"Oliver," Cindy says. "We're in a new relationship. We like each other enough to take it further. It's none of your business."

"Yes," I say when she stops talking, never taking my eyes off Oliver. "Yes, I love her." When I look over at Cindy, she's smiling. Maybe even blushing. "I do," I say. "You just took over my life and now that you're here, I can't imagine I would ever be happy if you left."

"Awww," Ariel says. "See, Oli, you've got nothing to worry about. Our little baby sister has won the heart of big, bad Mr. Mysterious."

"What about your *job?*" he says to that. And he sneers the word job. "You can't possibly—"

"I'm out," I say. "I'm partnering up with Cindy in her detective business."

"I guess that's why you showed up here in a trench coat and then locked yourself in Nolan's office?"

Ivy actually laughs on the other side of Cindy. Everyone is listening now.

"Yeah, that was kind of a dick move, Mysterious," Nolan says.

"Oh, stop about your stupid desk, Nolan," Ivy chastises him. "It's no big deal. Three months ago we were sneaking away too. So stop being judge-y."

261

"It's *my* office," Nolan says. "And I never fucked you in there."

"Jesus Christ," I say. "I'm done here." I'm about to get up when the chef and servers appear with dessert, and Cindy places a calming hand on my arm to keep me seated.

"Ten minutes," she says, leaning over to whisper in my ear. "Ten minutes and we can go back to our cabana and be alone."

"I heard that," Oliver says, as he is served a plate with a single chocolate-covered strawberry with some kind of filling spilling out the top.

My plate is put in front of me and I look down at it, just as the chef says, "Please enjoy the cheesecake-filled chocolate-covered strawberries. Who would like coffee?"

Fuck that. I pop the whole strawberry in my mouth and stand up before I get roped into twenty more minutes of conversation. "It was great, Elizabeth," I say to the chef, tossing my napkin down, and chewing through the words before I swallow and continue. "Sorry I wasn't dressed for the occasion, but I was traveling all day and now I'm pretty tired. So Cindy and I"—she is wrapping her strawberry into a hastily constructed takeaway container made out of her napkin—"are going to bed. See you on the other side, my friends."

I grab her hand and we flee. I practically drag her through the busy-as-fuck resort—how the hell did Nolan get so many people booked in so short a time, anyway?—as we make our way out of the main building, past the pool, and then off to the left where the private bungalows are.

262

"What room are we in?" I ask, as we walk along the elaborately landscaped path that leads to the private pool and little huts.

"Eight," she says. "The last one. But Pax—"

"Shhh," I say. "Just wait until we're alone, OK?" Corporate's kid and Perfect's dog, along with a nanny, are swimming and splashing in the private pool as we pass it. Cindy waves and smiles at the greeting we receive from the kid, and then she's got her keycard out and she's flashing it at the door.

I open it up and we escape inside, closing the door behind us.

I smile at the sight of her bohemian backpack, missing her completely in that moment of recognition, even though she is right next to me and still has hold of my hand.

"Pax—"

"Cindy, look. I'm fucking sorry for dragging you into this. Oliver is right, dammit. It's really not safe for you."

"Pax—"

"But I do love you. I have never felt so sure of something in all my life."

"Pax, listen—"

"We need to be careful, OK? We need to be very careful. I think it's best if you go home to the farm. Your crazy dad is there, and your mom, who probably shoots better than I do. So they can—"

"Pax!" she yells. "Stop talking and just listen to me!"

"It's my mother, Cindy!" I shout it and she startles. "Sorry," I say, pulling her close to me and wrapping my arms around her in a hug. "Sorry."

263

"No, listen to me. I know your mother has something to do with this, obviously. The Silver Society—"

"Right. I'm so fucking sorry for dragging—"

"You didn't drag me into it. Just listen! A silver envelope was delivered to the dating site office today, Pax."

"What?" I grab my hair with both hands.

"And it was addressed to me."

"Fuck!" I say. "What the hell was inside?"

"I don't know," Cindy says into my chest. "I couldn't open it in front of the other girls. Victoria called it junk mail and snatched it away. And then it flew onto the floor and I kicked it under the table in the kitchen before Ariel thought too much about it. But she's—"

"On to us," I finish. "That's why she wanted you to go to the bathroom with her, wasn't it?"

"Yes," Cindy says, pulling away from me so she can look up at my face. "But I lied. I said it really was junk mail and told her I threw it away. It was just good luck that the kitchen staff compacted the trash and got rid of it, so I think she bought it."

"Oh, no," I say. "I don't think she bought anything, Cindy. She's going to tell Oliver and everything is going to point to my mother."

"It's not your mother, Pax. I know it. I feel it. She knows... things. She told me, Pax. She told me about The Silver Society and I was supposed to warn all the girls about it, but—"

"The girls?" I ask.

"But I wanted to talk to you first and I didn't know what to say. I don't think your mother is the one behind all this bullshit. Or the rape charge, for fuck's sake. Just… no."

"Why is she interested in the *girls*?" I ask. "What the fuck?"

Cindy places her hands on my cheeks, stares into my eyes, and says, "It was never about you guys, Paxton Vance. It never had anything to do with the Misters. The only people who matter in all this twisted shit are the Misses."

CHAPTER THIRTY-ONE
CINDY

"Everything that's happened over the years is about the *girls*, Pax." But he's just staring at me with a funny look on his face. "Do you hear me?"

He takes a deep breath and then leads me over to the small couch and sits down, pulling me into his lap. "What girls?" he asks. "What's going on?"

I sigh, so fucking sorry I have to be the one who finally has the answers he's been looking for these past ten years. "Your mother went to Dartmouth. She's from a very important, very old money, very prestigious and public family."

"Yes," he says, staring straight into my eyes.

"She wasn't the first to be invited in."

"In?"

Poor Pax. I lean down and kiss him on the lips. "Don't worry. It's going to be OK. We are all smart and strong. We will find a way out."

"Out of what? Cindy," he says, raising his voice. "What the fuck is going on?"

"Out of the Silver Society. You were invited, sort of. Men really don't get invited, Pax. The women do. It's an all-female society. Secret to everyone, except the five new women tapped for membership from each Ivy League school at the beginning of senior year. I never went to an Ivy League school, as you know. I went to Irvine." I stop and try to make

267

myself brave. "But my sister Rory did. A long time ago, Pax. She's almost fifteen years older than me. And your mother told me she got an invitation."

"Your sister?" he says. "The princess?"

I nod, swallowing down my fear. "But she didn't understand what it was. And… well, she got out of it."

"Got out of it?" he asks, his voice soft now. "What do you mean? What does that mean, Cindy?"

"She's been missing ever since college. She disappeared, Pax. I haven't seen her, or talked to her—"

"She's *dead*?"

"I don't think so. I don't know," I say, struggling not to cry. "I don't think she's dead. We never found a body or a note for ransom, or anything like that. I was way too young to understand what happened, right? I was six years old. I barely knew her. I barely remember her, Pax. But she is a giant gaping hole in my life. I've watched my parents grieve over the years on the anniversary of the disappearance and it's been killing me. I've watched Five become so distant and withdrawn, he's barely a member of the family anymore. He loved her." I choke back a sob. "He loved her so much. And she loved him back, *so much*. They were destiny." I sniff the sob away and sit up straight, forcing myself to hold it together. "That's part of the reason why I became a detective, do you understand? I've been looking for her all this time."

"But your parents," Pax says. "Your parents talk about her like she's alive. I swear, I know they do. I have never gotten the impression that she was… gone."

"It's sad," I say. "They have never given up hope."

"Fuck," he says, rubbing his forehead with his hand. "Fucking hell." And then he looks me in the eyes again. "And my mother is responsible for that?"

"We don't know that, Pax. We can't jump to conclusions. We need to get that envelope out of the kitchen. We need to see what it says."

"It's filled with fucking cooks and servers right now," he says.

"I know," I say, my eyes filling with tears. "I know. So we just have to wait until tonight when everyone goes to sleep. And then we go back, get the envelope, and try to put these last few pieces together."

"I need to call her," he says, pulling out his phone. He presses a contact icon, then holds the phone up to his ear. Even I can hear the call ring through to voice mail. He tabs the end button and looks at me. "When did you last see her?"

"This afternoon. She was here, I thought she was staying. She told me we needed to come here and she said she'd explain tonight."

"It is tonight."

"I know. Maybe she just got caught up in something? She'll be back, Pax. If not later tonight, then tomorrow for sure. She can explain everything. And we can show her my invitation—"

"What if she *sent* the fucking invitation?"

I shake my head. "Just... don't stop trusting her now, OK? We don't even know if it *is* an invitation."

He looks at the window where the sounds of people in the private pool can be heard. "What time do you think they close up the kitchen?"

269

I shrug. "I dunno. Eleven, maybe? Out by midnight?"

"So we have like five hours."

"Yeah." I snuggle into his chest, inhaling his scent as I try not to freak out about everything that's happened in the past several weeks. "We could get all the answers in just a few more hours. I might even get answers about Rory."

"But they might not be the answers we want, Miss Cookie."

"No, Detective. But I guess that's the chance you take when you go searching for the truth. It's better to know than not know, right?"

He's silent for several seconds, his fingertips rubbing small, gentle circles on the bare skin of my upper arm. I lean into him even more and he tightens his arms around me, kissing my neck and inhaling me, just the way I did him. "An honest enemy is always better than a friend who lies. Do you know who told me that?"

"Who?"

"Your brother. The night we all had to disappear and not see each other again. I wasn't crazy about Five taking over. I was pissed, actually. I said a bunch of shit, pointing out why we shouldn't trust him, especially since he wasn't even a lawyer and he was making us all look very fucking guilty when we knew—*I knew*—I did nothing wrong that night. I didn't rape that girl. It was a fucking game, OK? I didn't even ask to play. I just got that silver fucking envelope and I was twenty-one years old. What guy isn't up for a game like that at twenty-one?" he pauses and then says, "Don't answer that. I'm sure Oliver would've said no. Five would've definitely said no. Perfect would've said no. Corporate would never be interested in games, his whole life was a goddamned game. Hell, I bet Romantic would've even turned that shit down."

"I believe you."

"'Five will never lie to us,' Oli said. 'And isn't it better to have an honest enemy than a friend who lies?' What could I say? I'd rather deal in facts any day. The lies—" He leans down to kiss my head. "I've had my fair share of lies from my fucking father. So yeah, the friend who lies is far worse than the enemy who tells the truth."

"Five *won't* lie to us," I say. "I will vouch for that. He's not even capable, I don't think. He's weird. Wired all wrong. A freak in many ways, just like his father. But he's honest. And he's loyal. I don't think you can ask for anything more than loyalty in this life. Love comes and goes. People change. But family is family, not through blood, but through loyalty. My dad used to tell us kids that all growing up. He's got a circle of friends so tight, no outside force could ever break it. *The strength of bonds comes from within*, Five's father, Ford, used to say. He's kind of a nerd. And there's this framed quote in Ford's house back in Colorado. It says, *Look out for the people who look out for you. Because in the end, they're the only ones who matter.*"

Pax grunts, but I can feel his smile against the bare skin of my cheek.

"So that's what we do, right?" I turn in his lap to look at him. "Right?"

He nods, slowly.

"We just look out for each other whenever we can. And that includes your mom. She's good people, Pax. And we

271

should not doubt her until she gets her chance to tell the rest of the story."

"I don't know if I want to hear it."

"You do," I say, placing both my hands on his cheeks again. "You do."

"And what if we find out your sister is dead?" he whispers. "Will you love the truth then?"

I slump against him, unwilling to even think about it. "I'll deal with that when it happens."

We are silent for long minutes after that. We just sit there, listening to the dog bark, and the kid squeal, and the splashing of the pool water. Eventually we hear West and Victoria talking. Then Mac and Ellie chastising the dog for something that probably involves a lot of long, wet hair. And Nolan and Ivy laughing about names for the baby she's carrying.

The only Mister voice missing is Oliver.

I guess that's because he has no Mrs. and doesn't feel comfortable around all the other couples. Or maybe he's still pissed about Pax and me and can't bear the thought of seeing us together?

"Miss Cookie?" Pax finally says, breaking my thoughts and the long silence at the same time.

"Yes, Detective?"

"Would you like to go bed with me? Waste a few unnecessary hours? Forget about later?"

I look at the clock on the wall. It's barely eight. "I certainly would, Detective. In fact," I say, getting to my feet and taking his hand so I can pull him up, "I can't think of a single better option than lying naked next to you right now."

"Naked?" he asks, smiling down at me. "I never said anything about getting naked." He reaches for the hem of my t-shirt and lifts it up over my head, his big hands cupping the lacy bra that outlines my large breasts. "But now that you mention it, it's just what the detective ordered."

He takes off his own shirt, drops it on the floor, and then leads me into the little bedroom at the back of the cabana. I watch the muscles move along his back in the dim light. The way they stretch and become taut with each step. The little twin shadows of dimples just above the waistband of his jeans. The curve of his ass and the length of his stride.

Everything about Paxton Vance screams power. But it's funny. With me, he's so gentle and sweet. He's really nothing like the man I imagined him to be all these years as I plotted and planned my way into his life.

He's so much better.

CHAPTER THIRTY-TWO

PAXTON

I just look at her. She's not even naked yet and I can't take my eyes off her. So fucking beautiful. But so much more than beauty. "You're so strong," I say, reaching around her back to unclasp her bra.

"I think I get it from you," she says, letting the satin and lace slip down her arms and fall to the floor.

"You're so brave," I say, placing my hands on her thighs, just underneath her flirty little skirt, and letting them travel upward to the round curve of her ass.

"I learned from the best," she says. "It's easy to be brave when everyone around you is a role model. I love your loyalty, Paxton Vance. To your mom, and your friends, and my brother. Loyalty is handsome on you."

"I will always be loyal, Cinderella Shrike. Never doubt me. Ever. I'm on your side, Sugar. Everything in my life from this moment on leads to you." I gently urge her towards me, so her breasts are up against my bare chest. I just want to feel the life inside her. The beating of her heart that I hope will be mine from this day forward.

"I feel the same way. I don't think we have anything to worry about with your mother. But whatever is going on, we stand by her until we know the absolute truth."

"Thank you," I say.

"You don't have to—"

"I do, Cindy. You have no idea what it will do to me if she's behind all this. But until I get that proof I can't turn my back. And I already know—I can already predict—all the fights between the guys and me over this. I totally understand now why Corporate refuses to talk shit about his parents. They were good to him."

"I know," Cindy says, frowning up at me.

"She was good to me."

"Don't think about it yet, OK? Just wait. This feels like the end, ya know? We're so close."

I feel it too. It's like we have one more corner to turn and then everything—all the elusive answers—will come into view.

"Let's go to bed," I say, unbuckling my belt and opening the button and fly on my jeans. I let them drop to the floor and then Cindy starts tugging on my boxer briefs until I can step out and kick all my clothes aside. I'm not fully hard yet, but that's only because I don't feel the rush of lust right now. I feel the glow of love.

I get in bed and sit up, my back against the headboard, then pat my lap for her to sit. She faces me, her legs straddling my thighs. Her long blonde hair falling over her shoulders, reaching down past the tips of her hard nipples and the curves of her breasts. Swinging against my chest with just the lightest tickling sensation.

I take her hair in my hands and place it over her shoulder, making her shudder. Making her already firm nipples bunch up even tighter. "I want to see you," I say. "I want to look at you. Watch the expression on your face. I want your hands on my shoulders, your nails digging into my skin as we move together."

Her tongue darts out and brushes over her lips, making them glisten. "You don't want to spank me, Detective?" she asks, gracing me with a smile.

I shake my head slowly. "No," I say, placing both hands on her hips, urging her to lift up so I can place my now-hard cock right at the opening of her wet entrance.

She gasps, then closes her eyes as she lowers herself back down without any signal from me. I close my eyes too. The pressure on my shaft, the small friction we create as we meld together, and the heat from her body is all I need right now. Just the feel of her is enough.

I think it's the same for Cindy, because she rounds her back and places her head on my shoulder, like she's seeking comfort.

"It's OK," I say, turning my head so I can whisper in her ear. I trace a feather-light touch down the curve of her spine with my fingertips, which makes her shudder again and slowly begin to move on top of me. She lifts her head and looks down, her eyes on me. Only me. The blue just barely visible in the low light emanating off the digital clock on the nightstand.

"I know," she says back, her breath coming faster as I begin to move too.

But there is something very sad about this moment. Something I can't quite put my finger on. It's not her. I think between Five, and Oliver, and me—I think we can keep her safe. And I'm not worried about me. I'm not worried about *dying*. I don't know what's happening to me and my friends, but it can't come back to *killing* us. It's something worse than death, I think.

And there are such things. There are many things worse than your own death. You can lose a loved one. That explains Oliver's reluctance to be in a relationship and why he doesn't want Cindy involved. You could lose your identity. Which explains Weston and his lies trying to cover it all up. You could lose your reputation, like Mac, and take on the world trying be a saint and get it back. Or you could lose your self, like Nolan, and turn yourself into the monster people expect you to be.

All these things are worse than death because you have to live with it. You have to get up every day and face the world you created, or succumbed to, or surrendered to and live with it. Does it matter? How it ends? Does it really matter when we all leave this life the same way? Dead?

No.

The only thing that matters is how you live.

So… what do I have to lose? This is the question on my mind. What can they take from me that I will miss, beyond what they've already stolen?

All those same things for sure. But don't we all live with that potential loss? The risk isn't in losing all those things my friends have. The risk is losing the few things I still have left.

If I lose my mother… or Cindy…

"Shhh," Cindy says, still rocking slowly in my lap as she reads my thoughts. It's only then that I realize a tear is falling down my cheek. "Don't," Cindy says, a tear falling down her cheek too. "Don't get lost."

If I lose my mother everything else goes with it. Who could I possibly trust after that kind of betrayal?

"We're fine," Cindy insists, her words barely a breath, not even a whisper. "It's fine."

I wrap my arms around her, holding her tight and close. Ashamed to show her my emotions. I keep her there, like a prisoner against my chest, and let it all go so we can escape for a moment.

I take my full attention back to the woman on top of me. I get lost in her instead. And when we come together, I let it all go.

I let my mother go, I let the past go, I let the shame go, I let the life go… and I become dead.

So now, there is no more risk. There is no more fear. There is nothing left to lose because there is nothing left to take.

Cindy slides off me, her back pressing up against my chest as we lie in bed. I hold her prisoner again, just a little bit longer, until she falls asleep.

And then I get up, get dressed, and go looking for Oliver.

CHAPTER THIRTY-THREE

CINDY

I sit up in bed, confused, my heart racing before I can make sense of where I'm at and what's going on.

You're at Mr. Romantic's resort.

Someone sent you a silver envelope.

I swing my legs over the side of the bed and go searching for my clothes.

"Pax?" I yell into the other room as I put my bra on and then tug my shirt over my head and slip on my panties and skirt. "Pax?" Where the hell is he?

I walk into the small living area and find it empty, then look back at the clock on the bedside table. It's only ten thirty. Did he go looking for the silver envelope without me?

I open the cabana door and find a whole crowd of Misters and Misses still at the pool.

"There she is," Ariel says, some kind of fruity drink in her hand.

"What the hell is going on here? Where did Pax go?"

Ariel walks towards me. "He left," she says. "Went looking for Oliver."

"Well, where's that?"

"Probably the bar," Ivy says. "It was a while ago. Oliver was in there getting drunk the last time I saw him. I'd leave them alone for a while. Let them work it out."

That's actually good advice. Except I'm not worried about Oliver anymore. I'm wondering what the hell Pax was thinking, going out without me.

"Thanks. But I'm just going to go check, just to make sure." I start walking towards the little path that leads back to the main part of the resort but Ariel follows me, yanking on my arm hard enough to make me stop.

"You're keeping secrets, baby sister. And I don't like it. You need to tell me what you know."

I turn and face Ariel. "You know," I say, "if I had any answers for you, I might do that. But since you're trying to bully me into submitting to your big sisterly bullshit, then I'll pass, thanks."

"Why are you so angry?" Ariel asks, blinking her blue eyes at me innocently.

"Me?" I say, pointing at myself. "I'm not angry. That's always been you, Ariel. You've always been the angry sister. I just want to find Pax, so if you don't mind—"

"If you don't mind, I'll go with you," she says.

"I do mind, Ariel. I'm not the baby anymore. I'm all grown up, see? And I'm looking for my boyfriend, so just go back to the party and leave me alone."

I'm being mean. I realize that. But I need to get the fuck away from her right now. I need to get into that kitchen and see if Pax found the envelope without me. And I need to find him. And Oliver. Why did he get up and leave?

"I'm just trying to help, Cinderella."

I sigh. "I know, Ariel. But butt out, OK? Just mind your own business. I'll be back in a little bit with Pax and Oliver."

I start walking again, willing her to stay put. I look over my shoulder just as I turn the corner and she's still standing there, arms folded, drink in hand. But at least she doesn't follow. So I hurry faster along the walkway, then push my way past a crowd of people at the pool. This place is super busy tonight. There must be two hundred people partying around the pool.

I finally get to the steps that lead to the main building and get inside. The bar packed too. And a live band is playing. But I do catch sight of Oliver and Pax, back near the pool table.

I stop and watch them for a moment, wondering if I should join them or go grab the envelope first. They are smiling and joking, our problems temporarily forgotten. So I opt for plan B and head down the hallway towards where I think the kitchen is. I know there are two of them, the main one used for the restaurant and bar orders, and the catering kitchen used as spillover for the private parties.

The main kitchen is still working, but it's slow. I keep going until I'm in front of the stainless-steel double doors that lead to the catering kitchen and know that no one is in there, because there's two little windows and both are dark.

I glance over my shoulder, just to see if anyone is looking. All clear. So I push my way through.

Inside there's a little bit of light coming from various outlets that have some kind of nightlight hooked up to them, but other than that, it's pretty dark. Which is perfect, since the last thing I need is for someone to see me get that envelope before I have a chance to read it.

I stop and look around, trying to orient myself and figure out where I was standing earlier, my eyes adjusting to the dark. The way the dim, blue lights make the stainless tables glow as I make my way down the aisle towards the back of the room.

This one, I decide, looking at the table in front of me with pots and pans hanging from a rack above it. This was where I was standing.

I bend down and start feeling on the floor for the envelope.

Nothing!

Jesus Christ, what if they really did throw it away? Like the kitchen staff found it? Or what if Pax got here first?

I stand up and a shadowy figure is standing on the other side of the room. I squint my eyes, trying to make out who it is. "Pax?"

A sharp pain shoots up my neck, my hand going there instinctively, only to find a small, needle-like spike sticking out of my skin. "What the hell—" I pull it out and throw it on the ground, and then gasp when the shadowy figure starts moving towards me.

"Who are you? Pax?" My heart is beating abnormally fast all of a sudden. "Pax?" My vision starts to go blurry as it gets closer. I back up, but hit the stove, and just stand there like I'm paralyzed.

"What's—"

But I know. I don't even need to ask.

I've been drugged.

I turn around, try to take a few steps, stumble, and have to use the stove to hold myself up.

When I look behind me, the figure is only a few steps away.

"Not Paxton," the figure says. "Fortunately."

"Who are you?" I squint my eyes. But no matter how hard I try, I cannot make out the form. It's not until it's almost upon me that I realize it's not some shadowy figure. It's a woman in a long, silver robe with a hood over her head.

"I would hate to kill him before we had to," she says as I slump down to the floor, unable to move.

"What—" *did you do?* But the last part of my sentence doesn't happen anywhere but in my own mind. I cannot talk. I slump down, and the last thing I feel is a few strands of hair being tugged from my head as they catch on the stove on my way down.

I cannot move.

"We like him, Cinderella Shrike. We approve of him, so very good job, young lady. Thank you for being so cooperative."

And then everything goes black.

CHAPTER THIRTY-FOUR

PAXTON

"Ten thirty," I say, checking my watch. "Cindy might be up now."

"Good," Oliver says, taking his shot at the pool game we're playing. "We need to figure this shit out." He stops talking to watch the seven ball go into the side pocket and then straightens up and looks me in the eye. "Tonight, if she can find that envelope again."

"I hope we were just looking in the wrong place and it's still there."

Oliver looks around the room, frowning. This place is so busy tonight. Three hundred guests. The resort is totally full to capacity. Apparently Nolan's sister, Claudette, booked this event months ago, long before all that shit with Nolan went down back east and she disappeared. "This whole thing gives me the creeps."

"I agree." It's a Zeta Phi Beta sorority reunion and after everything my mother told Cindy and I out at Del Mar, it's just... *weird*.

"Let's go get her and get to the bottom of this silver envelope thing."

We set our sticks back into the rack and then push our way through the people, out of the bar, then outside and have to practically fight our way through the people at the pool.

The quiet of the path that leads to the private family bungalows is a relief. And it's a welcome sight to see

287

everyone is still up so we can get all this shit out in the open and put our collective heads together.

The secrets need to be over now. Oliver is willing to talk about what happened to him That Night and I for one, cannot wait to hear it. Then we're going to give everyone else a chance to come clean with any other secrets so we can put this bullshit behind us.

As a team.

Fuck this silence. There is a time and a place for that, but it's long past now.

"Hey," Ariel says, coming up to us as we come into view from the path. She stops talking, then squints her eyes, looking past us. "Where's Cindy?"

"Still sleeping, I think."

"No," Ariel says. "She got up like ten minutes ago and left to look for you guys."

"What the hell is wrong with you, Ariel? You don't let her go off by herself at a time like this!"

"She was not friendly, Oliver. She basically told me to fuck off and mind my own business."

"So?" Oliver grabs his hair with both hands and turns to look at me.

"It's fine," I say. "She's fine. Come on, I think she probably went to get that envelope."

"I knew that envelope meant something! That little shit lied to me!"

Oliver and I start walking, but Ariel jogs to catch up and says, "I'm coming too. I told her to go look for you guys in the bar."

"Well, there were a shitload of people in the bar, but we didn't see her. If she just left, we might've crossed paths in the crowd of people." I say the words, but I have this really sick feeling in my gut. And when no one agrees with me, the feeling grows.

We push our way back into the crowd at the pool, then fight our way back to the bar. "You go check in there, Ariel," Oliver says. "We'll go look in the kitchen. We'll meet right here in five minutes. Do not," he says, stressing the words, "go anywhere else. Just wait for us. Even if she's not in there."

"Got it," Ariel says. And takes off.

"Do you think she'll listen?" I ask.

"No," Oliver says. "Do you think my sisters ever do what they're told?"

We have a small laugh at that. But we stop quick enough when we get to the dark kitchen and find it empty.

"Where's the goddamned lights in here?" I ask.

"I don't fucking know," Oliver says. Probably some master switch. "But she's not here, so let's go back to find Ariel. Maybe she was in the bar after all."

I don't move.

"Come on," Oliver says, grabbing my arm.

"You go meet Ariel."

"What the fuck, Pax?"

"I just don't want to miss her. What if—"

"What if *what?*" I can hear the fear in his voice all of a sudden. And I feel the same way.

"I think we need to search, that's all." I look at him in the glow of light flowing up from the outlets on the wall. "She could be here, right under our noses, and we'd miss it." I know I'm implying she's hurt, but I do this for a living. I fix shit. And when you're fixing shit, you don't skip the details. "We need to search."

We spend whole minutes looking for the lights, and when Oliver finally finds the switch, hidden behind a rack of stainless steel bowls, and the whole room is illuminated, we have to concede, she is not here.

"That's good," Oliver says. "Now let's go meet Ariel."

But I stand in place, just looking around. "I can smell her," I say. "She was here."

"You cannot *smell her*, asshole."

"No, listen. She smells like a bakery, Oliver. Some perfume or lotion she uses. She smells like a bakery. And I can smell it right *now*. She was in here. Very recently."

"So maybe she left. And went to the bar. And she and Ariel are waiting for us in the lobby?"

"Go then," I say. "Go meet them if you think that's the case." I stare at him, his blue eyes nearing panic. "But I don't think she is. We need to look around."

Oliver looks longingly at the door and I can practically read his mind.

He wants that possibility to be true.

But it isn't.

And when he looks back at me, we both know it for sure.

"Footprints," I say. "She has those cute boots on. Look for a scuff on the floor or—"

"What the fuck is this?"

"What?" I say, making my way around a table to where he's bending down. He stands back up grasping something very small and thin in between his fingers. He holds it up and the light glints off the slender piece of silver.

"A needle?" I ask. "Give me that." I hold out my hand and Oliver drops it into my palm. "There's blood on the tip."

"Dude—" Oliver says.

"Don't," I say sternly—I've found enough bad evidence in my day as a fixer to know what's coming next from him—"panic."

"Someone *drugged* her," Oliver says, talking very fast. "She came in here looking for that envelope, bent down right here, where we're standing, and then stood up, and someone fucking drugged her. And then she pulled it out, threw it down…"

"There's a scuff mark," I say, pointing to the floor. "Look. Her boots."

"What's that?" Oliver asks, pointing to the stove.

I bend down and see a piece of long, blonde hair stuck in a red stove knob. I pull it free and hold it up in the light.

"Jesus fuck," Oliver says. "Someone fucking took her."

CHAPTER THIRTY-FIVE

CINDY

My eyes flutter uncontrollably, and all I can think about is how weird I feel. What the hell… A clinking of ice in glass, very close to my face—so close I can feel the coldness on my cheek.

"What?"

"I'm sorry," a woman says. She's very close too. "I do apologize for our methods. It's always uncomfortable when you bring someone new into the fold. We can't avoid it, or we would, I promise. This will pass in a few seconds. The drug is reversed very quickly."

She's right. From the start of her sentence to the final word, everything goes from slow and sluggish to crisp and clear.

I try to lift my head and see who is talking, but a shooting pain makes me cry out.

"The headache and muscle control takes a little longer. It's just a precaution. So you can sit still and listen as your future is explained."

"What… the fuck—"

"Oh, now." The woman laughs. "We don't use words like that in this organization, Cinderella. And that name of yours, I'm sorry, it's going to have to be changed. You're OK with Cynthia, though? Right?"

CHAPTER THIRTY-SIX

PAXTON

"I need a gun," Oliver says, staring at the few strands of his sister's golden hair I placed on the table. "Like, right the fuck *now*."

"Just relax," I say, pulling out my phone and tabbing a contact.

"Who are you calling?"

"Five," I say, when he picks up. "We have a problem. Get Nolan and meet us in the catering kitchen. If you see Ariel out by the bar, tell her Oliver and I want her to go back to the private area immediately and everyone else should stay together in Perfect's cabana. And Five," I say, looking at Oliver as he tries not to freak out. "Bring the guns I know you have. One for each of us." I end the call and shove the phone in my back pocket. Oliver is still staring at the hair.

"It's gonna be fine."

"How the hell can you say that?" Oliver asks, his anger replacing his shock. "Someone drugged her and then took her away, Pax."

"I realize that, Oli. But it's not going to do any good if we freak the fuck out, OK? Now, look. I do this shit for a living. We need to stay calm. We need to look at everything in here and try to figure out where they took her. Nolan knows this place. Every inch of it. He built it, right? He's got the plans. He's got security cameras. We're gonna find out who did this, where they went, and we're going to get Cindy back."

"How long do you think she's been gone?"

"It can't be more than twenty minutes. Thirty tops. Let's look around while we wait. There has to be some kind of clue. People always leave something behind."

CHAPTER THIRTY-SEVEN

CINDY

By the time I can finally lift my head and focus my eyes enough to see her face with some sort of clarity, I know one thing for certain. "You're not Mariel," I say, coughing like my lungs are full of fluid.

The woman laughs and pulls the silver hood off her head, revealing short blonde hair that curls along her shoulders. "I never said I was, Cynthia."

"But you're calling me Cynthia. Like she does."

"Like…" The woman tilts her head, like a dog who's heard an unfamiliar sound. "You spoke to Mariel Hawthorne?"

Oh, I think, taking a deep breath to try to clear my mind of the grip the drug had on me. So she's not as well informed as she wants me to believe. "Several times," I choke out, still feeling the pressure in my lungs. What the hell did she give me? I turn my head to look around, figure out where the fuck I am, but everything spins and I have to fight down nausea.

"Don't move too fast," she cautions me. "The side effects of that are particularly uncomfortable. Just relax a little longer. You're going to be here for a little while."

I straighten my head again, look her straight on. I'm sitting at a small round table with a silver tablecloth, table set with fine china. There's a small silver dome, like the kind you see on a room service table that conceals a few small pads of butter underneath. And a bottle of champagne sits next to it.

She notices me staring at the bottle. "You're not ready for that just yet. Try the ice water first. If you're satisfied with my offer, then we'll have plenty of time to celebrate later. After we're all done ironing out the details."

"Details?" I ask, reaching for the cold glass that woke me up and taking a sip. My mouth is so dry; I feel like I've been lost in the desert for days. The table is lit up by a small chandelier hanging over the center. Just enough light to see and not enough to reveal what's hiding in the darkness surrounding me.

"All the things you're going to do for us, Cynthia. And all the things we're going to do for you in return."

She reaches into her robe and takes out a silver envelope. The one I dropped in the kitchen earlier, from the address label on the front. "You should be more careful with this," she says, placing it on the table between us. "I saved you this time. But if anyone gets a hold of this, Cynthia, the ramifications will be unpleasant."

"Define… unpleasant."

"Oh, I'll explain our bylaws, don't worry. I'm just trying to warn you. If anyone finds out that you're now a member of the Silver Society, well…" She chuckles and looks away, shaking her head, like this is so funny. She gives me a sidelong glance as the laugh dies. "You will forfeit your family." She holds both hands out, like it's just this simple.

"I'm not a part of your little secret group," I spit, furious at this whole situation. "And I won't join. So sorry, lady. You're gonna have to find yourself another little puppet. I don't play games like this."

"You know," she says, placing a perfectly manicured fingernail up to her mouth like she's trying to be cute, "your sister said the same thing."

I cannot hide the gasp of shock that comes bursting out of my heavy lungs. "What?" I whisper.

"Aurora Shrike had her chance. Don't make the same mistake she did, Cinderella. Or your parents might find another one of their daughters has gone missing."

CHAPTER THIRTY-EIGHT

PAXTON

We find eight more clues, including a few more strands of Cindy's hair and a long gash on the floor of the catering kitchen, probably made by her boots, and most likely indicating she was dragged.

"She didn't leave the kitchen," Nolan says, phone in hand, showing us the security footage. "Look," he says. "She went in here, through that door there"—Nolan points to the large double doors that lead to the hallway—"and she didn't come out."

"Then where the fuck did she go?" Oliver asks.

"Well." Nolan sighs. "I don't know. But she didn't leave by the connecting kitchen either—it was still being cleaned up for the night."

"I already asked them if they saw her," Five says. "They said no."

"So you're telling me," I say, "she never left the kitchen."

"Yes," Nolan says. "We have no cameras in this kitchen, but we do in the regular one. And they don't show her in there either."

"Why no cameras in this kitchen?" I ask.

"I dunno," Nolan says. "Claudette designed it as spillover for catering and large parties. It wasn't meant to be used every day."

"Claudette?" Five asks.

We all look at each other. Then Nolan.

He sighs, then nods. "She was in charge of the construction out here while I was working in San Diego.

"So there's a hidden room," Oliver says. And he's not joking. Most people would think that's a little too Scooby-Doo to be taken seriously. But if there's one thing I've learned from being Oliver Shrike's best friend, and by extension, inside Five's outer inner circle, it's that the weirder shit gets, the easier it is for them to accept it to be true.

Some might call that paranoia.

They call it the "real world".

"And all we need to do is find it." Five starts walking the perimeter, eyes searching the walls for any indication that something is hidden behind them.

"You think there's a hidden room?" Nolan is still in Scooby-Doo land.

But I have learned to trust Five and Oliver over the years, so I don't waste my time asking questions.

"Guys," Nolan says. "Come on. There's no hidden room. I have the plans right—"

"Found it," Five says, standing in front of an open electrical panel. "Stand back."

CHAPTER THIRTY- NINE

CINDY

"Don't look so horrified, Cynthia," the woman says. "It's very easy to prevent another family crisis."

"Just join your little *cult*," I say, sarcasm practically dripping off my tongue.

"We're not a cult. Did Mariel tell you that?"

I say nothing.

"Well, she's lying. We are the most prominent citizens of this country. We are the leaders, the innovators. We are doctors, lawyers, judges, mayors, governors, and many, many other things, Cynthia. But we are not a cult. We are a sororal society."

"A secret society, you mean," I manage to say. "I have to be honest Ms.—" I let the title hang there to see if she volunteers a name.

"You may call me Claudette."

Her name rings in the air like the lingering tone of a bell after being struck.

"Our sisters run this country, Cynthia. And you will be one of them." She looks me up and down for a second, tsking her tongue. "Of course, we will need to clean you up and make you presentable. And you won't be wasting your time as a private detective anymore." She smiles. "We will lift you up, Cynthia. You will run a city, then a state, and then, perhaps, if you spend a decade or two as a loyal and hardworking sister, we will reward you with the ultimate prize."

She's talking about the presidency. Overkill much? Like I'd ever be the one they'd put in the highest office on the planet. She must think I'm the most naïve girl ever.

And why not? It's the blonde hair. I'm the palomino racehorse on the track that day.

The only thing people see when they look at me is my looks.

Well, that's fine with me. I like being underestimated.

I want to say so many things. Like, *Lady, you are bat-shit crazy*. Or, *I'm going to rip your head off if you don't tell me what happened to my sister*. Or, *Just wait till my boyfriend gets here, you stupid cunt. And then we'll see—*

"What do you think of that?" She smiles at me. Calmly. Coolly. Certain she is in control.

"I think," I say, really, *really* wanting to give her a proper Bombshell response that would make my mother proud, but thinking better of it at the last second. "I think I'd like to know where I am."

Another indulgent smile. And then she snaps her fingers and lights begin flicking on, one by one, around the perimeter of the room.

CHAPTER FORTY

PAXTON

Five flips a switch and the lights go off, then come on again. But nothing else happens.

"Yeah," Nolan says. "Nice hidden room."

"You know what?" Oliver says. "You can just go back to your little fucking—"

"*Oliver*," Five snaps. "Shut up. He hasn't seen what we've seen over the years. Don't blame him for thinking this is some crazy, fucked-up shit. OK?"

Oliver looks like he might punch Five. But Five stands his ground and meets his gaze and Oli turns away from Nolan.

Nolan sighs. "Look, you guys—"

But before he can finish, there's a beeping sound and we all look behind us.

The shelf filled with stainless-steel mixing bowls is moving backwards into the wall, revealing a dark, empty hallway.

"What the fuck?" Nolan says.

I put a hand on his shoulder. Because I get it. When Five and Oliver started telling me about the secret hidden world they lived in, one I had no clue about, I felt the same way. "Just trust them, Nolan. Your sister is part of something much, much bigger than you can even imagine. And it all makes sense now, doesn't it? She came into your life when you were just starting this resort project. Offered up some of

305

her own money. And now you know," I say. "Now you know *why* she did that."

"She was planning on using this place as some… some…" But he can't even make himself say the words.

"Secret headquarters," Five finishes for him. "Come on, Cindy has to be in there."

We all have guns, even Nolan. He looked at the rifle Five was handing him like there was no fucking way he was ever touching another weapon again after what happened out on Martha's Vineyard. But then he had a second to finish that thought. And he knew Ivy would be dead right now if he hadn't taken action when he did.

So he took his rifle. We all took our rifles, plus a handgun, sticking the pistols in the waistbands of our pants.

And now Five goes first, his rifle at high ready. Nolan and I go second, both of us mimicking Five's weapon position. And Oliver brings up the rear so we have someone at our backs.

CHAPTER FORTY-ONE
CINDY

Mirrors. The room is circular and the walls are lined with mirrors, so that when I look at them, I see nothing but an infinite reflection of me, sitting at this table, with Nolan's crazy sister, Claudette Delaney.

"We call them infinity rooms," she says.

"You have more than one?" I ask, trying not to get lost in the reflections. It's like black magic, right? The only true representation of infinity in real life.

"Oh, yes. I'm going to destroy this resort when we leave here, Cynthia. Every outside recruit is honored with an infinity room that is only used once. After all, it isn't often we pluck a girl from obscurity and deliver her infinite possibilities. It's very special. Not meant for the masses."

"Why me?" I ask, swallowing hard, my mouth dry again. I want another drink, but I finished the glass of water I was offered and there isn't anything left but ice.

"Because your sister declined, sweet thing. And we really, *really* wanted her. We've evaluated your other sisters over the years. Jasmine is what, a tattoo artist, like your mother? Hmmph," Claudette says, clearly unimpressed.

"She's damn good at it."

"She's not worthy, Cynthia. And Belle takes after your father."

"She's an *accountant*," I say, getting more and more pissed off as this fucking witch of a woman evaluates my family. "She runs my father's entire empire."

"And Ariel never even finished college." Claudette pauses, to see what I have to say about Ariel. But I know better than to tell anyone anything about *that* sister. "No comment?"

I stay silent.

"Aurora was the perfect candidate. Star student at Princeton, beautiful, almost as beautiful as you. And in love with a man we dearly wanted to recruit."

"Five," I say, before I can stop myself.

"Five," she repeats. "But you, dear, are about to deliver a man we have wanted since his mother betrayed us thirty-one years ago."

Pax. I take a deep, measured breath, my whole body shaking as I let it out. "You killed my sister."

"She killed herself." And then Claudette lifts the little silver lid off the tiny platter sitting in the center of the table and reveals a single white wafer. Like the kind you'd find in a Catholic mass.

I look at Claudette. "What is that?"

"That's one of your choices. You can eat it, take the path your sister took many years ago and be left in this room as it goes up in flames. Or you can drink the champagne and leave here with me."

I stare at the bottle of champagne. Then the wafer.

"You give us something—"

"Like what?"

"Little things. We set up meetings. We deliver you contracts. You sign them, of course. It's just business. We help you rise to the top and you help us *stay* at the top."

"So I basically give you my life either way. If I join you, I do your bidding and then you control me like a puppet. And if I say no, you kill me."

"When you put it that way, it's such an easy choice. Isn't it, Cynthia?"

"Stop *calling me that*," I say, anger pouring out of me. I hate her. I hate her, I hate her, I hate her. *I'm going to kill you*, I think in my head. *I'm going to kill you very slowly.*

"Shall I pop the cork?" Claudette asks. "Or should I allow you the opportunity to eat that wafer and die painlessly after I ignite the room?"

I hesitate and while I do that, Claudette takes out her phone and tabs an icon.

Beneath the mirrored wall panel directly in front of me, flames erupt. Then another eruption, and another, and another. Until the whole room is nothing but an infinite circle of flames.

"Time's up, princess. I need an answer. *Right now.*"

The room is already filling with smoke. Smoke my lungs, damaged from whatever that drug was, can't handle. I stand up and try to scoot the chair back before I realize I'm chained. There are shackles around my ankles and I'm chained to the chair. "I'll join," I choke out through my wheezing, desperate to breathe. "I'll join. Just get me out of here!"

Just as the words come out of my mouth, an alarm sounds. Claudette's eyes go wide, then relax. Her hand comes up from under the table, a gun in her grip. She points it at my head and says, "Perfect. We'll continue our celebration in the car." She tosses me a key with her other hand. "Unchain yourself."

I scramble for the key and bend over, thankful for the fresher air that is still hovering low to the ground as the room quickly fills up with smoke.

One foot shackle is open. Then both.

When I'm free, I place a hand over my mouth and try to hold my breath. When I look at Claudette, she has an oxygen mask over her face.

"Come with me," she says in a tinny voice coming through the filter on her mask. "And bring the champagne with you."

I get up, still wobbly, and weak. My head is spinning and I have to take a moment for it to stop. I grab the neck of the bottle and stumble forward into the thick smoke.

"Go," Claudette says, coming around behind me, gun pointed at my head, and pushing me on the back.

"Go where?"

But one section of flames disappears and the same section of mirror slides down into the floor, revealing a dark hallway.

I take a step, slowly, carefully. We walk forward and when the darkness surrounds me, the opening closes at my back.

CHAPTER FORTY-TWO

PAXTON

An alarm sounds, wailing in our ears as we move through the corridor.

"What is that?" I ask.

"Fire," Nolan says, looking down at the security app on his phone, which is screaming the alarm from its speaker in unison with the alarms behind us back in the kitchen.

"Hurry," Five says. "This is when they make their escape."

"*Who?*" Nolan and I say together.

But Five doesn't answer, just starts running ahead of us. The only light coming from the beam attached to his rifle. But only a few seconds later, we come up against a concrete wall.

"Now where?" I ask. "It's a dead end."

"No," Five says. "Look." His rifle light is pointed at a seam in the wall where smoke is pouring out. "They lit it up already," Five says.

"Who?" Nolan asks.

"Nolan," Five says, ignoring the question once again. "There has to be an exit. Look at the plans. Find the exit."

"There's nothing but a ventilation shaft leading out to the east side of the property half a mile away."

"That's it. How do we get into it?"

"It says it's only a twelve-by-twelve shaft. We won't fit."

"The plans are wrong, Nolan. Now tell me how we get in there or Cindy is dead!"

Nolan studies his phone, turns around in a circle, like he's trying to get his bearings, and then points to the ceiling. "There. It's up there."

We all look up to see a hatch in the ceiling. Oliver drops his rifle and jumps up, grabbing on to one of the exposed pipes a few feet away. He swings his body back, then lifts his legs and gives the hatch a two-footed kick. Over and over again, until the panel buckles from the stress and the tiny door collapses.

"If we climb up there—"

"We won't fit," I say, suddenly hating my size for the first time in my life.

"I will," Ariel says behind us.

"We told you to go back!" Oliver yells.

Ariel smiles sweetly. "Don't you remember what Mom always said? You're not the boss of me, little brother. I'm the boss of me. So quit wasting time and lift me up."

Oliver and Five do that and I turn to Nolan. "Nolan, go back into the resort and get someone to the end of that tunnel. *Right fucking now!*" He turns to leave, but I grab his shoulder with one more thought. "And Nolan? Don't be afraid to shoot if you get there before us."

Nolan takes a breath, nods, and then he's gone.

"There's another shaft up here, you guys," Ariel calls back to us. "But there's smoke pouring out of it. Whatever's behind that wall is up in flames."

"There's another shaft, Ariel. Somewhere close by. The one that leads outside. Can you feel a draft? Something that tells you air is leaking through?"

Silence for almost a minute.

"Ariel?" Oliver yells, jumping up to grab the pipe again and then swinging his arms to grab another so he can poke his head into the hatch. "Ariel?" he screams.

"I found it!" she finally calls from some distance off. "It's off to your left. Hold on."

A few moments later the wall to our left begins moving back.

"Nice funhouse," Ariel says, standing on the other side. "Whoever built this place is a complete freak."

"Claudette," Five, Oliver, and I say together.

We go through the passageway and end up in a tunnel.

"It's a road," Ariel says. "Nolan will be on the other end. They left here in a car and Nolan will head them off at the other end."

"Fuck that," I say. "He just left here five minutes ago. There's no way he can get out to the end of that tunnel in time." I take off at a run and leave all three of them behind.

"Pax," they all yell after me.

"Pax, stop! There might be more of them!"

"You won't make it in time!"

"Pax!"

I don't stop. I don't even consider stopping. I run harder, my long legs finally good for something. They will not take Cindy. They will never take her away from me. I don't care if I die trying, she will not end up under the thumb of whoever these sick Silver Society assholes are.

CHAPTER FORTY-THREE
CINDY

There's a limo waiting in a tunnel once we get through the passageway. A tall guy, about Paxton's age, stands waiting for us dressed in a dark suit.

"Let's go," Claudette says.

"Who's that?" I ask, once I get inside the car and the driver closes the door.

"You'll find out soon enough, little pretty." Claudette's smile is sickly sweet like the perfume that permeates this car. It makes my stomach heave. "But now we can celebrate."

"What about all the people in the resort? There's hundreds of people there tonight, including my sister and brother. And Pax."

"All expendable, dear." She pats my leg.

"I thought you wanted Pax alive? I thought—"

"We did."

"What do you mean you did? You just told me Pax and I could be together."

"Oh," Claudette laughs. "No, no, no. You sweet, sweet innocent thing. I said we wanted him. But I never said *alive*."

I punch her in the face. Right in her fucking teeth. Blood goes spurting out of her lip and her hand comes up, eyes wide with surprise.

"You little bitch! Stewart!" she screams. "Stop this car right now and come tie her—"

I grab Claudette's hair, bring my knees up, and then smash her teeth again. I think I knock one out this time.

But she's fighting back, ignoring my attack. Her eyes rage at me as she drags her nails across my cheek. The sting shouldn't be enough to stop me, but she clips the corner of my eye with her nail and it fills with blood.

That one pause is all it takes to give her the advantage. I'm still half-drunk on the drugs she woke me up from. And the guy she called Stewart has both my arms and Claudette is sitting on my legs. She throws a hood over my face and then ties my wrists together.

"Get back in and drive," Claudette says, out of breath. "Now! We need to get to the gate before my worthless brother figures this tunnel out."

CHAPTER FORTY-FOUR

PAXTON

Up ahead I see brake lights. But before I can celebrate or even aim my rifle at the man I see struggling with someone in the back under the dim glow of the inside dome light, he closes the door, gets back in the driver's side, and they take off again.

Oliver catches up with me, panting and breathing hard from his sprint. "Was that them?" he asks.

"Yes," I growl. "That was them. Come on, we're not done yet."

We take off running again. Oliver keeps pace beside me as the car slows, then stops once more.

We keep running until we're within a hundred yards of them, when we realize what happened.

The tunnel has a gate.

And it is closed.

I will kiss you, Nolan Delaney. If I see you again, I will kiss you right on the fucking lips for coming through for me.

CHAPTER FORTY-FIVE
CINDY

"Why are we stopping?" Claudette asks. "Keep going!"

There is so much blood inside the hood, it's running into my mouth.

"The gate," the guy called Stewart says. "The gate is closed."

"It cannot be closed! I opened it myself when we got in the car."

"Well," Stewart replies, "your program appears to have been overridden."

"You're not going to escape," I say, choking my words past the blood. "Not this time, you stupid cunt."

She whips the hood off my head and grabs me by my braids, bashing my head into the seat in front of me. "If I go down, Cinderella, you go down with me."

"I'm OK with that," I say, looking at her through one eye. "I'm so OK with that."

"My brother did it," Claudette says, looking away from me. "He must've found the tunnel on the security system. But there's a manual switch on the side of the wall over there." She points to a faint glow coming off an electrical panel. "Get out and open the gate."

Stewart doesn't exactly complain, but he doesn't exactly hop to it, either. He opens the door and gets out, shooting Claudette a very dirty look as he does it.

"Hurry, you stupid piece of shit—"

And then Stewart's head explodes.

Claudette doesn't even blink. She opens her door, grabs me by my feet, and starts dragging me out of the car.

I give her a two-footed kick, but miss everything except her shoulder. She is not deterred.

"Stop right there!"

It's Oliver!

"I'll kill her," Claudette says, forcing me to my feet. "I'll do to her exactly what you just did to my driver." She pushes the gun to the side of my head, making her point.

Oliver comes into view, rifle out in front of him, laser scope mounted on top. The red dot hits me in my bloodless eye, making me blink, but it's gone when I open it back up.

"How about we make a deal, Claudette?"

"No deal."

"Just listen, OK? It's a good one. You let her go and then we'll kill you." And then he starts laughing. Like one of those crazy, madman laughs.

"You stupid, arrogant—"

"Shoot her!" I scream. "Shoot her, shoot her, shoot her!"

I swear to God, I can *hear* her finger tighten on the trigger of the gun. I close my eye, waiting for the moment when the explosion blows my brains out.

It comes.

Blood, and bone, and tissue. I'm covered in it. I stumble back, fall, my head hitting the pavement. I can hear screaming and it takes me a second to realize it's me who's screaming when I open my one good eye.

Pax walks out from the shadows off to my right, his gun still raised, smoke flowing out from the end of the barrel.

"Fuck that bitch," he says, kneeling down to smooth the blood-soaked hair off my face. "She deserved that."

"Yeah," I whisper, as Oliver unties my legs and Pax takes care of my wrists. I lean into him and he hugs me. Nothing has ever felt so good before in my life. "Fuck her."

My head swoons. Things go blurry and gray as Pax lifts me up. People are shouting now. Sirens and helicopters are blaring in the background. I hear Ariel talking to me at one point, chanting, "You're going to be OK. You're going to be OK…" over and over and over again. But I can't see her because my eyes won't open. Only my ears work.

And then… even that stops.

That's all there is.

Story's over, Miss Cookie, I hear the detective say. *Story's over.*

CHAPTER FORTY-SIX

CINDY

I wake up of course. In the ambulance just a few minutes later.

Paxton shot cunty Claudette, she didn't shoot me.

I never doubted him.

The drugs Claudette fed me have some kind of weird side effect that sticks in your system for a while and can cause you to flow in and out of unconsciousness for up to forty-eight hours. So they brought me to San Diego General Hospital for observation.

It's not so bad being injured in battle. I mean, it's a hell of a lot better than being Nolan and Ivy, who are stuck out there in the desert answering questions about why there was a secret unpermitted tunnel underneath their five-star resort.

Not to mention the fire in the room of mirrors. The cops actually asked Ivy if she was a devil worshipper.

That conversation was a hoot to listen to.

I'm still privately cracking up about Ivy Rockwell being painted a Satanist.

Or Pax and Oliver, who were taken into custody and are being held for questioning in the shooting of Claudette Delaney.

Five's handling that. Turns out Oliver and Pax were filming the whole thing using cameras mounted on their rifles, so there's plenty of proof to back up our story. That fucking Five. He thinks of everything, doesn't he? Even gun cams.

Or West and Mac, who took the Mister jet back to Mac's house in Colorado, trying to wait the investigation out. They're totally out of the loop.

So I get stuck here in the hospital with Ariel, Ellie, and Victoria.

"Bitch," Tori says. "Are you even listening to me?"

She's been talking incessantly since she got here this morning. I'm stuck in bed. What choice do I have?

"My plan is still a good one."

"True," Ellie says, eating my canned peaches off my hospital tray with a spork as she lounges next to me in bed. "I'm inclined to agree with her, Cindy. We should give it a vote once Ivy gets back."

Ariel answers for me. "Well, I'm in too. I say these Misters have taken far too long to figure this shit out. It's time they step aside and let the women take over."

"I love you," Tori tells my sister.

"Love ya back, bitch."

I crack an eyeball open as they fist-bump. I get to stay silent because I'm pretending to be sleeping off my drugs to make them all leave me alone so I can plan my next *Miss Cookie Meets Detective Mysterious* encounter.

I kinda like these crazy bitches, but they are not very good at taking hints. Ellie is gonna stick around as long as they keep delivering me trays with peaches on them. Tori is going to stick around until I agree to her plan. And Ariel... well, she's my sister. She's always around, even when she's not.

We didn't get all the answers. We still don't know where Mariel is. Or what part she played in all this. And Oliver, well… Tori says that he's next. That every Mister has been fucked with and now it's his turn. Not to mention all the lingering questions about my sister, Rory.

So that really sucks.

But I did get the one thing I went after before this whole thing started.

My Mister.

And I'm happy with that.

For now.

PAXTON

"Why, Miss Cookie," I say. "What brings you to my bedroom tonight? I thought your case was solved?"

Cindy is leaning against the window of the Malibu house terrace, backlit by the orangey-red sunset behind her. She places the back of her hand up against her forehead with a dramatic flair Vivian Leigh would envy. "No, Detective," she says, with an exaggerated Southern accent. She swings her head to look at me, then resumes her despairing pose. "It wasn't solved, merely... halted in place." She comes towards me, her long, coral-colored dress splitting all the way up her thigh with each step. "I need answers, Detective. And I need you to get them for me."

"Hmmm," I say, looking her up and down lewdly as I grab my dick through my pants. "But you're broke, Miss Cookie. Dead broke. How will you ever manage to pay my fee?"

"I have heard through the grapevine, Detective"—I raise my eyebrows in anticipation. I've been waiting to play this game with her all damn day—"that I can suck a man's cock like the wind blows across the Gulf during hurricane season."

I chuckle and then bite on the stem of my unlit pipe to stop it. It's a nice prop, I think. Making its debut *Miss Cookie Meets Detective Mysterious* appearance right now. I still have the trench coat. And the hat. But the pipe is still a nice addition.

I take a step towards her, making sure to admire her tits in that low-cut gown. "Well," I say, stuffing the pipe in my pocket so I can fondle both her breasts at the same time. "How could a man turn that down?"

"He can't," she says, leaning in with pouty, seductive lips like she's going to kiss me, but pulling away at the last possible moment. "No man," she says. "Not even the great Detective Mysterious."

I come to her this time. And I don't pull away at the last second. I kiss her. Deep, and hard, and soft, and seductively... all at the same time. Trying to forget all the many, many things that still haunt me.

Where is my mother? She hasn't answered her phone since last week when all that shit went down in the desert.

What was in that silver envelope? Cindy said Claudette had it in the infinity room, but the cops insist they never found it on her person. There's no telling if it went up in flames.

It's just so frustrating. We were so close. "What if we never get any answers, Cindy?"

She bows her head and looks up at me, batting her false eyelashes to try to keep the scene going. But I can sense the moment she gives in. "We're all still here, Paxton. And the number of people on your side has doubled in size since last year when all this shit started happening. We'll get to the bottom of it."

"There are just so many mysteries."

"That's OK," she says.

"What if we never get that happily ever after?" I ask. God, I just want to make her happy. She refused to sign the paperwork that gives her ownership of the house, but I forged her signature. So it's a done deal. But it's not enough. It's just not enough to make me feel like no matter what happens to me, she will always be taken care of.

"Do we need it?" Cindy asks.

"Don't you want it? Doesn't every Cinderella deserve the happily ever after?"

"Well," she says, resuming her dramatic character voice. "Maybe most princesses like that tired, old happily ever after, Detective. But me"—she stops to bat the lashes again—"I prefer the 'till death do us part' ending, myself."

I chuckle at that. "You would."

"Why, Detective, I do believe you're calling me a troublemaker."

"If the shoe fits, Miss Cookie."

"That's right," she says, placing both her palms flat on my face as she leans up on her tip toes to kiss me on the lips. "The shoe does fit, Pax." Her dramatic accent is gone, and in its place is just... her. "I'm Cinderella, you're Prince Charming. And no matter what happens, we'll be together till the end."

She picks up two mint juleps off a side table and hands one to me. We lift them in the air and clink them together. "To Mr. and Mrs. Mysterious," she says.

"Till death do us part," I say. "Till death do us part."

End of Book Shit

Welcome to the End of Book Shit where I get to say anything I want about the book you just read.

Well here we are at the end of Book Four and only one more to go. I hope you got some satisfaction in this one. I hope you don't hate me for what I did to Princess Rory. I hope it was fun to revisit Cindy, Oliver, and Ariel Shrike. (and Five. Hey – did you notice Five said he had a baby sister? And Sasha's name came up!!!)

For those of you who have never read my Rook & Ronin and my Dirty, Dark, and Deadly series you're not missing anything big. Cindy was six months old last time we saw her in the Happily Ever After book. Oliver was five and I can't even remember how old Ariel was. Possibly eight. (I keep a cheat sheet for all their ages but I don't have it on me right now)

So if you've never read anything else by me—no worries. You don't have to.

I'm not going to say anything else about Rory and Five because as some you might know Five is getting his book next year. I have it on my calendar for a September 2017 release. So whatever opinions you have about that little twist, just hang on to them until the book comes out. I can tell you two things about it now:

It takes place while Rory is in college. (so long before any of this Mister stuff happened)

Five comes to see her for the first time in four years.

Is it a second chance romance? A love triangle? A murder mystery?

You don't really expect me to tell you, right?

Hahahahhahahahahahahahahahahahahahh

;)

But back to Mr. Mysterious. He's sorta cute with his Mother Complex, and his weird job, and his cool houses and boats. If there's one thing I wish I could've put in here it was a scene where Cindy gets to go home and see Pax's family farm in Kentucky. I really (like *really*) wanted to write about that farm. But alas, characters don't always accommodate the writer the way we wish they would.

So maybe a bonus scene will come up after all the books are done. I mean... no one has gotten married yet, right? Well, Nolan did. But he and Ivy did that on the sly and her father is none too happy about it. So there has to be at least one wedding in the future. Maybe Pax will offer up his family farm for the ceremony. ;)

If I write the bonus stuff it won't be until next year. I don't have time to get it out in 2016. I mean, it's fucking OCTOBER, bombshells! Where the hell did this year go??

Mine kinda got swept up in this series and the farther I get into the story the more I love it. When I finished Rook and Ronin (after Guns) I was so sad because it was over. I felt the same about Social Media, and Dirty, Dark, and Deadly. Especially Wasted Lust because that was the real end, right? Jesus, it was sad.

And then I wrote a bunch of standalones last year. I wrote 321, Meet Me in The Dark and Wasted Lust (sorta standalones, but also in the R&R world). Then Sexy, which has no spinoffs at all. Then 18 (another true standalone). Then Anarchy Found, which is a series but I didn't write any more in that world this year, so it's basically standalone at the moment. And then early in 2016 I wrote Rock.

I like writing standalone books but honestly, how do you really (like *really*) develop the world and characters?

You get one shot to build it up and give your characters a back story and then poof. It's all gone and you have to build a new world with new characters.

I don't mind building new worlds and characters at all. I think I'm pretty good at it. But when you have a series like the Misters, then there's five total opportunities to build that world up. So I can mention a silver envelope in book one and it has no meaning whatsoever. I mention it again in book two and some readers who know me might start to wonder if there's something to that. Book three has them scratching their heads. And now – boom.

It's all about the silver envelopes, people. All about the silver envelopes.

And it's not even about the men! Ha!

Who runs the world?

Girls.

Duh.

It's great to have a large world to work with. To have a whole cast of main characters. I get this little writer's rush when I need something in a plot—a red herring, or a diversion, or maybe just some random character that has to interact with one of the mains in a chapter or scene— and I can pull one out of another book. Or sometimes even another series. I did that Social Media. Damian Li (Ashleigh's father from the Ford books) sticks his nose into Vaughn Asher's business during a card game.

I mean why not use him again? I have already set up his character, his background, his business, his past. He was the perfect choice.

This is something you don't get much of writing standalone books. Also, if you don't have thirty plus books written to choose characters, or settings or leftover plots from other stories it's kinda hard to pull off.

But I'm lucky. Have all these worlds, all these characters, all these places, all these stories to choose from. So I like use them.

I used to be a really big Stephen King reader back in the day and he does this especially well in his books. I can remember reading one of those Dark Tower books (Maybe Wizard and Glass—but don't hold me to that) and someone from another book suddenly appeared and I was like, *Gah!!!!!!!!!! I know that guy*!

lol. I swear to God, that was me.

I'm sure there are some people who read my books because they enjoy the simplicity of my sentences, I almost never totally fuck a story up, and they usually come out the other end satisfied. Right? It's just a good book to most people.

But then… there are the fans. People who do scream *GAH!* when Five shows up, or Oliver shows up. Or Ariel or Ford's name. Whatever.

I try not to "write to" any one group. In other words I'm not aiming for only fans when I write a story. Or only new readers or casual readers. I try to balance it out. I like to give you a hint of a "bigger world" without overwhelming you and I do that with these cool little Stephen-King-esque callbacks, which is a literary device called allusion.

Allusion is when information is implied. In most cases artists, like filmmakers and authors, use allusion to redirect the watcher or reader to the world outside the story—something that exists in the world of the reader. Something big or little. Sometimes it's nothing but intellectual minutia used to pat all the other intellectuals on the back and assure them they are smart.

But I mostly use it as a way to redirect readers to the overarching storyline of other books I've written where the characters or plot might cross, however briefly.

If the reader doesn't understand the reference then my words are merely decoration. If you read Wasted Lust as a standalone (and you can, if you want. I swear, all the information you need for that story is in there) then you miss the allusion and you end up with a very different perspective of the story.

Some readers don't like internal allusion. But fans usually dig it. So the allusion is for the fans even when I'm doing my best to write for both the reader and the fan.

This book was kinda hard to write because of the time line. Mysterious has been in all the books, but he had huge parts in Mr. Romantic and Mr. Corporate. He's much more than a side character. So when it came time to write his story I wanted to account for all those actions.

If you picked up Mr. Mysterious first and read the series out of order you might be thinking – this is not a standalone.

I sort of agree—BUT—I did give you everything you needed to know for THIS book. So I consider it a standalone. Yes, you're missing info, but what the fuck could I do? That info is all in the other books. You get the gist of it, right? If you need details go back and read the other Mister books. Start from the beginning this time.

One cool side effect, if you will, of writing this way is that there's almost two ways to read some of my stories.

There are lots of places to jump into the Rook and Ronin world. You could start at the beginning with Tragic and read them all in order. In that case you get all the allusion and you get it fed to you in the "standard" order. But you could also start at Dirty, Dark, and Deadly—read those three books, then go back and read Rook and Ronin and you've gonna have those *Gah!* moments when you realize how they connect. You can also start with the Ford books. Or Meet Me In The Dark, or Wasted Lust. Each of those books can be interpreted two ways because of the allusion.

Some people like to connect the dots… some people don't. I try to keep it all balanced and hopefully I'm doing a good job.

I also hope people don't get too sick of me going back and forth in time. I don't use this "literary device" lightly. In other words I don't do it just for the fuck of it. I only do it when it's necessary to tell the story a certain way. Usually I'm hiding something from you—I write romantic suspense, after all.

But I remember getting a complaint about it in 321 from someone. They said the time jumping was confusing. But the only time jumping in that book was in the prologue and the last few chapters. If that is confusing I can't help people with that. It really wasn't hard to follow. There was almost no allusion in that book at all. It's a straight standalone.

BUT… this book was sorta difficult. So if this time line confuses you, sorry. I try my best to keep the story as simple as possible but sometimes this is just how the shit shakes out.

Story comes first and this story required a full accounting of Paxton Vance's actions in the other books as it relates to the plot in *his* book.

When I first envisioned Mysterious, while writing Mr. Perfect, I really didn't know who "his girl" was. I think I told you that in the last EOBS for Mr. Corporate. That I plot the books when I'm nearing the end of the prior book. But I figured out Cindy Shrike was Mrs. Mysterious while I was writing Mr. Romantic. God, it just fit into the story so perfectly. And while I was writing the end of Mysterious I was thinking about Five. Because Five is in this world now and he's in another world too. Even more so that Oliver and the rest of this gang because he was born at the end of the Taut book and he had his own epilogue at the end of the Guns book. And I will say this about Princess Rory—I wasn't sure if I wanted to mention her at all. If you've been a fan for a while you know I've been promising a Five Book for two years now. More than two years, actually. And my reason for not writing it yet was because I just didn't have the right story figured out.

But it all came together for me while writing Mr. Mysterious and that book will be out next year.

As far as Oliver Shrike goes… well, I already know who Mr. Match's girl is and I know what kind of guy Oliver turned out to be after his whole Mr. Brown experience, so we're good to go there. He's a dirty motherfucker, ladies. So be prepared. His book gets epically erotic in chapter one.

Two months. That's all you have to wait. Just two more months and all the mysteries will be solved.

Well... sorta.

;)

If you'd like to hang out with me on Facebook I have a private fan group called Shrike Bikes. Just ask to join and someone will approve you as soon as they see it. I am in that group chatting with the fans every single day and we have a lot of giveaways and fun stuff going all the time. Especially around release days. I usually do a takeover and give away all kinds of stuff related to the new release, so come on by and say hi.

If you enjoyed this book please consider leaving me a review where you purchased it. I'm still indie. And the success of each and every book I put out depends on readers like you leaving their thoughts and opinions about the story in a review.

Thank you for reading, thank you for reviewing, and I'll see you in the next book.

Julie
JA Huss

About the Author

JA Huss is the New York Times and USA Today bestselling author of more than twenty romances. She likes stories about family, loyalty, and extraordinary characters who struggle with basic human emotions while dealing with bigger than life problems. JA loves writing heroes who make you swoon, heroines who makes you jealous, and the perfect Happily Ever After ending.

You can chat with her on Facebook, Twitter, and her kick-ass romance blog, New Adult Addiction. If you're interested in getting your hands on an advanced release copy of her upcoming books, sneak peek teasers, or information on her upcoming personal appearances, you can join her newsletter list and get those details delivered right to your inbox.

JA Huss lives on a dirt road in Colorado thirty minutes from the nearest post office. So if she owes you a package from a giveaway, expect it to take forever. She has a small farm with two donkeys named Paris & Nicole, a ringneck parakeet named Bird, and a pack of dogs. She also has two grown children who have never read any of her books and do not plan on ever doing so. They do, however, plan on using her credit cards forever.

JA collects guns and likes to read science fiction and books that make her think. JA Huss used to write homeschool science textbooks under the name Simple Schooling and after publishing more than 200 of those, she ran out of shit to say. She started writing the I Am Just Junco science fiction series in 2012, but has since found the meaning of life writing erotic stories about antihero men that readers love to love.

JA has an undergraduate degree in equine science and fully planned on becoming a veterinarian until she heard what kind of hours they keep, so she decided to go to grad school and got a master's degree in Forensic Toxicology. Before she was a full-time writer she was smelling hog farms for the state of Colorado.

Even though JA is known to be testy and somewhat of a bitch, she loves her #fans dearly and if you want to talk to her, join her Facebook fan group where she posts daily bullshit about bullshit.

If you think she's kidding about this crazy autobiography, you don't know her very well.

You can find all her books on Amazon, Barnes & Noble, iTunes, and KOBO.

Made in the USA
Coppell, TX
27 September 2020